Murder in
Madison County

International Standard Book Number 13: 978-1-60452-081-1
International Standard Book Number 10: 1-60452-081-7
Library of Congress Control Number: 2015935791

BluewaterPress LLC
52 Tuscan Way Ste 202-309
Saint Augustine, Florida 32092

http://www.bluewaterpress.com
This book may be purchased online at

http://www.bluewaterpress.com/MIMCO

This is a work of fiction. All characters, organizations, and events portrayed in this novel are either products of the author's imagination or are used fictitiously.

Cover information:

Front cover - One of the final PA-18 Super Cubs produced by Piper Aircraft of Vero Beach, FL.

Back cover - PV-1 Ventura of Lockheed's Vega Aircraft Company. Originally built for the U.S. Navy and used during World War II, the airplane was modified for use in the civilian market. Photo credit, Howard 350 executive standard, RuthAS, Creative Commons 3.0.

Dedication

I dedicate this book to my dear friend James Gillis.
Without whose help I would have never gotten the first
thing published.

May God be with you Jim.
May He always give you the patience to help others
as you have me.

More important though,
may He give you the wisdom to always
keep your powder dry.

A Short Note to the Reader:

Just to let you know, I have taken the liberty to locate my first ever non-western novel, in my home county of Madison. I also once lived in Natrona County, Wyoming, where some of this story takes place.

It has been quite a journey and a lot of fun to write this. I hope you have as much fun reading it.

It is a novel through and through, and not one incident mentioned herein ever took place, to my knowledge. It is strictly from my imagination, as are the law enforcement personnel, as well as all of the characters for that matter, except three.

There is mention in here of a Judge Wetzel Blair. He was the County Judge of Madison County at the time the story was written, and because of his unique distinction, and he being the only judge in the whole state to have this distinction, I felt obligated to speak of him. Of course, I speak very kindly of him, but that was not hard to do. He is a kind and just man and I hope should I ever have the misfortune to come before an officer of the court, it would be in front of his bench.

I also have given a small portion of this to my friend Jim Good, in hopes some of you might enjoy touring his Airplane Museum as much as I did. I also must acknowledge it was Jim who taught me how to keep the tailwheel to the rear, where it belongs.

Additionally, I want to say that Sandra Norris is a very real person who worked for many years at Elmer's Library. She is a wonderful lady and truly a great friend. It is she who not only helped me find many of my own ancestors, but also was most encouraging in my writing.

The photograph of the Super Cub on the front cover was given to me by my close friend Paul Davidson to use herein. Paul bestowed unto me the rare privilege of going with him to the Piper factory and picking up his brand new Cub. A treat I will never forget.

There is also a picture of an L-4 military Cub that was sent to me by the owner, Sandy and her husband Phil McKenzie, to use herein.

Sandy is not only a very good commercial pilot, A&P, and I. A., she also is cute as a button. The Murphy Rebel pictured in the story was built by Sandy and Phil and is a beautiful piece of craftsmanship. I am eternally grateful to them for allowing the photos to be used here.

I also want to thank my friend Myrtle Wallace for her time and labor in helping with the editing of this story.

If I have forgotten to mention others that I should have, please forgive, and lay it down to old age.

Elmer Spear, who founded Elmer's Genealogy Library in Madison, Florida, gave me some very good advice, which I would like to share with you. Having written and published several books of his own, he pointed out one very important fact, which had slipped by my simple mind. Elmer said, "There are some people who read books because they are required to, and some because they need to fill a void in their otherwise bored lives. There are some people who read books because they wish to increase their knowledge and some who read simply for the pleasure of it. Then there are some who read to satisfy their desire to find fault with other's work."

It is in wanting to fulfill everyone's needs that Elmer always makes a few intentional errors in spelling and grammar, so the last group may also find something to please them in reading his material.

I have followed in his leadership and done likewise. So if you find the mistakes, just smile and realize they were left there on purpose.

Murder in Madison County
INTRODUCTION

Most everyone has either seen Clint Eastwood in the movie *The Bridges of Madison County*, or read the book. This story has nothing to do with that Madison County. It is in fact, a story that happened a thousand miles away from the location of that book. This is a story of greed, power, and lust in what was once called Middle Florida.

Some would say it began when Nathan Rugg made his first million buying surplus B-25s and selling them to the CIA at a 500 percent profit, who in turn used them in the initial assault during the Bay of Pigs invasion. Others would say it really began when Blue Rugg left Colorado for Vegas.

However, I think most will agree it truly began the day Wall Roberts was dispatched to locate the cause of the power outage, which had been reported by Jeremiah Gaston. Not that all these other events didn't in some way play a part in bringing our characters together. Even so, this event would have never taken place had not the gust blown that water oak limb across the power line rendering the scattered homes on the Old River Road without electricity that sunny morning in late March of 1995.

This little strip of land had originally been homesteaded by Jeremiah Gaston's great, great, grandfather, for whom he was named. Perhaps another "Great" could be added to that list, you see Jeremiah was never sure about the true number, even though he researched it many times. Unfortunately, each time he came up with something new.

Way back in Bible days, as Deacon Jeremiah liked to say, all of this was a part of Georgia. However, sometime later, a new survey was made and the state line moved north several hundred yards to the south bank of the Withlacoochee River and Georgian Jeremiah Gaston the First became a Florida resident with the stroke of a pen in the hand of a man he had never met, nor ever would.

Being a Floridian really didn't mean much to him. In those days, North Florida and South Georgia, was the same for all practical purposes.

It was some ten years after the war when Old Jeremiah III or IV inherited this homestead and both states were in deep depression.

There were three peoples living in the region at the time. The freedmen, the rich immigrant recently moved into the area from the north to take advantage of land that could be bought for back taxes; and the dirt poor native. Jeremiah Gaston was one of the latter.

It was a surprise to most that the former Third Sergeant of Company G, Second Florida Infantry was able to keep the homestead at all, since he had given his loyalties to his native state during the war. However, he did keep it and now over one hundred and twenty five years later, several of his descendants still worked a portion of the original tract.

It was perhaps at or near the time Old Sergeant Jeremiah was struggling to feed his family by farming this sandy soil, the acorn dropped from the parent tree; a small green seed that sprouted into the mighty trunk.

It was from that trunk this offending limb had fallen, during the fast moving thunderstorm that passed through the hammock an hour before sunrise. When this huge limb fell, it took the power lines with it all the way to the ground and started a short-lived fire.

Wall Roberts worked for The Withlacoochee Co-Op for two years to the day on this now sunny Monday morning, and he was glad to be out of town and in the backwoods north of Pinetta. He had never liked the business of a town, no matter how large or small it might be.

He was a man's man, a man who grew up on Rayonier Land in Flagler County. His father had been a forest ranger for the company long before the ITT Corporation created the City of Palm Coast.

As a boy, Wall knew little about towns, except for the Flagler County's seat, Bunnell. Its population of 1500 was the only settlement of any size between St. Augustine and Daytona, and Wall considered it a necessary pest, where the only school was located.

Other kids in his class yearned to become of driving age so they could race down to Daytona and cruise the beach. Not so Wall. He only wanted his license to be able to legally drive the old military Jeep his father had parked in the decrepit shed behind the house after a rod broke, freezing its little engine back in the summer of '68.

Another thing, unlike most of the kids his age, it was important to young Wall to do it legally, too. His father had instilled in him the belief that a land without laws was the fertile soil where tyranny would sprout, and where there were laws, a man was obliged to obey them.

Wallace senior had been a Marine sniper in Vietnam and had personally witnessed what corruption and lawlessness can do to a nation. He never let Junior, as he called Wall, forget it.

After the politicians lost that conflict, his father came home and left the Corps for the ranger job with *Rayonier Timber Corporation*; a job that produced a pitiful paycheck, but one that included a small frame house in view of the tall, galvanized tower off U.S. Number 1.

Before the Mouse moved to Florida and air-conditioning became an economic standard in homes, which is to say, before Florida became over populated, every county had at least one fire tower. These were usually located on the outskirts of a town, sometimes up to five miles distant. Along with the steel structures higher than 100 feet, was a cluster of small frame Jim Walter homes to house the employees, and garages to house and maintain the equipment necessary in preventing and putting out forest fires.

It was at such a location in Flagler County that Wall had spent his youth. There, in the forests, he learned to enjoy a life of being outdoors most of the hours of any given day when not in school. The art of a hunt, the eye to read tracks, both human and animal, and the ear to identify woods noises townspeople have never even heard. Each and every one of these traits was honed there, in the piney forest north of Bunnell.

He never lost his love for the smell of pine and the interruption in the still morning air of a cat squirrel barking loudly, claiming his territory. In a pine forest in a part of Flagler County, few of the pilgrims who now cover the land like six-legged little critters swarming over an anthill after a cleansing rain, realize they even exist there.

However, this sunny morning in late March, Davy Kerr, driving the Co-Op pickup, had located the downed lines and radioed in for a boom-truck to aid in the restoration of power. Wall was driving that truck this sunny morning and soon was headed up The Colin Kelly Highway[1] towards Old River Road.

Davy called over the radio and told him the trouble was in the thick oak hammock on the west side of Nate Rugg's property adjacent the little sod airfield.

Wall knew pretty well where it would be. He had flown out of the field a few times, some three years past, and even thought someday he might get his pilot's license.

As he drove along, he wished after they had made the necessary repairs to the lines, he could conjure up some excuse to get Ray Swift to give him a ride in one of his little Cubs. However in reality, he knew it was only a fantasy, this being a workday.

Davy was sitting in the pickup smoking a cigarette when Wall arrived. Immediately a distasteful humor swept Wall's mind when he saw this.

'Davy knows full well the company has regulations against smoking while in the forest, especially when on private land,' Wall thought. Wall detested the use of tobacco. He had watched his best friend's wife struggle through her last days, desperately trying to gasp enough

---

1 Colin Kelly: A Madison County son who became America's first hero of World War II.

oxygen into her scarred lungs to get the strength to walk from her recliner to the toilet.

She had never smoked a single cigarette in her life, yet she died a horrible death, because the people in the office where she worked had filled the air she had to breathe with their smoky poison. All day, five days a week for nearly twenty-five years, she breathed it. Now he simply could not understand why anyone would deliberately suck such poison into their bodies.

Neither did he understand anyone wanting to sit in the cab of a truck when they could be out on this wonderfully clear morning, ingesting the many options nature provided to those who chose to recognize them.

"Where you been?" Davy asked when he stepped from the truck.

Wall noticed he still was wearing the lined jacket he was snuggling in when they crossed the parking lot before six that morning.

"You still wearing that damn coat?" was his only reply.

"Well, I ain't no Damn Yankee, like some folks."

Ignoring the insult, Wall looked to the power lines and then to the two hundred or so square yards of freshly burned needles and black-sided trees. "You get the breaker off?"

"Naw. Can't get to it, 'cause the way the limb fell. That's why I called for you to come. Figured you would appreciate getting out of town for a while."

"Well, I am obliged to you for that," Wall admitted, as he walked back to his truck.

"Good thing that shower put the fire out," Davy added. "Might have been bad up here."

"Ground is pretty damp yet, from last week's rain," Wall suggested as he stepped back in the big rig and started the engine before moving the truck into a position so he could swing the cherrypicker around to where he could reach the circuit breaker arm.

Wall was really enjoying the warm morning air as he stepped into the bucket and began gently manhandling the levers that would hydraulically lift him up above the transformer.

Slowly he maneuvered the bucket into the position he wanted; then when satisfied, he released his grip on the levers. At that moment a fox squirrel began barking a few trees away, displaying his anger at the distraction these invaders were bringing to his territory.

Wall turned his head hoping to catch a glimpse of the colorful little critter. It was at that moment he first saw her.

Chapter One
Blue

She was a mistake. Everyone knew it, even though no one ever mentioned it in front of Doggy or Dottie. All their friends knew her brother had been born twenty years before, when her mother was only twenty-three herself. Then after her sister came along five years later, there were no more children. Doggy and Dottie accepted that their little family was complete, and they lived their lives as fully as two hard working people could.

It was in February of 1962, when Doggy had persuaded his wife to accompany him on a trip he was making up in the high country. He had been given the assignment to try to retrieve a cattle truck that some of the Mexican hands had abandoned on a dim mountain road.

Doggy had gone up and checked on it only a day or two after it had been left back in early October. He immediately discovered the problem to be a broken axle, but snows came in force before he could get back with the new part. Mr. Cobb told him just leave it until spring and then hopefully it would still be salvageable.

The old cab-over Jimmy really wasn't worth much to a big outfit like *The Cobb Cattle Company*, but it had been the first truck of any size they owned and Miss Nell Cobb loved that faded old '49 GMC.

The first week in February had been exceptionally windy on the east slope of the Rockies and Amos Cobb was worried the hard chill would cause a small disaster among his herd of Black Angus. However, it turned out his worries were for naught. It even became a blessing, to some degree.

Trooper Johnny Norris, of the Colorado Highway Patrol, stopped by the ranch house to tell Mr. Amos he had been dispatched to work a wreck at the intersection of Highway 40 and the mountain road, near where Ole Red had been left. After finishing his investigation and being so close to her, he thought he would try and get back and see how the truck was fairing. When he located the old cab-over, to his surprise, he found the strong winds had blown the snow mostly off the road and she sat there faded, yet seemingly with the pride of a strong knight of the Cobb family.

"I think you may be able to get the old mascot of the Cobb Ranch out, if you hurry," he said to Mr. Cobb.

It was on this endeavor that Doggy Belle had persuaded Dottie to accompany him. She hadn't really wanted to go, but he convinced her she would love the sights of the high country in deep winter, and she knew he was right.

She did love the high country. It was in these same mountains, somewhat nearer Steamboat Springs, they had spent their honeymoon, or at least, that was what Doggy called the winter they had stayed in the old cabin just after they had been married. He was making his living trapping coyotes at the time.

Doggy had always been a cowhand, ever since he was old enough to hold a job. The trouble with that line of work was, and often still is, the outfits lay off the younger men after fall round-up, and the boys have to do the best they can throughout the winter months.

They had tied the knot the second day of November 1941 and Doggy reasoned that the two of them could stay in the high country that winter and trap the little wolves for a good profit. A prime coyote pelt was worth a dollar or two, sometimes more. He figured they could have three hundred pelts by February or early March, enough money to give them a fair stake. With that they could, just maybe, get a little spread of their own come spring.

It was in that cabin their first-born, Roy, was conceived. It wasn't until late March when they came down, did they learn about the unprovoked bombing of Pearl Harbor by the Empire of Japan.

Doggy's brother, Alvin, was aboard the USS Arizona that fateful morning and for the remainder of his life, Doggy never again said the word Japanese. To him, anyone who would spring a sneak attack upon another nation to which they were not at war, were people without honor. No, to Doggy there were no Japanese, there were only Dirty Japs. Or on occasion when he felt exceptionally bitter, Dirty Nips.

The pelt money didn't get them the spread they wanted, but it did get Dottie by while he was away fighting in the war.

Mary was born in late '46, and soon after, the Belle family moved into one of the hands' houses of *The Cobb Cattle Company.*

Doggy had the new axle in and a fresh battery installed just as darkness fell on them. Their plans had been to come home that night, but some reckless ya-hoo had shot out both headlights sometime after she had been abandoned. Now Doggy dared not try to drive down the mountain using only the lights of the pickup Dottie would be following in.

As is the case of all who live in the Rockies, a good tent and provisions to sustain life were kept in the lower section of the pickup tool box. In less than an hour, just as the last rays of sun dropped behind the western mountains, he had the tent up and was building a small camp fire so she could prepare their dinner.

"What's for supper, old woman?"

"Pork n' beans over pan biscuits, with canned peaches for desert, old man," she spat back.

"Sounds like a feast to me," he said, and slapped her on the seat of her jeans as she walked past.

The moon was almost full, bathing the surrounding snow-topped mountains in a pale cream, which contrasted sharply with the blackness of a clear sky.

They sat there beside the little fire and watched the stars sparkle above while the after dinner coffee was boiling. It was when she

Doggy in front of the mountain tent

was pouring them each a cup, Doggy suddenly remembered something. Standing, he walked over to the old GMC.

"Where are you going?" she called out, demandingly.

He didn't answer. Instead he opened the driver's door, climbed up, and began rummaging around inside. Less than a minute later, he stepped back to the ground and slammed the door, a sound that thundered in the quiet night. Almost immediately, a dog sounded off, some distance away. Then, before he returned the few steps to where Dottie sat, another responded, closer.

"Here, let's liven up this party a little," he said, holding out a mason jar, nearly full of a clear liquid.

She looked at him with a surprised expression, as he added some to her coffee.

"Where did that come from?"

"I just remembered. I put it there last summer, when we were over to Laramie."

"What on earth were you doing in Laramie in Ole Red?"

"Oh, we went to pick up that new bull Mr. Amos bought from them Lathrops up in Wyoming. Anyway, I got this little jug on that trip and wrapped it in my old shirt and put it behind the seat yonder. Plum forgot all about it till just now," he replied with a wicked smile. "Pretty smart of me, eh?"

Just then, the sound of a coyote howled close by and again another answered almost immediately, further up the slope.

"Don't you just love this high country?" he said, as much a statement as a question.

"I do. I really do. It puts me in mind of our cabin, back in '41," she said, looking off towards where the remains of the old, one room log structure must be.

"Puts me in mind of how you looked trying to wash up without freezing your tits off," he said, and she immediately slapped him hard on the arm.

In a flash, he had her in his arms and started kissing her strongly. Her reaction was to part her lips and press her tongue forward.

When the long passionate embrace ended, she took a deep breath and then a long swallow of her coffee before she said, "Doggy Belle, I do believe you plan to get me intoxicated," she paused before adding, "And then have your way with me."

"The thought was creeping up in my mind," he admitted.

"It better be," she said back, this time reaching for the Mason jar and drinking the smooth whiskey straight. "Ah," was her expression as she lowered the jar, appreciating the strong liquor that rushed down her throat. Then after taking a breath she added, "That's good stuff."

Later as they snuggled under the blankets in the tent, she laughingly said, "It was just such a night that brought us our first child, wouldn't it be a sight if we done sprouted another."

"Don't even mention such a thing," he scolded. "I might have done a mite a' bad things in my life, but I ain't never been so bad that the Good Lord would put a newborn child on me at my age."

"Hellfire, Doggy Belle, you're only forty-four."

"Yeah, and that means I'd be a hundred and four when the kid was full grown," he replied, before rolling over and drifting off to sleep.

The following November, Dottie gave birth to a bright, blue-eyed daughter.

The first time Doggy saw her, his heart swelled up in his throat to where he almost couldn't speak. When he did, he said, "We got 'a name her Blue. Virginia Blue. Virginia after my Ma, and Blue 'cause a' those beautiful eyes."

So it was to be, on November 2, 1962, Virginia Blue came into the lives of Doggy and Dottie Belle.

He would be very disappointed when, as Dottie had warned, the color in her eyes began to change. However, as the blue was replaced with the brightest emerald green anyone had ever seen, he just couldn't feel bad about it at all.

At age six, Blue Belle was a pretty, green eyed, red haired little girl. However, she was so skinny her father often would say, "She has to run round in the shower to get wet."

Everyone knew Blue was the pride of her father, and she went with him everywhere, whenever she could, whether it be in his old Dodge pickup, or on horseback.

Four years later, Dottie was killed by a drunk driver as she stood beside the mailbox, looking through the recently delivered envelopes. The loss was a blow to Doggy from which he would never fully recover. Despite all her protest and crying, the following year he sent Blue to live with her sister in Denver.

In early fall of 1980, Doggy shot a cow elk up in the high country. He was riding his favorite mount, Buttercup, and was leading a pack animal back to camp with the meat. Suddenly his horse slipped on some loose marl, and threw him. The fall broke his right leg and severed the femoral artery. The pack horse bolted, but Buttercup stayed close by as long as his master was still breathing, then later came back to camp alone. It was the next morning before they found Doggy's body.

Blue was devastated.

She and her older sister never had gotten along, and now with her father no longer alive to run interference, she lived a life of misery and depression.

Mary realized she resented her little sister, but she just couldn't help it. She had been the baby, and had received most of her father's loving attention as his only daughter. In her eyes, that ended when Virginia Blue came along. "After Blue, a change came over him, and he forgot all about me, for the new baby," she often hatefully complained.

There was also the fact, with each passing year, baby sister had become more and more beautiful, and Mary only became older, with more children of her own.

A year after Doggy's death following a heated argument with Mary, Blue packed her bags and headed out on her own.

Right after she graduated from school, Blue got a job as a waitress in *The Hungry Bear Restaurant* and was putting away money for college. However, with her father gone, she spent all her savings obtaining a small apartment.

Nonetheless, her strikingly beautiful face, exceptional height, and voluptuous figure, made her tips come often, and usually large.

Blue learned how to tease the ranch hands from an early age, and now as a waitress, she knew just how much to flirt, without being considered a tease. The many businessmen who came to Denver's finest eatery loved her, and let her know how much they appreciated her attitude and beauty.

During the next ten years, she worked her way up to assistant manager of the restaurant. She also put herself through two years of college and was in her second year with *The Denver Dance Troupe,* which gave performances twice a month.

That month, as the troupe was performing at the annual Cherry Creek Fiesta, Willis Cunningham spotted the beautiful redhead who stood a head above her fellow dancers.

Willis had no desire to be in Denver; he was there because his boss wanted him there. He had much rather remained in Vegas where he had a fine room in the casino, and practically his pick of the girls; young, beautiful girls who were desperately trying to maintain their well-paying jobs.

It was his responsibility to keep the showgirls in line and ready to perform at the boss's beck and call. This gave him a power most men would kill for. It also offered him the ability to recruit new talent when he found it.

That night when he saw the exceptionally beautiful redhead dancing, he knew he had to have her, and immediately set out to accomplish that very thing. Before the night was over, he secured an invitation for the party being given at the Governor's Mansion, and had it delivered to her dressing room.

Normally Blue never responded to such invitations. Several had come her way before. However, by chance that afternoon, her sister telephoned with bad news from home. She knew it would be so when she recognized the voice on the phone. Mary never called, unless she could deliver some news that would depress Blue. This time it was of Salty dying.

Salty had been a ranch hand for the Cobb outfit as long as Blue could remember, and it was he who had found her dad that morning after he had been thrown.

She had always felt terribly close to the little lanky guy, even though he was older than her father. Now he, too, was gone.

Mary also had found a way to mention that one of the younger boys who worked for her husband had been showing her a great deal of attention. She admitted she was considering having an affair with him while John was away on a well up in Wyoming.

Blue doubted a younger man was showing Mary that kind of attention, unless she had been the invitee. Anyway, she allowed her sister to carry on in her fantasy.

However, it was what Mary said about her new admirer being the nephew of the Governor, that caused her to accept the invitation to the party. Blue realized when her sister found out about her being invited to the Governor's Party, Mary would cringe with jealousy.

Willis spotted her the moment she stepped from the long, black Lincoln he had sent for her transportation. He immediately stepped forward and introduced himself as the person who had been assigned as her escort for the dinner.

She was a little skeptical, but the invitation had come from an unknown source, and she figured she could handle this little man, should he become a problem.

That, he never did. Instead, he had shown himself to be a perfect gentleman. Surprisingly, he was really fun throughout the night. When he asked her to dinner the following night, Blue heard herself accept.

They spent the next three evenings together, and on the last night he was to be in town, she invited him to stay with her. Instead, they went to his suite.

The next afternoon, Blue found herself sitting in the window seat of a Boeing watching Colorado slip away, 30,000 feet below.

Chapter Two
Vegas

It all happened so fast. One day she was happy working as an assistant manager of a restaurant, secure in her twenty-five thousand dollar a year profession. Then, less than a week later, she was headed for Las Vegas with a man she had so recently met, for a position that would earn her four times that much, or so he promised.

Willis Cunningham provided Blue with two very valuable pieces of life's experiences. First, he introduced her into the reality that her true power lay in her beauty and her body. Second, he hardened her into a person who knew no limits when she decided to accomplish a new goal.

By the time Nate Rugg saw the woman who would capture his life, she was something to behold. She waited for five years, expecting Willis to marry her as he promised. However, it was the night he had agreed to have her entertain two bosses who had come in from New York to inspect the casino books, she realized he was not her fiancé, as he liked to tell everyone, rather her pimp. She also realized she was little more than a very high-priced whore.

In the year following that night, she entertained several special guests, and received as much as a thousand dollars a night for such an engagement. Once, she was tipped five thousand dollars when she entertained two of them at the same time, but she was not happy with this kind of money.

Also, Willis had begun to treat her differently. She was still considered his property at the casino. Nonetheless, she knew to him, she was only a means to climb his ascending ladder, and if he found someone who could help him more in his ambition, she would be finding another source of survival.

That was when fate brought Nate Rugg to the strip.

Three days later, once again, she found herself high above the desert looking out of a small window, only this time it wasn't in a Boeing. It was in her new husband's Cessna Citation.

Chapter Three
The Peeping Tom

Wall saw her as she came through the sliding glass doors onto the pool patio. She was wearing a white bikini over her pure white skin causing him to think she was nude and the sight took away his breath.

"Hey, Davy, is that old transit in this truck, or in Huff's?"

"I don't know. I think it's in here," his partner replied, without bothering to look.

Wall lowered himself back to the ground and walked over to the yellow pickup, where Davy was now sitting on the tailgate. "You get her turned off?"

"Not yet," Wall replied, without looking at Davy. Instead, he headed straight to the toolbox and began rummaging through it, removing rope, spare gloves, three hard hats, and some chalk, before he could get at the leather handle of the old wooden box. Lifting it clear, he sat it on the front seat and raised the top.

He gingerly lifted the old Gurley Transit and removed the lens covers. First, he blew gently at the dust that could be seen there. Then looking back in the box, he found the soft cloth folded neatly where he had left it months before.

Satisfied with his cleaning job, he then searched around the truck until he found the angle clamp. Without saying another word, he returned to the bucket and climbed in.

"Hey, what you doing with that?" Davy asked.

Wall ignored him, lifting the hydraulic handles. As soon as he was at the proper height, he immediately looked to make sure she was still there.

He was happy to see she was using a long-handle net to scoop some fallen leaves from the pool water.

Carefully, he attached the clamp to the side of the bucket, then screwed the old instrument to the top of the clamp.

Turning the long tube to the north, he lowered his eye to the lens and began twisting the knurled knob to bring her into focus.

He now could see she was not nude. He brought the scope down to her feet and then ever so slowly inched it up her body. Her skin was alabaster white and her hair was long and flowing over her shoulders. He tried to think of something that was the same shade of red, but he could not think of anything in nature that fiery. Not the head of a woodpecker, or the breast of a robin. A cardinal was all wrong. Nothing he could remember was that color. "It must come from a box," he said aloud.

"What did you say?" Davy asked.

"Nothing," Wall replied, without taking his eyes from the transit.

"What are you looking at?"

"I'm not sure. I think maybe an angel," he paused then added, "or perhaps a She-Devil."

"What?"

"That's Nate Rugg's house yonder, near the river, ain't it?"

"Yeah, that's about where it is all right," Davy agreed, looking off to the north, seeing nothing but thick underbrush among the scattered oaks and pines. "God, I hope he ain't home," Davy added. "If he's out a' power, we had better get this fixed and be quick about it."

"You ever see his wife?"

"Think so, a couple years back, over at the Governor's Mansion in Tallahassee. Back when I wus working fur Florida Power," he replied, and then looking up at his friend he asked, "Why?"

"What does she look like?"

"A real knockout. A big red head that's about twenty years younger than he is, and a foot taller," he said back, then asked, "You never seen her?"

"Humm," was all Wall uttered.

"Yeah, she is a real looker. Got tits the size a' watermelons."

"Mush melons," was Wall's only reply.

Blue had placed the net back alongside the brick wall and removed her bikini top a second or two before he answered Davy.

She then eased the bottom of her two-piece down and Wall again found himself short of breath.

"That didn't come out of no box after all," he said, not really meaning to be communicating with Davy.

"What are you talking about?"

"Red. I'm talking about the color red."

"What?"

At that moment, she dove into the water and swam around a few minutes before getting back out and walking over to a lounge and sitting down.

Although he was two hundred yards away, he could see through the transit the cold water had caused her long nipples to harden and stand out proudly from her breasts.

She turned around, adjusting the chair, giving him a perfect view of her round hips, before she turned again and sat down. Then she leaned back with the bottoms of her feet pointed straight at his scope. He watched another several seconds before he gasped, as she opened her legs to where each foot was at the side of the lounge. Wall tried focusing the old scope again, hoping to somehow increase the magnification or the clarity, but it was already at its optimum.

Finally, he decided he had better get to work, and he reluctantly raised his head from the scope before moving the bucket to where he could disconnect the circuit breaker. When he lowered himself to the ground, Davy asked again, "What were you looking at, for so long?"

"Oh, one of those red-headed woodpeckers. You know the ones the Audubon Society tries to convince everybody into believing have been extinct for a hundred years."

"The ones that are about a foot tall?" Davy asked, taking the transit from Wall.

"Yeah, a tall red-headed one."

"I know the ones you mean, look like Woody Woodpecker."

"That's the ones alright," Wall agreed, nodding his head slightly with just a hint of a smirk on his face.

"Hellfire, they ain't extinct. I see them every once and a while."

It took them less than an hour to put in temporary wiring and then just before they left, Wall again ascended in the cherrypicker to reconnect the circuit breaker. Looking over at the house, he could see she was sitting on the lounge with her legs over the side rubbing her arms. *'Applying sun screen,'* he surmised.

"Well, I tried to get in on the radio, but can't seem to get anybody, you want to try yours?"

"No need. Mine just barely could receive you until I was a couple miles away," Wall lied. "Better head back to the store in Pinetta and call in on the landline."

"Yeah, I guess so."

"I think I will ease over to the airstrip and see if Ray Swift is around," he said.

"Well, don't be long. They may have some more work for us."

"Cover for me for a few minutes, and I will be along directly."

"Okay."

As soon as his buddy was out of sight, Wall turned his truck through the gates and up the paved driveway, which led to the Rugg mansion.

He stopped in front. To his left he could see the Withlacoochee River winding its way slowly towards a rendezvous with the Suwannee, some twenty miles south.

The house was a big two-story structure, with the first floor made of brick, and the second from Cypress logs.

There was a large overhead veranda covering a portion of the circular drive. This porch was supported by four huge, white columns that extended above the porch to a large roof. The whole scene brought to mind the homes he had seen in paintings of the Old South.

'There is money here, a lot of money,' he thought as he walked up to the front door and rang the bell.

Half a minute later, a small, mango-skinned woman appeared asking his business.

"I need to speak to Mr. Rugg."

"He not home," she said back sharply.

"Then I need to speak to Mrs. Rugg," Wall sternly said to her.

The maid took a deep breath, showing her annoyance at his request before she spat back, "I see if Mrs. Rugg can be disturbed."

"What is it, Famalie?" he heard a soft voice call from the rear of the house.

"Mussy be some tarpree[2], in work clothes," was the only announcement he received.

"I'll speak to him," she said, as she walked through the large open room.

"Yes?" she asked.

'Here she is, standing not three feet away in that white bikini, and barefooted, and she is looking me straight in the eyes, and I'm in my work boots. Not only is she the most beautiful woman I have ever seen, she is the tallest.'

"I ah', I just wanted to tell you the electricity is back on."

"Yes, I realized that when I saw the ceiling fans begin to turn, and the lights suddenly brighten up."

"Well, I thought I should inform you, that when the lines were knocked down, they started a fire back there in the forest," he stammered out.

"Am I in danger?" she asked, lowering her chin and turning it slightly to the side just before she blinked her eyes.

"Oh. Oh no, Ma'am," he replied. "I just thought I should tell someone," Wall paused and then he added, "It's only temporary."

"The fire?" she teased.

---

2 Tarpree: Bahamian slang for low class.

"No. No, Ma'am. The electrical repair, we'll have to come back and install new cable. What I did today is only temporary."

"I see. Will it be out long, the next time?"

"An hour or two, no more."

"Will you be climbing back up in that tree then?" she asked, looking him straight in the eye.

"Tree? Oh, no Ma'am, I weren't in no tree. I was in my bucket, there in the cherrypicker," again he stammered, twisting his body towards his truck outside, but never taking his eyes from her face.

She looked at the boom-truck through the large front window, and then back at him.

"Well, my cherry was picked long ago, so no need to bring it next time," she said, then turned and walked away without closing the door.

He wanted to say something to stop her. Anything to try to explain, but he couldn't think of anything to say. Before he had much of a chance, the maid returned and closed the door in his face, giving him a last second, "Pooh."

All the way back to Pinetta, he thought about what a fool he had been. She obviously had seen him spying on her. *'I wonder if she saw me before she took the swim or after. Maybe when I let the bucket down, it did jerk some then. I'll bet that's it. She saw me, just as I was going down.'*

"I never should have gone up to the house," he said aloud, with only himself to hear.

'If she calls in, I'll have no excuse, and if Davy tells them about the transit, I could be labeled as a peeping tom. You stupid jerk!'

Throughout the remainder of the day, his stomach was uneasy and when they returned to the yard that afternoon, Andy, the maintenance man, said, "The boss wants to see you before you leave."

"Crap!"

He put his equipment away. However, he kept out his personal belongings, expecting full well he was headed for a pink slip. *'At the very least I'll get a first class ass chewing.'* Something Wall never took well.

Walking in, he nodded to Ash, the receptionist. "You can go on in, Mr. Miller is waiting for you," she said, and buzzed him through the interior door.

"You wanted to see me?" he asked, standing in front of Miller's desk.

Wall had never liked Miller, not that the man had been a back stabber or needler, but he just wasn't friendly, and seemed a little indifferent to the problems the men in the field experienced.

"You go to the Rugg house today?"

Taking a deep breath, he answered, "Yes."

"Roberts, you must be better at public relations than I gave you credit," the seated man said.

"What?" Wall said back, narrowing his eyes at the man across the desk.

"Mrs. Rugg called and wanted to know your name. I thought you must have made a nuisance of yourself, but she said that you had been the perfect gentleman, and she wanted to let someone know that you had taken the time to come and inform them of a burn on their property."

"Yes, Sur. I did that," Wall replied, still not believing what he was hearing.

"Well, I don't know if you know this or not, but Old Nate Rugg was instrumental in the Co-Op being headquartered here, instead of in Jefferson County."

"No. I didn't know that."

"Well he was, and had it not been for him, Tri-County would be the only electrical company in this area. Thanks to Nate Rugg, we all have a job and Mr. Collins will be pleased to know you went out of your way to show extra courtesy to the Ruggs."

"Yes, Sur. Thank you, Sur."

"Bye, Wall." Ash said, as he passed her desk.

"See ya'," he replied, and gave her a smile.

Walking across the lot to his truck, he said to himself, "She asked for my name."

Chapter Four
Carpetbaggers

Shortly after the War Between the States, Nate's family acquired a large tract of land in Madison County, Florida. Although Nate's parents spent many winters in Madison, Nathan Rugg had been born in Savannah Beach, back during the years when the world was struggling with a great depression. He was named after his grandfather's grandfather, who had come to the island in 1866 from New Haven, Connecticut, taking advantage of the newly opened land that had been confiscated from the secessionists through war taxes.

The Ruggs had been a seafaring family for generations, and the love of the sea and all things nautical had earned Nathan the first a position in the navy yards early on in the rebellion. It was on the very same Carolina beaches Nathan found himself when the conflict came to an end, having been sent by the War Department to inspect Fort Pulaski after its capture.

He very much liked the area and after a short time back in Connecticut, he returned to stake out a large portion of the north-end of the island for his winter home.

His son also made his fortune from an income from the sea and migrated to Jacksonville in the early nineties to establish a fairly large repair business in the shipyards upriver from Mayport.

Eventually, the remainder of the Rugg family all migrated south, either to Georgia or Florida, except one or two.

Nate's father was a high-ranking member of the Kaiser Manufacturing Corporation for several years, before the Big War. In early 1942, Kaiser transferred him to the west coast to work in the building of the Liberty Ships their yards were beginning to manufacture.

He left his pregnant wife with his mother there on Savannah Island, to give birth to Nate's sister Ellen.

Although the sea had been the family tradition for two hundred years and he had joined the navy at 18, young Nate discovered his love to be aviation, and he applied for duty as an airman.

However, his eyesight eventually washed him out of flight training in Pensacola. He was, however, able to remain as an aircraft mechanic. Unfortunately, once more bad fortune plagued Nate when an accident left his foot crushed and he was medically discharged during the second year of his naval career.

Nate's disobedience to his father's wishes of nautical versus aviation brought on a bitter feud between the two. Even as a young man, he often expressed his belief that the only purpose a battleship had in a modern navy was to give support to the aircraft carrier. When the war proved Nate correct, the split between him and his father became even greater. As a result, he received little or no support from the family fortune. All that would have gone to him was directed to his mother by a change in the will only two months before his father died in 1960. This did not hamper Nate in his desire to fly and he pursued that ambition with a passion.

Even after he had proven himself capable, and earned the necessary hours, because of his limp, no airline would have him. Finally, he secured a job with Southern Air Transport as a right seat driver in C-46's hauling freight to the Caribbean and Africa.

Years later, on one of these hops with Southern, he spotted the twenty-two Mitchell bombers sitting alone and looking quite deserted on the airstrip at Santiago. With a little detective work, he learned they belonged to the government of The Dominican Republic, and that they could be bought, as is, where is, for a song.

Soon thereafter, the name Rugg was all too common among certain halls in Washington, no matter which political party the people of this country thought was controlling their government. During the next thirty years, he continued his relationship with America's covert organizations.

He arranged for the equipment and vehicles to transport arms to third world nations in this hemisphere and others. He supplied the aircraft to introduce and retrieve assassins on more than one occasion. He even was given the opportunity to deliver smuggled gold from Yellowknife, NWT, past the Canadian customs, and on to Mexico. There, the proper officials would then look favorably on the selling of Mexican oil to the U.S. at a price that would cause the OPEC leaders to cringe, all taken care of from the comfort of his American offices, without ever leaving the country.

However, after Senator Al Gore and the Democratic Congress attacked Oliver North with such vigor, his sources in Washington became somewhat afraid of the wrong people finding out about a few of their business acquaintances, and Nate's income from that source began to dwindle to almost nothing.

Too, when a friend of his was killed in an airplane accident, Rugg himself began to be somewhat skeptical. Everyone assured him Harry's death had been an accident, but Nate Rugg was not so sure. He had seen other situations happen over the years, when the company had done their work so well everyone was convinced it had been an accident. Many of these times, Nate knew damn well better. By 1991, he was looking over his shoulder all too often.

Blue Rugg, on the other hand, enjoyed his discomfort. The years of their marriage had not been the rose garden she thought it would be, nor what Madison County society believed it to be.

Blue had become Mrs. Nathan Rugg because she saw he was a man of considerable wealth who seemed to be totally infatuated with her beauty and charm. She had never fooled herself into believing he was truly in love with her, any more than she was with him. It was a very comfortable relationship and each knew their limits with the other. She would be the perfect wife for him to present to his guests and business acquaintances, and she would live a life of such luxury few enjoyed, or even imagined.

It was not until shortly before the death of Nate's mother did Blue come to fully realize the true depth of his wealth. The properties that had been obtained by the family, from shortly after Mr. Lincoln's war, and over the next one hundred and thirty years, had become worth more than a hundred million dollars. Nate wanted no part in sharing any of this with his sister Ellen.

Only three days after Nate's father was paralyzed from a stroke, Ellen's husband, Bill Huntington, had been killed by a hit and run driver as he stepped from the family Cadillac on Dale Mabry Highway in Tampa.

The jolt of seeing Bill crushed before her eyes had been a traumatic shock to Ellen, and Nate immediately had her admitted to a hospital in Charlotte County. "A wonderful place where she can recover," as he referred to it. In reality, it was a hospital she would never leave, as long as he lived.

Eight years earlier, after an argument with his father over his being arrested for possession of drugs, Bill Junior disappeared. Then two years before Bill's death, their oldest son, Hugh, had lost his life while skydiving. These losses truly made Ellen Huntington unstable, and only the strong medication Nate had been able to secure had kept her from a breakdown when Hugh died. For some time, she only had her aging mother and brother to rely on, and Nate was seeing she would do that very thing.

Three months after Nate's father passed away, William Canton Huntington, Jr., was declared legally dead in the courts of Leon County.

Hester Rugg was no fool. She was not convinced Ellen needed to be so swiftly admitted to the Charlotte Institution, any more than she was convinced all of the tragedies that had suddenly plagued Ellen and her family were accidents. Regardless, her health was poor, and she also relied on Nate for her well-being.

However, it was Hester who had contacted Blue to come and see her at the family home in Madison. There, she opened up to her daughter-in-law for the first time about how the family fortune was managed and where most of it was contained, as well as some very personal family secrets.

When she first learned of the marriage, Hester did not readily accepted this girl Nate brought home as a bride, but over the years, she began to learn Blue was exactly what Nate needed. She also appreciated Blue as a woman all her own. One who would not be intimidated by the family power or fortune, a trait Hester admired.

She also, in a strange way, felt a sense of security with Blue, a feeling she perceived was slipping away between her and her son.

It was these thoughts about Ellen's state, as well as her own dependency, that brought Hester to request the rendezvous that day, a meeting with which she would always be pleased.

The grand old lady dismissed the servant and sat her daughter-in-law in one of the well-padded, white, wrought-iron chairs on the top veranda, and there they talked over a tall glass of sweet tea. "One of the South's true treasures," Hester often said of the drink.

It was there, while they watched the squirrels chase each other among the moss covered oaks down the street in The Four Freedom's Park, Hester spilled the story that would ensure Blue's future for years.

"Nate was seventeen years of age at the time. He was attending Bolles Military School in Jacksonville," she paused and took a sip from her tall glass. "He had brought a friend to our Savannah Island home for spring break, a Spanish boy of a good family, down in Venezuela.

"While there, they broke into the liquor locker and took a bottle of Scotch with them to a beach party," Hester paused again, and sighed briefly before she continued, "During this party the two boys talked a local girl into going for a ride with them. Quite quickly they had her so inebriated she gave little more resistance than saying *No*, before they _____," once again Hester paused, and took a deep breath and then said, "Well, the local deputy sheriff described it as, enjoyed the pleasures of coupling."

Blue could see in her mother-in-law's expressions, telling this, perhaps reliving it, was a great strain on her.

"Later, when Jorge began to sober up, his religious upbringing began to find its way back into his conscious mind and he felt obligated to confess his sinful deeds to his family. That would have been right, perhaps, but the foolish boy insisted he must also inform the local authorities." Again, Hester stopped and looking off into the distance she slowly shook her head. "This was something Nate simply would not stand for.

"Even though the girl had not told the Sheriff who the boys that forced themselves on her were, there was a big article in the local paper about a 15-year-old high school girl being raped at a wild party. The reporter made great inference to the fact that she had been given liquor to subdue her before the 'Fate worse than death' had been committed, as he put it."

Hester stopped again for a few seconds and Blue could see she was fighting back the beginning of tears. "Jorge would not listen to reason about his confession. He was a very religious boy, and finally in a fit of frustration, Nate shot him squarely in the forehead with an old pistol his father kept in the bedroom."

She wiped her eyes with a linen tissue before telling the remainder of her story.

"Young Nate, realizing what he had done, went straight to his father and confessed all.

"The story given to the police was the two boys were returning from a movie when they saw a man lying in the road. As soon as they stopped to check on him, two more men came from the palmettos beside the lonely stretch of road and the three men robbed the boys. When Jorge resisted, one of the robbers shot him before they fled in Nate's new Ford. Neither the car, nor the murder weapon, was ever recovered.

"The Sheriff found many holes in the story, but was never able to acquire enough evidence to make charges. The man searched for the remainder of the time he was in office for the murder weapon and the Ford, but never found either. To this day the case is open."

When Blue left her mother-in-law's home that day, she had in her possession that P-38[3] pistol and the knowledge of how the crime actually was committed. She also knew in which lake Nate's father had the car submerged, this little bit of information she kept to herself.

Unfortunately, one night after a long argument with Nate, while both she and he were too intoxicated to realize what they were saying, she revealed to her husband her security.

She went to the wall safe in her bedroom, retrieved a document and threw it in his face. "Read this, Little Man, and weep. Remember it well the next time you threaten me. There are another ten copies and all contain, in detail, the facts of the murder, as well as where the gun can be found," she screamed at him. As he read the paper, she added, "I have placed them with separate attorneys in ten different states, each with the instructions to be opened upon my death, or incarceration into some mental institution, like your sister, Ellen."

This time when he looked up at her, she had a satisfied smirk on her face as she gave him the final punch. "They are instructed to send a copy of this to both the authorities here, and in Savannah Beach, and to the news media. Also, I am enjoying great pleasure in informing you, your fingerprints are still on the Walther."

Nate went into a rage and charged her, grabbing her by the throat. For a moment, she thought he was going to kill her, but his age and her size made it easy for her to overpower him and knock him to the marble floor. "Best not to forget, I learned to shoot quite well while riding horseback with my father many years ago. You had better realize your own limitations, Little Man," she scowled, towering above him.

A week later, he approached her with a paper that would dissolve their marriage, leaving her with half a million dollars. The sum he claimed was exactly half his fortune. She laughed in his face and told him of the millions he had stashed away in various places she was aware of, and that if she found he was attempting to hide

---

3 P-38: A Semi-Automatic handgun of the Nazi reign. P for pistol and 38 for 1938.

any of it from her, she would send her evidence to the IRS as well as the Tallahassee papers.

Again, he went into a rage, but this time he kept his distance. He feared the papers as much as he did the IRS, and backed away from the fight.

Finally, a few days later, they together agreed to continue their relationship as before, only totally in separate bedrooms.

Both were relieved with the agreement.

Blue was somewhat ashamed of herself. She had not wanted their relationship to come to a point where she needed to show her ace-in-the-hole. She realized it would only be a matter of time before he figured out the only source she could have gotten this information from was his mother.

That fall, Hester was found dead one morning, still in her bed. She had overdosed on sleeping pills, which had been prescribed for her. The death was ruled accidental rather than suicide because there was no note found, and it was learned from the maid that Mrs. Rugg had drunk an unusually large glass of brandy before she retired. The police found no evidence of a struggle and the medical examiner found the brandy and narcotics in her system, as reported.

Blue never believed it for a second.

Chapter Five
Betsy's Crossroads

James Hancock grew up on The Little Withlacoochee River. His parents owned a small bar they called Betsy's Crossroads at the intersection of Corbitt Farm Trail and Jumping Gully Road, on the Georgia side of the river.

It was a little three-building enterprise that gave the locals a place to hide from those they did not want to find them. One of the buildings was a small one-room cabin tucked neatly in the grove of magnolias, which became an enticing rendezvous location for adulterous lovers.

On the southernmost portion of the thirty acres Cader Hancock owned, was a small three-bedroom frame house. It was built on stilts to protect its contents from the angry waters when the river overflowed its banks every five years or so. It was here Cader and Betsy called home and raised their three children. Cader referred to it as The River House, because he always intended to build Betsy a bigger home further up the bank, but he never did.

James had come first, followed in a couple of years by Barry, and then in another five years came a baby girl, Cindy. She was the pride and joy of her oldest brother.

Throughout her early life, Cindy always knew that James was there to protect her, and hold her, and show her more love than her father had ever been capable of. This is not to say Cader Hancock did not have strong feelings for his children, but love was an emotion he had found strange to understand. Life had been hard and he never felt the relief of knowing his obligations, which came due every month, would be taken care of unless he struggled to take care of them. This didn't leave a lot of time for showing emotions.

Cader was good with his hands, but he was the farthest thing one could imagine from a businessman. No one could call him an alcoholic, for he certainly never had the need to drink. He did, however, have the pleasure of it. Unfortunately, in the years they ran Betsy's Crossroads, he often drank most of the profits away, sitting and *'chawing the fat'* with the regular customers.

The Little Withlacoochee River
Betsy's Crossroads was to the Lower Left

Betsy was not an unattractive woman by any means. She was some fifteen years younger than Cader and many a man who had consumed too much had let her looks and friendly smile be mistaken for more than he should have.

More than once, Betsy was glad Cader was too far gone himself to notice the comments, and sometimes even bolder actions, of these drunk would-be lovers.

She knew quite well had Cader realized what was happening, something awful would have resulted. Something neither Cader nor the man would have liked seeing, once their livers had cleansed the alcohol from their heads. That is, if they were still breathing when that cleansing occurred.

Of the Hancock children, it was James who loved living so near the river the most. He spent many an hour in his little Coochee Boat[4] on the blackwater stream, relishing in the throwing of beetle spins or snagging Cooter[5] from fallen logs that spotted the edges of the river, all along its hundred-mile run. As much as he craved the pleasures of being on and about the Withlacoochee, it was diving in the river's many caverns that he loved the most.

He had an old steamer trunk nearly full of flint arrow and Cunningham points that he had scooped from the sandy bottom of this beautiful winding river.

The summer he turned fourteen, he landed a job working at the pulpwood plant up near Clyatt's Crossing and saved practically every penny he earned to buy a diving lung.

He proudly told his baby sister, "Now, I can really explore the river's hidden treasure, down there in many caverns."

The following year, he drove the ninety miles to Wakulla Springs, where he took the necessary lessons to become a certified diver. It was this that led him, years later, to join the service. His sole goal at the time was to become a Navy Seal.

---

4 Coochee Boat: Nick name for a Jon boat used on The Withlacoochee River.
5 Cooter: A stripe-necked turtle predominant in the rivers of the deep south.

Chapter Six
Cowboys

The money Blue now had in her lily-white hands offered her opportunities few people have enjoyed throughout history. At the drop of a hat, she could beckon servants for her wildest desires, or come and go to any place in the free world at her leisure. This last power had become her most used option after the final fight and ultimate agreement she and Nate had endured.

Blue Rugg was a woman who always appreciated and admired men. She had been madly in love with her father. Every ranch hand who hired out to The Cobb Cattle Company had been a friend to her. She liked to be around men. She liked the smell of them. Liked the way they walked and talked, and liked their mannerisms, when they were being polite.

On the other hand, she had no use for a wimp. There had been just such a boy in her school, Jason Fargo, who followed her around and tried to spy on her from the eighth grade throughout high school. Blue detested him and made no bones about it. Years later, when he had become the director of a local Colorado National Bank branch, she refused to enter their doors. The moment she learned of his new promotion, Blue had both her savings account, which Doggy and Dottie had started for her the month she was born, as well as her checking account, moved to another location, transferring from the branch the family had used for over thirty years.

Blue had enjoyed her first sexual experience during her senior year in high school. The boy's father worked as a hand on one of the neighboring ranches. His father and her father rode fence together many a time, back in their single days, and were fast friends. The two families often spent an off day together, riding the back hills or going up in the high country in the summers.

Doggy had Blue on a horse before she could walk, and she was an expert rider from the time she was ten. She won a barrel race at the local rodeo that same year.

She had known Keith Quincy, or Latigo, as everyone called him, for as far back as she could remember, and he had bought her a cherry coke that afternoon after her winning ride.

Eight years later when she made up her mind to have sex, she decided the first time it would be with Latigo. Not because she was madly in love with him or because she had a wild crush on him, rather because he was the boy who most represented what she thought a man should be, at least of the boys she knew at the time that were her age. The truth be told, it was Blue who seduced him, rather than the other way around.

Since that time, she had found she had a deep inner desire for sex and sexual things. Even when Willis Cunningham had turned her into a very expensive call girl, she had enjoyed the encounters, at least at first.

Now she realized the two men who had most changed her life after the death of her father, were both truly wimps. Neither Willis Cunningham nor Nathan Rugg looked anything like Jason Fargo, but when she suddenly became fully aware they both reminded her of him, she felt sick with disgust at herself.

As a result, now when she felt the need to wind her clock, she would leave town for a few days and hire her own escorts, as so many rich men had done her only a few years before. One thing she was very cautious of when she did, was to never let anyone know she was leaving, or where she was going.

Too many of Nate's acquaintances had met with accidents, especially after they had in some way angered him, and she knew of no one who had angered him more than herself. She truly had no doubts had she not let him in on her life insurance policy, she would be fertilizing some small patch of ground he owned, from not too deep a grave.

Nonetheless, life insurance or not, she wanted neither him, nor anyone else to know where and how she took care of her needs.

Blue bought a rather rusty Oldsmobile over the internet and had it delivered to a repair shop in Tallahassee, in the name of Ray Dunkin. She didn't think Salty would mind her using his name.

She had learned *Earnheart's Restorations* had the reputation for first class engine work, as well as being a top restorer of Muscle Cars from the days when Americans still had pride in their own designs and craftsmanship.

It was there she had the vehicle completely overhauled mechanically. She had Earnheart pay special attention in the balancing of the 403 engine, to which she had him add a second 4-barrel carburetor and a long duration camshaft. To handle this power, he found one of the rare 5-speed transmissions of the era, but was unsuccessful in locating a really good third member. Regardless, the Olds was a real sleeper and anyone seeing her on the street with her hood locked down would have never recognized her to be the Banshee she really was.

Blue had him totally rework the interior, removing the original upholstery and replacing it all in white glove leather. She also requested he apply dark coating to all the windows, with instructions to make them as dark as he thought she could get away with, considering Florida's law.

Before it was completed, she could have bought a new Beamer for less money, but she didn't want a new car. She wanted a car that was very reliable and also inconspicuous. This rusty and dented old girl fit just such a bill.

She also leased an apartment in *The Seminole Towers*, Tallahassee's only true high-rise. There, she could enter the parking garage without the fear of being followed by one of Nate's hired dicks; park her Eldorado, and leave in the dark-windowed 1977 Oldsmobile, without them or anyone else realizing she was gone.

1977 Oldsmobile

In the two years she had paid the rent on Suite 2404, she had never spent a night there.

New Orleans was a five hour drive to the west and Gulfport was half that distance. From Gulfport, she could hire a small charter and be in the Cayman Islands in only a few hours. She knew a native on Grand Cayman who gave the most wonderful massages, followed by hours of raw sex. In New Orleans, she had come in contact with two men in the business who likewise never seemed to quit once they saw the color of her money.

Although Blue knew between her fabulous looks, and unending supply of funds, she could have any man she ever dreamed of, she still enjoyed buying her sex. There was just something about having her own whores that seemed to justify the years she spent with Willis Cunningham.

Chapter Seven
Worm

His parents had moved to St. Augustine Beach from Rome, New York when he was only a small child. His sister, Charlotte, was born in the Ancient City when he was seven. Unfortunately, she had been accidentally killed in a fall ten years later, while on a school day-trip to the Jacksonville Zoo. Reata Estes never seemed to get over her daughter's untimely death, and her son suffered for her weakness.

Arthur Estes was embarrassed about Willard's friends calling him Worm, but it was a name that just stuck. Almost everyone knew him by that and nothing else, so his father did not openly object.

As soon as Willard turned fourteen, Arthur bought him a moped to ride to and from school. He thought that if Willard had his own means of transportation, his son's status would rise a little among the other boys and girls in school. Unluckily, this failed, as had everything he did for Willard.

When the war in Vietnam took his son away, Arthur was almost relieved in that he did not have to hear someone referring to his son as Worm every day. As fate often strums a strange tune, it was there in the rice paddies and the mud, the hills and the blood, Willard found two things that truly gave him pleasure - drugs and the taking of a life.

At twenty years of age, he stood five foot and one inch and barely tipped the scales at one hundred pounds. Everyone kidded him about his size and when a skinny Vietnamese whore giggled and pointed at his four inch, fully erect cock, he killed his first human.

Watching the warm blood flow from the slice in her neck gave him an orgasm and in the months to come, no one again snickered or seriously kidded him, at least to his face.

One of his favorite adventures was the tunnels that laced the jungles of the country. Anytime a soldier found a new entrance, Corporal Willard Estes would volunteer to inspect it; sometimes staying for hours waiting in the darkness until a VC of some importance would venture by his stealth location.

When his year was over and he returned to Florida, he felt lost. Suddenly, he was back to being Worm, the little guy on the moped, rather than The Tunnel Worm, killer of a hundred Viet Cong.

One of Walter Cronkite's reports from Viet Nam contained a short clip about The Tunnel Worm, Killer of a Hundred Viet Cong. The broadcast did not identify this particular American soldier, for fear a contract would be placed on him by the Communist Regime, nor was his face shown. However, millions who watched CBS that evening viewed a small GI slipping into the camouflaged entrance of one of the many tunnels. Cronkite did say this man had already been credited with over one hundred kills, many of whom were officers of the Viet Cong and the Viet Minh military.

Worm's stay at home was short; in less than three months, he had requested a second tour in Nam, and was soon once again increasing his notches, and reputation, as a man not to be crossed.

It was in January of 1970 as his company was being transported north to retake a hill that had been taken and then abandoned only two days before, that the Hughy he was riding in received a strong burst of heavy machinegun fire. The pilot was hit in the left ankle with a 50-caliber slug and they almost went down in the VC infested jungle. Somehow, that incredible pilot kept the chopper in the air until they reached friendly territory and crashlanded in a cleared field, before passing out from the loss of blood. It was this landing that ended Willard Estes' military career. Willard spent two months in the hospital in traction, and then came a medical discharge.

"Bim-Bam, thank you ma'am, the Army is through with you," he would say many times thereafter.

While recovering in a hospital in the Philippines, Worm met Vinnie Spindetto, a nurse from Chicago. It was Vinnie who would introduce him into an avenue where his special talents and needs, would both be met.

Vinnie Spindetto's uncle was connected with a family who often needed someone with Worm's talents, and since his own discharge came within a week of Worm's medical discharge, the two men soon found themselves living in a small apartment whose only window gave one the spectacular view of Chicago's I-90 expressway.

Only the never-ending burning of the weed gave any relief to the disabling shots of pain, which came without warning, to Worm's back. Although only lasting a few seconds and then disappearing as suddenly and mysteriously as they came, for that moment they were disabling. The other relief, brought about by always being high was a deaf ear to the never-ending roar of traffic outside their window.

They had been there nearly three weeks and were beginning to run dreadfully low on money when a call came from Vinnie's uncle. Worm was needed for a special job.

He never saw Vinnie's uncle. However, he did meet one of his Lieutenants and then only the one time. After the first job, every few months, a small envelope would arrive with a key to a safe-deposit box. Worm knew where this box was located. In the box would be a larger envelope containing the information on the mark. A week after confirmation was announced in the paper, another envelope with a key would arrive, and in the safe-deposit box this time would be between one and ten thousand dollars, depending on the importance of the target, or in some cases, the difficulty in carrying out the task.

Worm and Vinnie liked the arrangement. They could go and come as they pleased and the job gave them opportunities to travel to places they otherwise would have never thought of going. Soon, they moved to a much better apartment, with a great view of Lake Michigan.

Vinnie worked part time with a private nursing firm, and he talked his boss into putting Willard Estes down also as an employee, even though Worm never crossed his doors or ever met him. For a hundred dollars' worth of coke a month, Worm had a job, on paper, and W2 forms to send in with his income tax forms every year. This kept the IRS and other such worthless organizations off his back. He knew no one would believe he was living the life style he did on the disability check the government sent him. This so-called job was a good cover, and he was proud he had thought it up.

Chapter Eight
BB 60

Wall had taken Friday off and since Sunday was Independence Day, and the observed holiday was Monday, he had a four-day weekend, just enough time to go to Biloxi. Not that he was that much of a gambler, but it seemed to be the passion of several others at the Co-Op, and one of those was Dixie Marie Ragsdale, a bookkeeper in whom he had taken a keen interest.

Dixie Marie was perhaps 25 with a deep southern accent. He was sure her dishwater hair had to be natural. *'No one would have picked that color from a box when there were so many prettier shades of blonde.'* Nonetheless, she had a nice smile, and a better than nice figure, and most of all, he suspected she like him as much as he did her.

She married one of the local deputies the week she graduated from Florida State. However, their two-year marriage had been a rocky one to say the least. Her divorce was to be final the second week in July and she told Wall, "This Fourth of July weekend is an early celebration present to myself."

She encouraged him to come to Biloxi and hinted she would like to celebrate the holiday with him.

He liked the idea himself. However, sometime shortly after midnight there had been an accident on SR 53 just past the Cherry Lake crossroads. A new yellow Mustang had wrapped itself around one of the power poles, snapping it in the process, and Wall was called out.

It was well past nine in the morning when he finally got the truck back to the yard, and reminded Ash he had taken the day off. She gave him one of her knowing smiles and suddenly he realized why it had been him they called.

All of the others who were going had been Mississippi-bound for two hours before he got back to his house to clean up. It had been a tough pill to swallow when he called Dixie Marie to explain why he would be late. He was hoping she would say she would wait and ride with him, but when she asked, "Wall, have you fixed your air-conditioner, yet?" He had to admit that he had not. She immediately replied, "Well, thanks anyway, Wall, but I'll go on with Betty and Hugh. You can catch up in Biloxi."

He was two hours behind the others and in his old Ramcharger, which, after the odometer had turned 300,000, he promised he would not drive more than 55 miles per hour. *If she will just keep on keeping on, until I have enough money to put a new engine in my 'Vette.* Now, every second, his friends were increasing their head-start and distance on him.

None of this would have bothered him in the least, had it not been for the thoughts of spending the weekend with his face buried between Dixie Marie's huge boobs. He knew quite well there were others who would be there with the same idea, and all too often the early bird gets more than a worm.

The four o'clock traffic was just building for the holiday weekend when he reached Pensacola, and soon he was falling even farther behind his buddies. Finally, he was able to break free of the traffic near the milepost 8 sign and was just taking a deep breath when he saw the faded gold Oldsmobile pass him at a high rate of speed and he thought, *'That guy will be lucky if he gets to the state line without a Trooper pulling him over. He must be doing over a hundred.'*

The car was perhaps a quarter of a mile ahead when he saw the telltale smoke erupt from the left rear of the Olds and a second or two later, pieces of black rubber began to fly skyward. Wall tensed up, looking hard at the old car as it swerved back and forth from one side of the roadway to the other. Finally, its driver was able to get it under control and off onto the right berm.

"Boy, you are a lucky fellow," Wall said aloud, as he approached the older car. *'I should stop and help, but I'm already too far behind the others, and besides, that guy shouldn't have been going so damn fast.'*

As Wall was approaching the stopped vehicle, he changed lanes quickly when he saw the door suddenly fling open. He cursed sharply at the driver. However, when he saw the two very long legs swing out, his attention and attitude suddenly took on a different view of the situation.

She stood at the very moment he passed, and he immediately felt a sizable lump swell in his chest.

"Son of a gun, that's Mrs. Rugg," he realized and then added the thought, *'What is she doing in that old piece of junk?'* His foot was hard on the brake pedal at the same time he was creating the thought, and he soon was stopped and backing along the berm towards the rusty Oldsmobile.

When he got out, she was at the rear of her car bending over looking at what was left of the destroyed Goodyear Blue Streak.

He tried to look at the damage, but for some reason he simply could not take his eyes off her. She was not fabulously dressed. On the contrary, she was wearing a pair of short-shorts, not the kind where one's cheeks would hang out, but still short-shorts and a pullover button down collared shirt. Sitting on the top of that fiery red hair was a sailor's cap, the kind the boys wore back in the big war, as his father referred to World War II. Her heels were tall and thick-soled, which he didn't understand at all, considering she had to be over six-foot in her bare feet, and were as white as the rest of her outfit. In fact, the only color not white was the red polish on her toenails and the jeweled bobby-pins that secured the cap to her hair.

Her attire was truly not overly extravagant, still every inch of it oozed class. No, that is a bad statement. She oozed class, first class, and it made him feel a little weak ingesting her beauty.

She was cursing, not screaming or violently yelling, but still cursing the car, or her mechanic, or perhaps her bad luck, he was not sure which.

He thought it was about time to announce himself, for he realized she did not know he was standing there, "Mrs. Rugg."

Suddenly she looked up and saw him. For a moment, she didn't recognize him, then a slight smile broke the frown and she answered as she rose from the squatting position she had been in when he approached her. "The Tree Man."

He was glad she remembered him, although he would have preferred she had remembered his name. *'After all she had called and asked for my name.'*

"I am really sorry about that," he replied, which was not entirely true. He was sorry about being caught spying on her, but he was not in the least sorry for the view that the spying had provided, and the images now imbedded in his memory.

"Now, let us see what it will take to get you back on the road again," he said tearing his eyes from her, after finishing his statement. It was the gentlemanly thing to do, and although Wall Roberts possessed many faults, failure to be a gentleman was not among them.

When he forced his attention to the mangled tire, he squatted as she had done and it was only then he realized the problem might not have been Goodyear's responsibility after all. The tire was truly a shattered mess of processed rubber and steel wire, but it still somewhat surrounded the wheel, a wheel that was now slanted at a defiant forty degree angle from the fender.

Wall blew air between his lips, not so as to make a whistle, rather as an unconscious expression of concern.

"It's bad. I can see that," she said.

"Yes Ma'am. I do believe you have broken an axle shaft, and that is what caused the wheel to separate, and in turn, resulted in the blowout," he replied looking back up at her. *'God, she is a beautiful thing.'*

"And I paid plenty to have a reliable car. That damn Mike Earnheart will hear about this," she spat.

"I doubt he could have foreseen this," Wall replied in defense of the mechanic. "Looks to me to be a flaw in the metal, or perhaps a heavy foot." He let the final statement trail off without a great deal of inference.

"And just what is that supposed to mean?" she spat back at him.

"Well, you were going like a bat out of hell when you passed me," he replied, standing again. "I thought sure you were going to roll this thing before you got her stopped."

"The manner in which I drive is of no concern to a Peeping Tom!"

Wall took the dig and caught his breath before replying, "All right. I'm a Peeping Tom. You are a beautiful woman who was sunning herself nude and I looked you over. You are not the only beautiful naked woman I've seen, and certainly not the first, but that has nothing to do with this. Let's just stop this spatting at one another and see what we can do about getting you on the road again."

At that very moment a Peterbilt, pulling a long reefer, passed and blew his air horns at the beautiful woman standing there, and the sudden blast broke the mood each had found themselves in.

"What do you suggest?" she asked in a different voice.

"Well," he replied with a long sigh, "first I think we need to get off the side of Interstate 10, and somewhere cooler. There we could make some phone calls."

"I have a car phone," she said, nodding to the thin black antenna secured to the rear window.

Sliding his straw hat back on his head, he said as he used his forearm to wipe the sweat beads from his brow, "That will take care of the phone calls, but not this heat."

"You are right. Give me just a minute to call Earnheart's and I will be ready."

He started to suggest she just use a local wrecker. After all, Earnheart was some two hundred miles away, but decided against suggesting anything to her without first getting a request for his knowledge.

While she was talking on the phone, she called out to him, "Do you know where we are?"

"Yeah, I would say some five maybe six miles east of the Alabama line."

A moment or two later she stood and he overheard her say, "When you have it properly repaired, deliver it to the Seminole Towers' garage. The remote to open the gates will be in the glove box, the space is 2404. Be sure to lock it up. I have a spare set of keys."

When finished, she pitched the phone back in the front seat, and pushed the button that released the trunk lid. "Will you get those two bags for me?" she asked, walking back to where he still stood at the rear of the car.

He placed her bags on the backseat of his truck and then stepped back, extending his arm as a gesture for her to occupy the front bucket.

He had cleaned the interior before he left that morning, but since the air-conditioner was not working, he had the windows down and a fine layer of dust had settled on everything. He had not noticed the fine dust, but she did. Blue wondered if the dust would stain her shorts when she got out of the Ramcharger.

He immediately explained about the air-conditioner, or rather the lack of one, but she only nodded in reply. However, when they entered Alabama and neither had spoken a word since that explanation, finally, as only a silence breaker he said, "Can I ask you something?"

"Certainly."

"Why were you driving that old piece of junk?"

"Piece of junk! I'll have you know I have nearly thirty thousand dollars in Goldie." He raised his eyebrows and opened his eyes wide before nodding his head to her statement.

"And besides, this is certainly not the newest vehicle on the highway either," she shot back, looking around at the interior of the twenty-two year old Ramcharger.

He started to defend his faithful truck, but stopped and looked about as she had. *'She's right,'* he thought. *'This is not the newest thing on the road.'*

"Yes, you are right, Mrs. Rugg, Ole Green is not the newest thing on the road, but my Dad bought her when she was new, and she's been in the family ever since. She still gets me most places I need to go." Then as if he felt the need to add a little information about his financial status he said, "I also have a 1963 Split Window Corvette. He bought it new too, and a '43 Jeep that belonged to him."

"You like things that are old, don't you?" she replied, although this time her statement was not harsh, almost friendly.

"I like things that have class and this, 1974 model Ramcharger is the only year the top comes off to make a full convertible, without window frames, and '63 was the only year Corvette's had a split-window coupe. Both classy."

"Why then did you not drive the Corvette? I assume it has an air-conditioner that works," she said, feeling a bead of sweat run down into the valley between her breasts.

"No, Ma'am. He bought her as a street rod, no air-conditioner at all. She has a 340-horse 327, and is a real screamer, too."

"Well?" she replied as if to say, why are you not driving the 'Vette.

"I blew the engine a couple of years back and haven't gotten the money to have it overhauled yet," he replied, twisting his head slightly, not really sure why he needed to explain his personal misfortunes to her.

"Are you good at blowing engines?" she asked teasingly.

He was aware what she was referring to, but he did not go there, instead he simply said, "No, it was my first, and I made a real mess of it."

"Well, when you get your 'Vette repaired and I get Goldie on the road again, we'll have to try them out someday. Then we'll see which of us is the real screamer," she added, this time in a friendly challenge.

"Maybe we will," he agreed, and smiled at her. "But don't hold your breath, 'cause it will be quite a spell before I get the money to have that engine overhauled."

She looked over at him. It was the first time she really had ever looked at him, not that she had not appreciated his good looks and fine build the first time they spoke. Had she not, she never would have called in about him, but even then, she had not really looked at him, not the person, only the body.

'He is tall and well built, perhaps not quite as tall as me, but close.'

She liked the black curly hair protruding from his shirt where the top two buttons were not clasped. She also liked his tight jeans that failed to hide the muscular thighs inside them, and she especially liked the fact he was in pointed boots. *'Damn! He reminds me of the cowboys back home.'*

"Tell me, Tree Climber, what is your name?"

"Wallace Roberts," he said, looking over at her face, "but my friends call me Wall."

"Well, Wall, can we be friends?"

"I would like that very much," he replied, nodding his head several times, ever so slightly.

"Alright, Friend Wall, my friends call me Blue."

This time when he looked at her, she knew his voice was sincere when he said, "Hello, Blue."

From then on, until they were crossing the long bridge into Mobile, they talked friendly, and freely, to one another. He told her of his plans to meet his co-workers in Biloxi, and his hopes for a fun weekend with Dixie Marie. Not as brag, rather as a portion of the conversation a couple of friends were having. However, when he looked to his left and saw the big Battle Wagon berthed in all her grandeur at the dock nearby, he had to make mention of her. "You see that old gray boat over there?" he pointed to the ship.

"Yes."

"That's BB 60, the USS Alabama. My grandfather was a machinist mate on her during the big war.

BB 60

He walked onto Japanese soil from her decks in 1945, just after the surrender. I distinctly remember him telling me all about it and how proud he was when he and my father brought me over here to tour her, back when I was maybe ten or so." Wall thought for a few seconds before adding, "I have always wanted to do it again, but never seemed to find the time."

Blue could tell the boat had a deep place in his heart and she suddenly also felt something for the old battleship. "You mean, 'make' the time."

"Yeah, I guess it's all a matter of priorities."

"Tell me, Mr. Roberts, which has the greater priority to you, jumping that blonde's bones or your grandfather's ship?"

He looked strongly at her, questioning her meaning.

"Well, are we going to make the time to walk around that old bucket of bolts or not?" she asked.

He began to nod his head, this time more forcefully than before. "If you are game, Mrs. Rugg, we'll make the time."

"I'm game, Mr. Roberts," she replied, feeling totally satisfied with her suggestion.

The tour of the big ship took over two hours and then they entered the USS Drum, a WW II fleet submarine also berthed there.

Afterward they walked among the many airplanes on display in the little park.

Display of The USS Drum

The temperature was hovering somewhere over 90, but for some reason, neither complained about the heat. It was as if they just didn't want the little side trip to end.

Finally she said, "Back home, on the Fourth of July, we always would go up in the mountains, where it was cool, and have a family picnic. It was just wonderful. Now each year, when The Fourth comes around, I wish I had planned a trip back there, just for that reason."

"It's all a matter of priorities, I guess," he said back, mocking her for her earlier statements about his decisions.

She slapped his arm hard with the palm of her hand and then as if it was the most natural thing, she ran her arm between his arm and his large chest, before pulling herself close to him. It was in this same coupling they returned to his old green truck.

"You know, Mrs. Rugg, if I had the time and a new airplane, I would take you back to your mountains for your picnic."

She stopped there beside the Ramcharger and leaned back against it. They both realized something had happened to them during the last three hours, although neither wanted to admit it. Finally, she reached out, placed her palm around the back of his neck, and pulled him in to her. They locked lips like long-lost lovers. When they finally parted due to the need for air, she asked, "Is it really that important for you to bang that blonde tonight, or would a redhead do?"

"A redhead would be much better, if I knew where I could find one," he shot back, not entirely believing what he had just heard.

"Do you think they have a hotel in Mobile with a nice, cool air-conditioned room, and a king size bed?"

"I bet you they do," he replied, as he leaned forward to kiss her again. This time when they parted, she said, "Let's see if we can find that room."

That night she called for room service to bring up two New York strips, both cooked medium rare. This both surprised and pleased him. He had always found women wanted their steaks overcooked, a mortal sin to his way of thinking.

He was also surprised when she made no effort to get up from the bed and dress when the boy brought in the food, not that she was not covered by the sheet, but still there was something about her casual attitude in front of a stranger that surprised him, yet at the same time excited him as well.

He slipped on his jeans when the bell rang and tipped from his own money, although she had already checked in and paid for the room when he arrived from parking the truck.

The minute they finished eating, she went to the bathroom and soon he heard the shower running. A few minutes later, he heard her call to him, "Wall, come here."

"What?"

"Come here, I want to know something."

When he did, she pulled back the shower curtain, revealing her nakedness in all its splendor. "Is this the way you remember my wet body?" she ask lustfully. "I was wet the first time you saw me."

Immediately, he felt his manhood spring to life for the third time this day, and he dropped his jeans and stepped into the steamy shower, pushing her back against the tile wall. She instantly jumped up and locked her long legs around his hips and he entered her as if by design. This time, their sex was fast and furious, and she bit him hard on his left upper breast muscle, just before she screamed so loud he was afraid someone might call the police.

Later, while he slumbered, he thought he heard her talking to someone, but it might have been a dream. He was not sure all of this was not a dream.

When he awoke, she was again in the shower but he did not go in. Instead, he made a pot of bad coffee from the small drip-maker attached to the wall and was just finishing his cup when she walked out of the bathroom. This time she was dressed in a white jumpsuit, which contrasted with her red hair beautifully as it flowed over her shoulders.

"Good morning," she said joyfully.

"Good morning, pretty lady," he replied.

"Get dressed quickly. We need to be at the airport by ten."

"Airport?" he questioned somewhat disappointed, realizing this meant the past night was all of this weekend he would be spending with her. Even though it was obvious he was not going to get to enjoy sex with her again, he simply did not want their togetherness to end so soon.

"Yes. I've decided to go back to Colorado for the remainder of the weekend. As you said, it is all a matter of making the time; of priorities."

"Yes. I did say that," he agreed, remembering he had realized Dixie Marie was not as high on his priorities as BB-60. It was then he also realized he was not as high on her priority list as the mountains.

When they arrived at the airport, he turned towards the terminal, but she stopped him and instructed, "Go over there, to the General Aviation building."

He did so, and parked his truck. Then after opening her door for her, he removed her bags and followed her into the office.

"Yes, Mrs. Dunkin. The plane is all ready for you to board," the man behind the counter was saying as Wall approached.

"Good. I'm ready. I also want it understood I will need to return on Monday, without fail."

"Oh, yes Ma'am, without fail," the balding man assured her.

She then turned to Wall and asked, "Did you lock your truck?"

"No," he replied. "It'll just heat up."

"I think you should lock it. Mr. Wilkerson said there have been things stolen around here lately, and I saw that pistol in your glove compartment."

"Oh, yes, all vehicles must be locked at all times here on airport property, especially if they contain a gun," the man behind the counter agreed.

"Alright, I'll just be a minute," Wall said, turning and heading for the glass door. He felt this was completely unnecessary, it would only be a few minutes while she departed, and that would be just long enough for the temperature to rise another ten degrees in the closed-up truck.

When he returned, he saw her standing at the bottom of the extended steps of the Lear, waiting for him. "Come on," she beckoned.

He rushed over and stood there looking at her strongly. *'Damn, I hate for her to go,'* he thought, and then he said it. "Damn, I hate for you to go."

She looked at him before chuckling softly, "Come on, help me get seated," she said back, and immediately started up the steps before he had time to make a reply.

Reluctantly he climbed in behind her and looked about. There were two men in the forward cockpit, but no others on board. *'Damn, she has rented this whole airplane for herself,* he thought, shaking his head slowly.

As soon as she was seated, he looked at her and intended to say something clever, but just couldn't find the words. At that moment, the pilot looked back and seeing she was seated started the engines.

He stood there a few more moments, then shaking his head he leaned over and kissed her, and spoke softly, "I hope you have a wonderful picnic, Blue. You certainly have given me one."

"You silly boy, our picnic has just begun. Now sit down and buckle up."

"What?" he replied looking questioningly at her. It was at that moment he felt the plane begin to move, which caused him to grab hold of the seat back.

"You don't think I'm going to let this weekend end so soon do you?" she said, and then added, "You best get seated and buckled up for takeoff," nodding to the soft tan leather of the lounge beside her.

Shortly after liftoff, she unbuckled her seat belt and picked up the phone. "This is Mrs. Dunkin. Will you ring me when we reach five thousand two hundred and eighty feet?"

Frank Alvarez, sitting in the left seat, assured her he would do so, and gave a knowing smile to the lanky co-pilot as he motioned for his friend to close the door between the cockpit and the cabin of the jet.

Short minutes later, he switched to the intercom and pressed the push to talk switch.

"Yes?' came the soft voice,

"Mrs. Dunkin, we have just passed 5280, climbing to thirty-one thousand."

"Thank you," came the reply and then, "We would like not to be disturbed for a while."

"Yes, Ma'am," Frank assured her, and then he switched off the intercom and switched on the hidden camera that covered the cabin area.

"We are going to have some fine movies to watch tonight, Ken," he said, and smiled to his co-pilot.

"Do you know what the Mile High Club is?" Blue asked Wall.

"Mile High Club? No, I don't guess I do," he admitted.

"Well you are about to join it," she said, standing and slowing removing her jump suit, revealing that the only thing she wore under it, was a little bit of perfume.

Just short of two hours later, the intercom rang and she picked up the phone, "Yes."

"Mrs. Dunkin, we'll be landing at Jefferson County in about twenty minutes."

"Thank you, Frank. Will you call and reserve me a car with Hertz. I prefer a Jeep Cherokee, if one is available," she replied. After replacing the receiver, she began slipping on her jump suit again. "You had better get dressed, we will be landing soon."

"We're already in Colorado?" he questioned.

"We are," she said, not looking at him but with a smile just the same.

Moments after Frank switched off the camera, he called Denver approach for clearance to Jeff Co.

He had flown Mrs. Dunkin several trips in the past, although it had always been out of Gulfport, and always to Grand Cayman Island. This was the first time she had asked to be picked up at Mobile, and the first time she had a passenger along.

The camera had not been installed for her benefit, rather by the DEA, who also leased this jet from time to time, making it available to undercover agents posing as wealthy drug dealers in order to gather evidence on unsuspecting importers.

He considered it his good luck to be the only one checked out as the left seat driver in the company jets. This morning, as soon as he learned who was requesting a jet, he made sure old N24LJ was serviced and ready, including a fresh tape in the recorder, just in case. It had been a great move on his part, for that night he and Ken enjoyed watching some of the wildest sex scenes they had ever witnessed from non-professionals, including the one in which three oil company men and four of their secretaries had played naked all the way to Paris.

Just after touchdown, he called her once more. "Your Grand Cherokee will be waiting for you, Mrs. Dunkin."

Wall noticed she handed the pilot a fat envelope as she stepped onto the asphalt, in front of the big hanger. "Frank, I will expect you to be ready for a 7:00 PM departure Monday night."

"Yes Ma'am, you can count on us being here."

On Thursday, July 15, when Wall got off from work, he walked out to the parking lot only to find his truck missing. He looked all around where he had left it, and was just headed back inside to call the sheriff's office to report it stolen, when he suddenly spotted it at the opposite end of the parking lot from where he had left it that morning. Very confused, he walked to where it now sat and looked it over from bumper to bumper. *'Nothing appears wrong, but I am positive I left it on the west end. I always park there,'* he thought. *'There the shade from the tall pines keeps the afternoon sun off it, and here it is in the last space on the east end.'*

He just shook his head before unlocking the door and looking quickly in the glove box for his pistol. It was there, but something else was there also. He lifted the old Colt from the box and looked at what was taped to the grip. A small jeweled pin. This was even more confusing, until he held it close and read the tiny letters across the bottom of the pin:

MILE HIGH CLUB MEMBER

"Well, I'll be," he said aloud.

His next surprise came shortly after he started the old 440, and cool air came from the dash vents. This time when he spoke, he said, "Well, I'll be a son-of-a-bitch."

He had made no attempt to contact her after they departed in Mobile on their return trip. He drove home and she flew on to Tallahassee in the Lear. The last thing she said to him was, "I'm glad we are friends Wall Roberts, and I have not enjoyed a Fourth of July weekend more since I was a child with my father and mother."

He wanted to say something, anything that would stop their parting, but as he started to speak, she placed her finger softly against his lips and added, "I'll get in touch with you, when I can." Then she kissed him lightly on his lips, and turned and walked back up the steps of the plane.

He watched the blinking lights until they could no longer be seen, and only then, he walked over to Ole Green and cranked her up for the long drive home.

Wall realized she was already in Tallahassee, or close to it, when he looked over at The USS Alabama while crossing the bridge

The Old Depot in Hanson

eastbound, and taking a deep breath, he said softly, "Well, ol' girl, you served Grandpa well. I only hope you did the same for me."

Wall lived in an old house that had once been the railroad depot in Hanson before the line had closed down and the tracks removed. At one time, the structure had been condemned, but some years back, one of the Ashley boys bought the property and had the old habitus partially restored. Restored is not a correct description of the work that was done. Better said, young Ashley had rescued it and put enough money into the hundred-year-old building to keep it sound. He had converted part of the ground floor into a good size apartment. On the backside, there was a large door that allowed much of the non-living area to be used as a garage. It was in there Wall kept his Jeep and 'Vette.

On Monday, August 2, he returned home to find a large wooden crate at the rear of his place, blocking the garage door.

Wall had no idea what it contained or where it had come from. He walked over to the house in the rear, where the Johnsons lived. Mrs. Johnson was near ninety and spent most of her awakened hours in the living room glued to the Western Channel on her TV. She also was quite a snoop, and with her 8X Tasco binoculars ever present, little came or went in Hanson that she didn't know about.

"All I can tell you, Wall, is a good size truck came up and dropped off the crate, right where you see it."

"Do you know the man who drove it?"

"No. Never seen him 'afore, but I can tell you, he ain't from around here."

"How is that?"

"Cursed like a drunken sailor when he bumped his knee on that truck. None of our home boys would have done that, in front of me."

'I wouldn't be so sure about that,' Wall thought, but said nothing.

"It were a big truck, though, had a little tractor on the back. It wus what he used to unload your crate with."

"I just don't understand why it was left there," he said, shaking his head, and looking back at the rear of his place.

"You mean you didn't order nothing?"

"No. It must be he delivered it to the wrong address. I'll go back and see if I can find something on it that will locate the owner."

"Naw, Sur, it is yourn' alright. He come over here and asked me where you lived."

This time Wall really frowned in total confusion. "I just don't understand it."

After walking back, he got a crow bar from his tools, and pried off the top. Then with an astonished expression, he gazed upon a new, small block Chevy engine. There was a Crane Cam business card attached to the intake and on its back he read,

> *340 horse 327 Corvette,*
> *balanced and blueprinted.*
> *Tom P.*

Thomas J. Petitpren
Emissions and Fuel Economy Testing
Crane Emissions Laboratory

530 Fentress Boulevard
Daytona Beach, Florida 32114
Phone: 904-252-1151, extension 269
Fax: 904-258-6167

Also stuck in the carburetor venturi was another envelope with his name on it. Upon opening it he read,

> *"Mobile, Labor Day Weekend. Same Hotel. Same Room.*
> *Hope you can get that bucket of bolts running by then,*
> *Goldie is ready to take you on.*
> *If not, drive Ol' Green, you'll be glad you did."*

It was not signed, but it didn't need to be. The next morning he approached Mr. Miller and asked for Friday the third of September off. When Miller started stammering around, he said, "Look, my Grandpa was aboard the USS Alabama during the war, and he and The Alabama will be in Mobile that weekend. I have to go; it might be the last time I get to see him."

Miller reluctantly agreed and gave him the extra day off. On his way out of the office, Wall said a little silent prayer, asking for forgiveness, for his lie about his dead Grandfather.

Chapter Nine
The Left Seat

Francis Joseph Alvarez had fallen in love with airplanes, and everything aviation, at the age of five when his grandfather had taken him on his first adventure into the skies. It had been quite an adventure for Jose Alvarez also; not his first ride, but it was his first ride as a refugee. What little Francis did not know when they boarded the silver Lockheed 12 on that cloudy morning in late April of 1960, was that they would not land again in their home country.

Doctor Jose Alvarez was one of the most well respected surgeons in Pinar Del Rio and had accumulated quite a fortune during his many years of practice. Unfortunately, in 1958 one of Fulgencio Batista's children had developed a severe stomachache while visiting the tobacco capital of Cuba. It was Dr. Alvarez' misfortune to be the surgeon who removed the infected appendix. Now some two years later, Alvarez' friends informed him of more than one of Castro's new Secret Police Force asking about him, and questioning his relationship with Batista.

It was true; after Dr. Alvarez had saved the child's life, Batista summoned him to Havana to receive an award from the President himself. However, other than that, Jose Alvarez had no contact with any of the government officials. However, times were changing fast, and the wise doctor had seen the writing on the wall. This morning, he would abandon all his riches, all his fame, and take his grandson to America.

His only true connection in his newly adopted country was a cousin, who worked in a large cigar factory in Ybor City. It was there Doctor Jose Alvarez learned to be a common laborer. It was also there that young Francis learned to speak English without the slightest accent. He excelled in his academics to become the valedictorian of the graduating class of 1971 at Tampa Bay High.

Long before he entered the United States Naval Aviation Training at Pensacola, Frank had become a commercial pilot and instructor at old man Vandenberg's little strip in east Hillsborough County.

In early 1990, Lt. Alvarez found himself stationed at the United States' base at Guantanamo on Cuba's southeastern most point, flying front seat in Tomcats. Deep inside his heart and mind, he wanted to even the score, just a little, for the loss the communist leader had caused his family. On more than one occasion, he slipped dangerously close to the opposite end of the long island, from where he had departed so many years before. It was on just such an adventure that the Cuban government dispatched two Mig-21s to intercept the American fighters.

The next morning the Cuban News made all sorts of charges and challenges about Alvarez downing one of the Migs. Of course, the anti-Bush media in Europe, as well as in America, created a national scandal over the accusation by Castro that the American planes had violated his airspace, and thereby committed an act of war by shooting down one of his defending fighters.

The facts that the Mig fired first and its debris was located 15 nautical miles from the shore, more than three nautical miles in international waters, made little difference to the media. This information never appeared in any headline, anywhere in the world.

Still Alvarez, being a natural born Cuban, had caused an international scandal placing the Navy in a bad position, politically. When promotions came around the next year, Alvarez was passed over, and feeling unjustly condemned, the young officer resigned his commission and took a job flying charter jets for *Mississippi Aviation* in Meridian.

It was at *MA* he met Ken Martinelli, a lanky aspiring professional airline pilot, who was trying to build enough stovepipe[7] time to land a job with a major carrier.

Ken, unlike his left seat, was young and undisciplined, and Frank had a hard time keeping the lad in line, especially around the ladies who often were passengers on the chartered flights.

He also began to notice Ken seemed to have an unusually high number of head colds and other nasal problems, a sign that soon concerned Frank.

Unfortunately, Frank owed his right seat, not so much to Ken himself _____, but rather, to Ken's uncle, who had been Alvarez' wingman that day off Cuba's southwestern coast. It had been his testimony that neither he, nor Alvarez had entered Cuban airspace on the morning in question, which saved Alvarez' bacon. Now, when Frank would really like to divorce himself from Ken Martinelli, and since he really could not do this without giving a justifiable reason, he felt obligated not to give that reason. So he bit his lip, gritted his teeth, and kept his mouth shut, but not his eyes.

Ken, on the other hand, had no feelings of obligation to anyone, but he did sense that he had some unknown power over his captain, and he enjoyed that feeling.

When the state legislators approved casino gambling, *Mississippi Aviation* bought out one of the FBO's[8] at Gulfport/Biloxi International, and set up a sub base there. They soon had a deal with connecting FBO's in Mobile, Miami, Orlando, and Tampa to run weekend round trips to the gambling capitals of the south. Most of the aircraft used were Piper Chieftains, which the company also used to make regular runs to GBI[9], Marsh Harbor, and Grand Cayman Island. However, *MS* also owned two jets for the affluent, a Cessna Citation IV and the Lear 24.

Only the owner of the company and Frank Alvarez were qualified to fly left seat in the two jets. However, in early February 1995, Frank had come down with a severe intestinal virus and was

---

7 Stovepipe: Slang for Jets.
8 FBO: Acronym for Fixed Base Operator, or airport service station.
9 GBI: Grand Bahama Island.

temporarily grounded by the company's flight physician. During this time, Greg Winn was deep in negotiations on renewing his contracts with the FAA on these very routes and could not be there to fly. It was at this time he approved Ken Martinelli to be checked out as a command pilot in the Lear. His intention was for it to be a backup position and no more, because he did not personally like the young aviator. In fact, he had almost dismissed him after witnessing a very hard landing Martinelli made in one of the Chieftains, but Alvarez talked him out of it.

Ken would never deny he had a strong drive for the ladies, but his true addictions were cocaine and gambling, both of which he refused to admit to anyone, especially to himself. This combination would one day be the infection that would bring much sorrow to a great many people, not the least of whom was Ray Swift.

Ray had been an observation pilot in the brown shoe days, before our congress finally admitted we needed an Air Force instead of just an air branch of the Army. He trained in L-4's in Texas and Tennessee and spent a year in Europe flying his beloved Cub until a German 8mm spitzer entered his left leg, just above the knee, and exited the little craft through the Plexiglas windscreen.

This round, Ray always claimed to have come from a machine gun, ended his flying career with the army, but not with his life. Immediately upon mustering out, he applied for and was granted, his civilian private license. This was soon followed by a commercial license with an instrument rating, as well as an instructor's ticket.

Ray knew his severe limp would keep him from any good job with one of the major airlines, especially with so many of the four-engine boys coming home after the war, but he was infected with the flying bug and for the remainder of his life, he made his living near the smell of red gas[10] and butyrate dope. He worked for years as a crop duster in North Florida and South Georgia, and finally in 1983, he bought 50 acres from a retiring farmer. There, he laid out his own little piece of heaven he called *Swift Field*.

---

10 Red Gas: 80 Octane Aviation fuel.

It was the same year Nate Rugg built his huge home on the 1200 acres abutting Ray's east property line.

Ray, being the practical and professional pilot he was, put up a nice-sized hanger with a small apartment attached to its side where he could rest his bones after a day bouncing around over the unending fields of corn, beans, and goobers[11] that were the cash crops of the region.

However, by the time Wall Roberts came to him wanting to learn to fly, Ray was nearing seventy years of age. Not that most would have realized this by looking at him. He weighed perhaps 140 pounds and stood five and three quarter's feet tall, and was as wiry as a teenager in appearance, save for the limp courtesy of the German rifleman so many years before. Still, he knew his days were numbered with the FAA. Not that losing his medical would in the least keep Ray from enjoying the pleasures of flight, but it sure would end his ability to earn a living dusting or instructing.

He liked Wall Roberts and wanted to see the lad get his ticket before it was too late for him to help.

Ray also had another quirk that most in the modern aviation business found to be totally ridiculous. It was not ridiculous to Ray Swift though. It was his rule and as long as he owned *Swift Field*, he would enforce the rule. A large sign painted in Cub yellow with the notice — **No Tricycle Geared Aircraft On This Property** — inscribed in black was placed atop two twelve foot high poles he had bought surplus from Langdale's in Valdosta.

He had learned to fly in conventional geared planes and he saw no reason to have his students learn in any of the new-fangled airplanes. Besides, as he was quick to point out, if you must land off-field, a tail wheel plane is far less likely to flip over than a trike. Also, those who learn with all three up front never fully understand the reasoning or importance of a rudder. Ray was steadfast that none of his students would be so handicapped, or so ignorant.

Nate Rugg had originally leased an acre from Ray and built a large hanger for his Beach 18, but when he traded the beautiful

---

11 Goobers: Peanuts.

taildragger twin for a King Air 90, Ray refused him the right to land the propjet on his airport.

"No trikes!" Ray said firmly, and when he turned and walked away he added, "Besides them damn kerosene burners stink up the countryside."

Nate became so enraged he tried to get Ray's zoning changed and shut him down, but Ray had done a lot for the county over the years and he was a friend of every farmer within thirty miles. The county commissioners were soon to realize there were just too many voters who wanted *Swift Field* to remain, and so it did.

Swift Field
Note: Burned area at top right of photo.

Finally, Nate had his hanger disassembled and moved to Valdosta. It was actually better for him because he soon lost interest in the King Air and bought the Citation, which would have never been able to operate off of Ray's sod field. However, the wound

Ray had inflicted by refusing Nate landing permission would never heal and Nate cultivated his anger against his neighbor. He loved to say, "It's not wise to fool with Mother Nature ___, or Nate Rugg."

In the fall of '95, Wall decided he would again work on his private license and he began to hang around Swift Field most of his off time.

Ray had three planes, the Thrush he dusted in, and the two he instructed in, both Piper rag wings; an L-21, which was a Korean War version of his beloved L-4 that had served his needs so well in Europe, and a PA-12. The 12 was a three place Cub, thereby being much roomier than the L-21 and Wall preferred to fly it the most. Of course, circling the little Super Cruiser over Nate Rugg's home and wagging his red wings at the lady by the pool had nothing to do with why he wanted to fly again.

Worm Estes pitched an open zip lock bag containing a small amount of gasoline into the culvert around dark the night before. Now, just as the sun was coloring the eastern sky, he eased his small body into the same concrete cylinder.

The week before, he had bought the burlap sacks from the potato plant south of Bainbridge and made his new ghillie suit from them. He could have bought one which would have served his purpose almost as well, but he never left a trail where one could be avoided, and besides, he liked his own design better than those of Cabela's or Bean, or any other of the other commercial outfitters who sold this ultimate camouflage.

The slight odor of gas was still lying in the culvert, but this was greatly preferred to the reptiles that might have called this tube home before he tossed in the bag of gas.

Worm had sighted in his Remington to hit 4 inches high at one hundred yards and with the 55-grain sabot jacketed 30-06 rounds, traveling at over 4000 feet per second, he could simply hold on a target the size of a grapefruit out to 400 yards and be assured of a direct hit. He found this to be the ultimate killing weapon in this type of contract and used it often.

Worm had no idea who the man he was about to kill was and cared less. He suspected he had in some way offended one of Vinnie's family, or perhaps not. Why this man was to die on this sunny spring morning meant nothing. He was worth $5000 and that was all he needed to know.

The intelligence he had been given was the mark would be in the right front seat of a black Cadillac convertible. The Cadillac would be following a black, four-door Chevrolet, and that following a red Mustang. The small caravan would pass along this roadway between 0800 and 0810 hours on this day.

The culvert he was lying in was on the side road, which angled off the highway, slightly higher, and something short of two hundred yards from where his target would soon pass.

It would be a simple shot, and he would be in his car and headed away before anyone would realize what had happened, and that is precisely what took place.

The driver of the Cadillac slowed as he approached the intersection then sped up at the sound of the rifle report, and drove on for another half mile before stopping. The Chevrolet and Mustang never stopped at all, both continuing on towards Macon.

The tiny 22 projectile entered Will Grains' mouth and severed his right eyetooth before disintegrating in the palate to the left of his tonsils. The fragments tore away the rear half of the palate taking the tissue with them as they passed through the brain stem and into the left rear door. Will never knew what happened. One second he was reliving the argument he had with his wife that morning before he left for work, and the next second, he was knocking on the gates of hell.

"Just like turning off a light," Worm liked to say, taking pleasure in talking about his killings in Nam with his friends, or to others he wanted to fear him. It was often an expression he used with girlfriends who seemed to have lost interest in him. "A woman afraid makes a wonderful lover," he had once said to Vinnie.

With the $5000, he and his friend took a trip to the Caribbean for a few weeks to relax in the warm sun and swim in the crystal clear waters.

Ray Swift had taken off from work for a couple of days to go over to New Smyrna to attend the funeral of his old friend Glen Snyder. He and Glen had spent many a hell-raising night together in the early days while at Lamesa, Texas, with the Third Army Air Force Liaison Training Detachment.

Each had learned a slow roll followed by a gentle loop would open the legs of a female passenger faster than a double shot of Kentucky Bourbon. They often kidded each other over who had the most "unknown" children in west Texas.

This all had been before the army sent Ray to France to fly his beloved L-4, and Glen to Burma with an L-5 squadron. Now some 56 years later, it would be Ray who would scatter Glen's ashes over the vast Atlantic off the inlet east of New Smyrna from the open window of the L-21.

For just a split second, Ray had wanted to follow his friend into the dark waters below, but he didn't. Soon he was skirting the Daytona controlled airspace and headed back to Madison County.

It was while Ray was attending Glen's services that Nate Rugg had observed the red and cream airplane circling his place. He had seen this same plane many times before, as anyone landing to the south at *Swift Field* had to over fly his land. However, what gave him reason to take notice on this morning was the second pass. He saw Blue, who was lying out by the pool, wave and then peel off her bikini, giving the pilot of the low flying Cub a good look at her treasures, and he wondered.

A week later, Ray was visited by one of the 'Friendly Officials' from the FAA. They explained they had received a complaint about him flying too low over occupied homes. Of course, Ray had a low altitude waiver because of his crop dusting business, but still at his age, he wanted nothing to do with an FAA investigation.

To Ray's way of thinking, the FAA seemed to be the closest thing to totalitarianism he had known since the fall of the Nazi Party. The term, *Due Process of Law*, had never been introduced into the FAR's[12] of the Federal Aviation Administration. He was confident if it came to it, even though he was completely innocent of any wrong doing, he would surely be subjected to exceptionally strict flight medicals in the future. That was something that terrified every 70-year-old pilot. So, he simply showed proof to the Federal man that he was in Volusia County on the day in question and expressed total cooperation in trying to find the offending culprit. He also assured the FAA he would set up a right traffic pattern from then on, so no one would be flying low over Rugg's property.

When he confronted Wall a couple of days later, the lad agreed not to over fly the Rugg house anymore. This was a bitter pill to swallow for Wall. The only means available to him to get a glimpse of her was by flying over the house. Now he admitted to himself that perhaps 20 feet above the trees was a little low, even for a downwind approach and he should have not circled so many times. However, after the first time she had stripped naked, it just seemed the thing to do. Now he was forbidden to even fly over the house and it really angered him.

As a result, that afternoon he went up to Betsy's Crossroads for a few beers. He had not been there long before James Hancock spotted him and came over. They soon were in deep conversation, while they each emptied more little brown bottles than any two men should. Finally, shortly before sundown, James and Wall staggered down to the riverbank, where they each began to try and out-tell the other's last tale. One of these tales involved a drag race they had a couple of years before on the Nankin Road, not all that far from where they now stood. It had been on this run that Wall had blown the engine on his 'Vette, and as a result, James won the race.

The two had argued ever since on what the outcome would have been, had that engine held together. Unfortunately, neither would find out, as James had traded off his six-pack Challenger and it was no longer in the area.

12 FAR: Federal Aviation Rules.

One who did not know these boys would have thought they were ready to kill one another, but Betsy knew better. She had seen these two friends go at it many times over the outcome of those few seconds of acceleration and was not in the least bit concerned.

Blue was very concerned. She had no knowledge of any report to the FAA, and when she realized Wall was no longer over flying the house, she became quite disappointed.

Piper L4 with Bazooka Attachment

She had made a strict rule many years before to never become involved with any local man. Not even for one night. In fact, she had not entertained anyone from Florida or Georgia since moving to the area, except back when Nate and she shared the same bed on occasion with friends. Now she had broken her own rule and not only spent a few weekends with a local man, she knew she had strong feelings for him as well.

This really didn't make sense to her. He was certainly not a prize. He had no money, and little or no culture; two things she had become very accustomed to in the last few years. What he did have, she would have to admit, was the ability to curl her toes. Something no man had done since she left Colorado, save the whores she had bought.

He also was a symbol of everything she admired in a man. A no-nonsense, no put-on, no lies, kind of a man that her father had been. In fact, he was the closest thing to a real cowboy she had seen east of Arapahoe County; and to Blue, a real cowboy meant a real man.

Now, he suddenly stopped with the only contact they had, and it bothered her. No, it hurt her. A hurt she had not felt before, and she didn't like it. That weekend, she would fly to Grand Cayman Island for a massage.

At the same time Blue was stepping from N24LJ, several hundred miles to the east, Worm and Vinnie were boarding *The Admiral Karl,* a charter fishing boat owned by an outfit in the British Virgin Islands known as *Fishing with Fred.* There were twelve paying passengers that day as they worked around the reef near the Wreck of the Rhone.

The day had been windy and the sea too choppy for Worm's liking; his stomach was uneasy and he would be glad when they returned to Salt Island. Besides, Vinnie had caught several nice fish and Worm never liked it when his friend outdid him at anything.

A mood had set in hours before the sea fog rolled in. On their return to Salt Island Bay, the visibility became so bad the captain was navigating solely by radar. This might have been all that was needed on most vessels, but it lacked something on a boat owned by *Fishing with Fred.*

Six miles southwest of their destination, they collided with *The Flying Gypsy,* a shrimper out of Lee Bay. She immediately burst into flames, and soon *The Gypsy* went under.

The collision caused considerable damage to *The Admiral Karl* as well, and she, too, was taking on water, although there was no immediate danger of sinking.

All except one of the six who had been aboard *The Flying Gypsy* were hauled aboard, but they never saw Sancho Crespin after he jumped overboard with his shirt in flames.

Marco Pablo, the captain of *The Admiral Karl* that tragic day, immediately radioed for help. Every ship in the area was alerted of the collision, as well as the loss of one of the boats and damage to the other.

About forty minutes after *The Flying Gypsy* went under, Pablo realized it was now very likely they would share the same fate. This time he sent out a desperate call for help.

"Mr. Rugg, I hate to disturb you, but we have received a call for help from a sinking boat with several people aboard," Captain Barry Beal said, shortly after entering the stateroom of his employer.

"Yes," Rugg replied.

"Well, sir, we are only a couple miles away and most likely the only ship able to reach her before she goes down."

Nate studied this information for a few seconds before answering. He was entertaining several influential people from New York and Chicago and really didn't want his decks littered with the type of people who would be aboard a common fishing boat. On the other hand, for *The Savanna Witch* to be the rescuer of innocent lives would be positive publicity that could not be purchased for any amount of money. Turning to his captain he replied, "Mr. Beal, radio them we will be to their rescue as rapidly as possible."

"Very good, sir."

The fog was thinning a little by the time they arrived, some one hundred yards distance from the sinking vessel.

Nate ordered them to stop and for Beal to launch a small boat to pick up the survivors. It was obvious to all who now watched the rescue, the fishing boat would not remain afloat much longer and had it not been for *The Savanna Witch* arriving when she did, many lives would surely have been lost.

Among those who stood along the rail gazing at the frightened people as they came aboard, was one Lanzo Schade, a member of the Spindetto party.

Uberto Spindetto seldom left Chicago without two bodyguards and a member of the press he could count on. Schade was well accepted in the Cook County media and Uberto liked the young man.

The Savanna Witch was a 161-foot trideck luxury yacht, originally built by Warwick in New Zealand back in 1986. However, after its purchase in 1994, she had been completely refitted to Rugg's specifications. She now not only had six staterooms and a large master suite, but practically the entire second deck had been converted into one large conference/party room, with the addition of a heated Jacuzzi. Lanzo Schade considered himself very privileged to have been included on this cruise.

Worm Estes, on the other hand, decided should he survive the sinking of *The Admiral Karl,* he would never again set foot aboard another boat. Once aboard *The Savanna Witch,* he wanted only to sit down with a tall whiskey and water.

He did not want to talk to Vinnie. He did not want to even see Vinnie. It had been Vinnie who had suggested they spend the day fishing aboard that smelly boat to begin with. They could have spent their day with one of the beautiful English whores who were readily available on the island. It was not until Vinnie recognized his uncle Uberto that Worm would even look his way.

Worm was not too upset to realize where his butter came from these past several years, although he had never actually met this uncle before. *'That damn Vinnie could fall in a sack of shit and come out smelling like a rose,'* he thought when the elder gentleman was introduced to him.

Nate Rugg also had seen Estes and had formed a rather distasteful opinion of the obnoxious looking little man. He would be very happy when the entire bunch of inferiors were off-loaded, and the sooner the better.

When he found out the two worst looking of the whole lot were related to his longtime friend, Uberto Spindetto, he was taken aback. Nonetheless, Nate was a wise man and knew better than to offer an insult to an old ally, or his family.

Sometime later, after all the survivors of *The Admiral Karl* and *The Flying Gypsy* were safely ashore on Salt Island, Nate learned of Estes' special talents. A small piece of knowledge he would store somewhere in his vast working mind.

Blue learned of her husband's newfound fame while she waited for the Lear to land. She saw the news on television in the lounge at *Owen Roberts International Airport*. The BBC ran a full minute, including some video footage of the rescue, and a report by Lanzo Schade on the daring incident.

"Bull!" was her only comment, as she swirled the Glen Moray around over the two ice cubes in the short glass.

This trip had been a disappointment. Not that her sex partner had not been good, Greg was always good, and always earned his pay.

Greg Borden was a tall, lean 22-year-old whose family had been on the island for more than a hundred years. He was strikingly good looking, well-tanned, with deep blue eyes, genuine blonde hair and quite well built. He spent his days in the clear waters that surrounded the island, when not entertaining the bored wives of some of Europe's wealthiest aristocrats. He had become a professional masseur immediately after graduating from Pantheon-Sobonne University with a degree in political science, and for the past two years, received more in tips from his satisfied customers than he could have ever expected in a 'real job.'

Blue had found him quite by accident more than a year before and had made several trips to get one of his special massages. This time, however excellent it might have been, it was not satisfying; long and wild, but with no fulfillment.

She was depressed as she watched N24LJ taxi up to the private ramp. It was the first time she had returned after a couple of days or nights with Greg feeling this way, and would be the last time she would come to his Nirvana Table.

Ken Martinelli had seen whose name was on the charter papers and he immediately had a flashback of the tape he and Frank Alvarez had secretly shot of Mrs. Dunkin and her man-friend on the Colorado flight.

Ken considered her to be the best-looking woman he had ever seen, either with or without her clothes. He had masturbated several times while watching that tape. However, he knew she was really big money and he couldn't afford for her to make a complaint about him. As much as he hated it, he restrained from making a pass at her, thus far.

Regardless, Mrs. Dunkin was not the reason he had so desperately sought a way to captain this flight. He needed to make this run without Alvarez. His gambling debts in Biloxi had become excessive, and he had been visited by three very large black men two weeks before - with a message. *Pay up or disappear, and the disappearance would not be by your choosing.*

They left him semiconscious behind his old Mustang in the airport parking lot with a folded piece of paper stuffed in his mouth. The paper contained a telephone number. When he dialed it, an unknown voice told him he was to contact a Beda Rivers at the Owen Roberts Airport within two weeks; and what he suspected to be the reason, was something he knew Alvarez would never stand for.

Immediately after landing, he asked about Beda and the line boy sent him straight to her. She was one of the waitresses at the airport restaurant and lounge.

Once satisfied he was who he said he was, she gave him a brown leather attaché case and told him someone in Biloxi would contact him, nothing more, and he dared not look inside the package.

Instead, he placed it among Mrs. Dunkin's luggage, just in case they were visited by an inspecting customs agent on their arrival back in Mississippi.

That night Blue stayed in Gulfport and cried herself to sleep.

After arriving back in Madison County, she took her father's old rifle and put a bullet in the electrical transformer Wall had replaced a few months before. Immediately their lights blinked twice and then all power was lost. In a few seconds, the emergency generator cranked on, but she already reported the loss of electricity to *The Withlacoochee Co-Op.*

Satisfied with her shot, she set the battle-scared Winchester against her dresser.

Chapter Ten
MCSO

Dick Taylor had been a State Trooper for almost ten years when he was elected to the office of Sheriff. He served the county well for another fifteen years until one day, while walking out of his office in the county courthouse, he collapsed.

After three weeks in the intensive care unit of Shands Teaching Hospital down in Gainesville, the doctors told his family, "When we have to remove him from the heart pump, he will not live. Only 20% of his heart is left in working condition."

Ol' Dick proved them wrong and walked back into his office six months later. However, he knew the writing was on the wall. When the twenty-fifth anniversary of his law enforcement career arrived, it was also the last day of his active employment with Madison County. Dick turned the Office of the Sheriff over to his chief deputy, Aaron Coons. Three years later when the election came around, Coons easily won over his closest opponent. Everyone had liked Sheriff Taylor, and if he thought Coons was good enough to run the department, they would back his man.

The only problem was that Aaron Coons was not his man. Dick Taylor had turned over the office to Coons because he did not see anyone else in the department who was qualified for such a ranking administrative position. It was not because Coons would have been his choice had he felt he had another candidate.

He never liked Coons. Had he not been from one of the oldest families in the county, and the fact that his Uncle Dorsey was the local State Attorney, the young deputy never would have been hired in the first place. Dick owed many people over the years, and one of the ways he paid some of the favors to the State Attorney's office back, was in promoting Coons.

Now the man was the highest-ranking lawman in the county and it worried Dick from time to time. It was not that he thought Coons was dishonest or corrupt, but he considered him weak and easily led by others. Not a virtue Sheriff Taylor admired.

Aaron Coons also owed people in the area. Many who had placed pressure on Taylor to have Coons advanced over the years and he knew it. They had always made sure he knew it. Some of these people had kept him out of trouble more than once, and he knew he needed them to stay in office.

One of those Sheriff Coons owed was Madison Horry, a man considered by many to be the county's most powerful attorney. Another was Nate Rugg.

Although no mention was made of it in the news release, Horry was aboard *The Savanna Witch* the day she was used as a rescue vessel.

Back when Coons was a fresh graduate of Madison High, his father saw to it he was enrolled in the University of Miami. Unfortunately, while attending the university, Aaron had fathered a son with one of the exiled Cuban girls who also attended UM.

Shortly after Coons became Sheriff, Gilberto Mendoza was hired as a dispatcher. The following year when Gilbert graduated from the Police Standards Class at the local Community College, he was advanced to the position of Deputy. No one, other than he and the sheriff, knew Mendoza was Coon's bastard son.

Blue had seen the flashing of the spotlight among the trees, and followed the truck as it approached. Suddenly, a moment of near panic swept over her, *'What if it is not him?'* she thought. *'If it is not, whoever it is will surely see the bullet-hole there, and who knows what will happen then.'*

She whirled around and quickly ran back into the house. There she returned the old 25-35 that Doggy had used for so many years to feed his family, to its home high upon the wall on two antelope horns in the big closet of her bedroom. Then she watched from the window as the lights of the truck slowly came closer.

It had been their good luck that Wall was on call that night and when he received the notice that Mr. Rugg had reported a power outage, he was quickly dressed and in his 'Vette headed for the yard.

He decided at the last minute to take the boom-truck. Normally on a call-out, he would have driven a much smaller vehicle to locate the trouble, and then call back for additional help if he needed it. But something in his gut told him to take the cherry-picker and he did.

First, he drove into *Swift Field* and seeing the night security light Ray had near the front of his big hanger was burning, he was pleased. Ray had paid a considerable amount to have all the lines buried on his property, thus Wall was pretty sure he would find the trouble somewhere near the location he had been when he first saw her. *'The trouble has to be on Rugg property and that means I might just get a chance of seeing her.'*

Before he drove on, however, he noticed a yellow sheet of paper on the front door of Ray's office. Getting out of the truck, he walked over and using his flashlight, he read the note, then he returned to his truck and moved on out.

Driving around the perimeter of the airport so as not to allow the heavy truck to leave ruts in the sod runway, and by using the spotlight on the truck, he finally located the power lines where they came out of the ground and returned to overhead poles. Following them, he soon found himself in the burned out field to the rear of the Rugg Mansion. Knowing exactly where the transformer was located, he soon spotted the black spot on the side of the heavy cylinder. *'Strange,'* he thought.

After lifting himself high enough, he flipped open the large breaker rendering the line beyond free of juice, and then he disconnected the useless transformer and brought it to the ground. There he inspected it closely. *'No doubt about it, someone shot this thing,'* he immediately concluded, and slowly he looked towards the big castle some two hundred yards to the north.

There were lights on in the house. He was not surprised, *'Certainly, Nate Rugg would have an automatic generator as a backup in times of storms and such.'*

It was then, as he looked towards the big house he saw her. She was running towards him and he dropped his tools and rushed to intercept her.

Their meeting was hard and furious; she clung to him like a child would to a parent on a stormy night. She kissed him hard on his lips until she bruised them against his teeth, but he didn't feel any pain. He only felt the woman who had been torturing him for months, now he could think of nothing else.

Finally, after a full minute of her locked to him she pulled back and asked, "Where have you been? You never fly over anymore. Are you angry with me? Did I do something?"

Her questions were fast and unending, never giving him a chance to answer. "Wait, wait a minute. Your husband complained to the FAA about me flying over and they put an injunction against Ray Swift. Now we must do right patterns into his field so as not to fly over Rugg property."

"That bastard!" was her only reply and then she was kissing him again. Between breaths and kisses, she said, "I'm so horny, so very horny."

He turned and looked about and then he took her by the hand and led her back through the dim trail of the power line, then across the landing strip to the hanger. Opening the door, he didn't bother to find a light switch. The glow of the pale green security light was enough to find their way between the aircraft until they were at the tail-plane of the Thrush.

There he stopped and began fumbling with the zipper of her jump suit, but she stopped him and did it herself. "You're taking too long," she said breathing heavy. He was pleased to see she wore nothing beneath the white coveralls, and in an instant, he had her sitting on the horizontal stabilizer and was entering her. She leaned back against the cold aluminum and lifted her legs, placing them over his shoulders, and soon was screaming at the top of her lungs.

The night before, at sometime after midnight as she lay in bed awakened from a nightmare, she wondered about him. She knew she had easily entertained many times over a hundred men in the fifteen years she had been having sex, and with the exception of her paid whores, she never climaxed with any of them. Even with the men she bought, she had never experienced the multi-orgasms she did with Wall Roberts. It was like the moment she felt him inside her, she would flow over a great falls and enter an unending river of white-water that with every splash brought a climax of some degree, each becoming greater than the last. Sex with him was like no other man she could imagine. She even wondered if her father had provided her mother with such pleasure. *'Surely he had.'*

This night it was better than she remembered, and for twenty minutes she continued to explode over and over. Finally, she felt him grow tense and she knew he was close and suddenly she heard the echo in the hanger of someone shouting, "Yes, shoot it in me. Please shoot it in me. Shoot it deep in me."

It was a full minute before they recovered enough to speak, and when they did, neither really knew what to say. Finally, he took a deep breath and spurted out, "Boy, I almost came that time." It had been the right thing to say, it broke the ice, and she laughed and slapped him hard on his hairy chest.

Then she looked around and realized what they had used for a cot. "This wing, I hope I didn't hurt it," she said placing her hand down on the tail-plane.

"Stabilizer," he corrected.

"What?"

"It's a stabilizer, not a wing, and I doubt what we did would damage a Thrush. It's made tough."

"If you say so," she replied, as if it made no difference what the correct name for the improvised sex table really was. Then she added, "I do hope we didn't awake the man who lives here."

"If he had been here, we would have awakened him, I feel sure," Wall replied, remembering her screams.

"Wall, I want you to come back to the house with me. I want to spend the night with you."

"What about your husband?"

"Oh, he's gone somewhere. He won't be back tonight, that's for sure."

He was a little uneasy about going to her house. He could just see the headlines,

Lineman Shot Dead In Bed By Jealous Husband

"We can stay here," he suggested, "in Ray's place. He's gone to the VA in Gainesville for some test. There's a note on his door, he won't be back until tomorrow."

"No. I want you in my bed. I might even have you in Nate's bed, and leave the stained sheets on it for him to fume over."

"You are nuts."

"Yes. I'm afraid I am. Nuts over you. Damn you," she replied and then to encourage him, she dropped to her knees and began to bring him back to life.

"Wait," he stopped her. "I have to replace that transformer someone shot a hole in."

"I'm a pretty good shot aren't I," she teased. "That was a long way off and I hit it on the first try."

"You're nuts," he said again, and then he looked about for her jumpsuit. He started to hand it to her, but stopped and looking at her naked body one more time, he shook his head; then handed it to her.

"Where are my boots?" she asked after slipping into the pearly white covering.

As the two lovers strolled back across the airfield towards where he had left the truck, Ray Swift shook his head and said aloud, "I should a' took that note off the front door when I got home tonight. 'Course it would have been a might crowded in here with the three of us in my little bed." Then he turned over and went to sleep, entertaining fond memories of West Texas and his youth.

They did, in fact, have sex in Nate's bed, although Wall didn't realize it. As they were ascending the staircase she thought, *'My bedroom overlooks the back and east sides of the house, but from his window one could see an approaching vehicle.'*

Wall stayed as long as he dared, and then slipped out while she slept. He got the boom truck in the compound only half an hour before the morning shift would be arriving and he knew it would not be good for them to see him there. He was always to work on time, but never the first to arrive, so he headed over to Greenville where a cute little gal ran a breakfast and lunch counter, and there he ordered coffee.

"You're early," she said, setting a cup of dark liquid on the counter in front of him. Then before he could reply, she added, "Damn, Wall, you look terrible. You been on a drunk in the middle of the week?"

"Thanks, Sally. It's those little bits of encouragement that gets a fellow going in the morning," he replied, giving his head a few short nods as if he approved of his answer. "And no, I ain't been on no drunk. Got called out last night and spent most of it repairing a line north of Pinetta." *'Well that's partly true,'* he thought.

A week later, he was called to the office. When he stopped at Ash's desk he asked, "What's this all about?"

"Don't know," she said, raising her shoulders, but he knew she was lying. The girls in the office always knew everything that was going on, and some things that weren't going on.

Passing Dixie Marie, he gave her a wink, and she returned it with a big smile, and then pointed towards Miller's office door.

"What's he want?" Wall whispered, but she too just raised her shoulders as if she didn't know.

After a knock on the smoked glass, he heard Miller call out, "Come." *'What an arrogant way to answer your door,'* he thought, as he opened it and walked in.

Upon seeing who it was, Miller picked up the phone and made a call. It was obvious to Wall the call was not important, at least not so important that it could not have waited, and this angered him. However, he realized there was little he could do about it, at least at the moment.

Finally, Miller replaced the receiver back in its cradle, and looked up at Wall as if to say, "You want something, Roberts?"

Wall lifted his palms upward before saying, "You called for me."

"Oh, yes I did. That transformer you replaced at Rugg's the other night."

"Yes?"

"It has a bullet hole in it."

"Yes it does, that's why it quit working."

"Well, how do you suppose it got there?"

"I would guess someone shot it," he replied and then before Miller could jump him for his smart aleck answer, he added, "Rugg's maid said she saw some fire hunters shoot a deer across the river earlier that same night. We figured they must have missed with one round and it ended up in the transformer."

"You don't think it could have come from that little airport do you? I understand there is some trouble between Swift and Mr. Rugg."

"No. The bullet definitely came from the north. It's easy to see that if one was to look at the transformer and see the connector marks."

Miller immediately realized he should have done just that, before calling in a man from the field. "I guess it's possible a hunter done it. You don't think its vandalism then?"

"I'm sure it was not," Wall lied.

"Did you notify the game warden?"

"Naw, if they shot from across the river, it would be from Georgia most likely, and I ain't got no speaking relationship with the game wardens up there."

Miller nodded his head, showing his satisfaction, and then looked back at his desk and picked up a sheet of paper and began reading it to himself, and after a few seconds he replied, "That's all, Roberts," without lifting his attention from the sheet.

On his way out Dixie Marie stopped him, "You want to get a cup before you go back out? It's time for my break."

"Sure," Wall replied, and he stepped back and waited for her to go ahead of him.

She poured them both a cup of coffee and then sat down at the small table across from him. He watched as she dumped in her cup a large spoon of powered creamer, followed by the contents from several blue packages of artificial sweetener. The thought of such a drink nauseated him.

"Well, what did Miller-Diller want?" she asked.

"He was interested in night hunting."

"He was?" she asked back surprised.

"Yeah, but I warned him about the game wardens over in Georgia."

"Well, I would hope so. I can't imagine shooting a little deer anyway," she replied sipping her coffee.

"You know, Wall, my divorce was final several weeks ago."

"Yeah, I heard you have been down to The Stone Fox Tavern, most every night since."

"Pshaw. I only been there a couple of times," she shot back defensively.

Wall had to admit she was quite desirable and he would like to play loos'em between her mounds, but he had such a strong feeling for Blue, he just couldn't bring himself to ask her out. After a few minutes, he excused himself and left. Ash gave him a hateful look, as he walked out the front door. *'What the hell's the matter with her?'* he wondered.

Chapter Eleven
The Lodestar

Sheriff Coons had been persuaded by Deputy Mendoza to allow him to be trained as a K-9 officer and they sent off to the City of New Orleans for a dog.

Kurt had been well trained as a drug sniffer there in Louisiana, and had been the main witness in two large busts, but his partner had left the department, and considering Kurt's age, they decided not to assign him to a new man.

Coons, on hearing about the dog and that he could be bought for a song, finally convinced the county commissioners to allow them to buy the K-9. He sent him through the training classes again, this time with Mendoza as his new partner.

The local veterinarian warned the Sheriff that the shepherd already had some problems with hip dysplasia and it would only get worse. Coons, considering his limited budget, reasoned this dog would be the only way he could afford a good K-9 sniffer, and if the dog found just one good haul, it would pay for it all. Then he would have the money for a younger dog when Kurt had to be replaced, and he was right.

The second week after they finished school, Deputy Lang stopped a speeding Mark VIII on Interstate 10 west of SR 53. The Lincoln had all the windows tinted so dark they were obviously in violation of state law. The driver was an expensively dressed black; with him were two white women passengers.

As Lang was pulling in behind the black Lincoln, he heard Mendoza take a 10-8[13], so he radioed and asked him to bring the dog to where he was stopping the vehicle.

When the second sheriff's car arrived, Lang walked up to Mendoza and said, "It's a pimpmobile and a half. That Spook is wearing more gold than Queen Elizabeth, and he's got two whores with him. Out of Miami headed for New Orleans and the whole damn car smells of pot."

"That so?" Mendoza replied, "Let's let Kurt have a walk around."

Lang asked everyone to step out of the vehicle and to stand back beside his cruiser. When they had done so, after much complaining, Mendoza took Kurt out and placing him on a short leash and led him to the rear of the Lincoln. Immediately, the dog hit on the trunk area and Lang advised the driver and the passengers of their Miranda Rights before asking for permission to search the car.

Charles Dozer quickly replied, "Well, I don't guess I mind. Da' car don belongs to me no way, it's my cozen's."

"He says, go ahead," Lang called out to Mendoza and the K-9 Officer took the keys from the ignition and opened the trunk. There were four suitcases and an attaché case in the trunk. Kurt hit heavily on the attaché case and upon opening it, they gazed on stacks of twenty-dollar bills.

Lang immediately placed all three suspects under arrest and had the Lincoln towed to the Sheriff's compound by Stewart's Garage.

By the time the trial was over, Coons had confiscated the $40,000 and an almost new Continental, which he reasoned should be the personal transportation of the High Sheriff.

Yes, his gamble on the old sick dog had paid off, and before the year 1994 was history, Kurt brought in another $10,000.

The local paper was singing Coon's tune and he did look like a shoo-in at the next election.

---

13 10-8: Radio call advising the unit was in service and ready to work.

When Mendoza was promoted over other senior Deputies, most just considered it a 'thank you' for the success he had brought to the department.

There are three airfields in Madison County, *Swift Field* up near the state line, *The Madison Airport,* which was along Highway 90 near the town of Lee, and *Sampala Lake Aerodrome* near the southern end of the county.

Sampala Lake Aerodrome was both a sod strip as well as a seaplane base and was owned by Sam Price. It was located on the west end of his 6000-acre plantation, where his property bordered Sampala Lake. The landing field was dredged from the swamp years before the EPA was organized, and was a very well groomed 4000' strip.

All three airports are privately owned, but Madison County leased theirs, and made it a public use airport. The other two required permission from the owners prior to landing.

On this day, Wall was cruising low and slow over the south end of the county in the little PA-12. Just before dusk when he made a wide turn to head back to *Swift Field*, he saw a large, twin-engine airplane slip into Price's strip.

It was too near dark for him to fool around, or he would have circled around and taken a better look at the big twin. It was one he had never seen before and was quite curious about it.

Ray was out on the strip, looking skyward, when he heard the familiar sound of the 0-320, far off to the south.

Back when Nate Rugg had been using his field, he paid for landing lights to be installed. However, once he moved his airplane, Ray had never again turned them on. He didn't like to fly in black air, and he didn't want others to do so in one of his planes. This night he decided to see if the lights still worked.

Wall already had the strip in sight and was preparing for a straight in approach, when all of a sudden, the lights came on. He immediately gunned the engine and climbed out. Having never seen *Swift Field* lit before, he circled the strip once, making sure he was not landing at the wrong airport.

Finally, convinced he was at the right place, he turned final again, and set her down from the south. Taxiing up to the hangar, he could see the anger in Ray's expression, and he knew he was in for a chewing out.

After they had the little bird in its nest, he asked Ray about the strange twin.

"Well from your description, I would saw it was a Lockheed, a 12 or maybe an 18. You just don't see 10's or 14's no more," the old man said, and then rubbing his chin with the palm of his hand he added, "Come on in here. I got a book that should have a picture of her." The younger man followed two steps behind the old flier into his office/apartment.

After moving several magazines and old *Trade-A-Planes* around, he found what he was looking for and opened the small black book. He flipped through several pages before he stopped. "Here, it look like that?"

"Yeah, only maybe bigger," Wall replied, looking at the picture of the old military airplane.

"How about this?"

"Yeah, that's it, that's what it looked like."

"Huh, I wonder what Sam Price would be doing with a Lodestar?" the old man said, more to himself than to Wall.

The next morning before sunup, Ray was in his L-21 flying high over Sampala Lake, but he saw no sign of the Lockheed.

He knew full well why a Lodestar would be slipping into a private field at or near dark, but he didn't want to get involved, so he told Wall he didn't want him flying over Sampala anymore.

"Me and old Sam never got along, and he might just complain to the Feds on you. I can't afford no more investigations," he said. Wall didn't question him anymore on the subject, although it didn't sound like a very feasible reason.

'That's okay,' he thought. *'There is plenty of airspace around these parts. I don't need to be flying over Sampala Lake, or Rugg's property.'*

Ken Martinelli had spent twenty-five hours at the old navy strip south of Meridian, learning to fly the big tail-dragger, and was really not all that comfortable in it still. Regardless, Hicks gave him an ultimatum and he really had no choice.

On the day when he landed back at Gulfport after returning Mrs. Dunkin from Grand Cayman Island, he was met by two men who simply said they were there to pick up the package Beda had given him. He quickly handed over the case, but before they left, they opened it. Ken was not surprised to see it filled with several clear bags containing a white powder and the larger man opened one of the bags and tasted the contents. He then handed Ken an envelope. Later, after they were gone, he opened the envelope and inside was all the gambling IOU's he had accumulated over the past year.

A week later, another larger package was waiting for him at the FBO office. In it was a video tape, and it scared the hell out of him.

Later that night when he had the chance, he slipped the tape into his VCR and waited nervously. Just as he feared, the tape was a visual record of a dark-haired woman handing him the attaché case, and clearly over his head, was a sign of the restaurant there on Grand Cayman Island. Soon the tape revealed him handing the attaché case to the two men at the airport in Mississippi. Again, the camera had been so located that the FBO shingle could be seen clearly in the background over his head. Throughout the short tape, his was the only face visible, but you could see very clearly, what the big man was doing when he tested the white powder, and also, when he handed Ken the envelope.

Here was unquestionable proof he had transported unlawful drugs into the United States from a foreign country, and he realized he had swallowed their hook, their line, and their sinker. Immediately he felt he was about to lose the Big Mac he had gobbled down while hurrying home to view the tape, and he ran for the bathroom.

Now, he was flying an old WW II bomber that he was not really sure was safe at all, but he did learn very soon that this was no ordinary Lockheed 18.

The old girl had once been the pride of Naval Aviation in the Aleutians. The PV-1 was fast, very fast for its size and vintage. Fully firewalled and down hugging the deck, he had seen 375 MPH on the old airspeed indicator, and he was very impressed. *'She can outrun anything short of a jet, and once in the air, she handles better than the Lear at low altitude.'*

He had taken off from Jeremy's unpaved strip and was not sure the short winged monster was going to be flying before it used the entire short runway. But when she became light on her wheels, she seemed to become an old friend.

The plan was to circle a ship located at the lat/longs he had been given. It would be squawking a particular transponder code for positive identification.

When he arrived at that location, there were several fishing boats down there, but one was sure enough squawking the correct code, so he circled until he saw the Aztec ease up beside him, and then he turned off all his electrical equipment and slipped in under the Piper's belly and they headed for Florida.

The Aztec pilot made all the right moves and was in contact with Miami Approach, so if he stayed close enough, they would look like one blip on the radar screen.

When they were 10 nautical miles southeast of Ft. Pierce, he dropped down on the deck and firewalled the big R-2800's, and raced in over Florida's coast, just above the waves faster than 300 knots. Then he slipped up the east side of the Avon Park Restricted Area, and cut the angle between Orlando and Tampa just east of Lakeland. From there, he was free and clear the rest of the way to Madison County.

The Company planned for him to arrive after nightfall, but Ken had kept his speed up and made it there a few minutes before full dark. Sam Price was not all that pleased when he saw the big twin drop in over the line of sweet gums located along the end of his runway, but he was happy to see nothing following. Soon, they had the Lockheed inside his hanger. Within the hour, several Mexican hands were unloading the cargo.

Before midnight, Ken was all fueled up and taxiing out for a takeoff to the west, over the lake. It had been a trying flight, but still exciting, and he had to admit the high of it all had been almost worth it, especially when Sam Price handed him the envelope containing one hundred Ben Franklins.

He did not know what had been his cargo; only that it had weighed a little over 2200 pounds, which was nothing to the useful load of a Navy PV-1.

Navy PV-1 converted by Howard for civilian use

Chapter Twelve
Middle Florida

F lorida is often sectioned up by those who want to brag about, or condemn, a certain location in the state. For hundreds of years, Florida had been separated between West Florida and East Florida, two different territories altogether. West Florida began at the Mississippi River and went east to the Apalachicola River, with Pensacola as the capital. East Florida began at the Apalachicola River and took in everything east of there, having St. Augustine for its capital.

However, when it was time for the newly acquired Spanish land to become two American Territories, there were too many abolitionists influencing congress to allow two more potential slave states to enter the South. When a final compromise was achieved, the vast majority of West Florida was given to Alabama, Mississippi, and Louisiana.

There was a small village of Tallahassee Indians who lived in the red hills south of Thomasville, Georgia. Since this village was approximately half the distance between the old capitals of Pensacola and St. Augustine, it was chosen as the location for the new Territorial Capital.

For many years thereafter, Florida was divided into three sections by the natives. West Florida, now beginning at the Alabama State Line and running east to the Apalachicola River,

Middle Florida running east from there to where the Suwannee River flowed south from the Georgia line, and everything east from there was considered East Florida.

None of this went very far south, because everything south of New Smyrna was considered unfit for human habitation, other than Indians of course. Many true native Floridians to this day, agree with this thinking.

However, as more immigrants moved south, especially after The War between The United States and The Confederate States, much of this southern region became inhabited by white families. Soon, these immigrants began calling the Indian land South Florida, and so it remained for about a century.

Unfortunately, the native Floridians suffered the disastrous results that have plagued their state since a California Yankee by the name of Walter Disney brought his mouse family to a small, quite cow town in Osceola County known as Kissimmee. Soon the population around there exploded and the wonders of old Florida vanished. Soon after Disney, there was a 'Central Florida,' as referred to by local television news stations.

Today, Central Florida begins at the coast of the Gulf of Mexico and runs east to the coast of the Atlantic Ocean. It is usually agreed the northern part of this new Florida is approximately where SR 40 crosses the state and south to the parallel road of SR 60.

Madison County is to the north, in the heart of old Middle Florida. The residents would like nothing more than to somehow segregate themselves from the rest of the state. There are less than 15,000 people who call it home and the vast majority of these can trace their genealogy back a century or more to this very location.

At one time Madison County was one of the most populated counties in the state. Of course, at that time there were very few whites living in Florida.

Madison was an extremely strong location of secessionists before the outbreak of the war, and when it was learned that Florida had seceded from the Union and become an independent nation, there was a turnout in the streets the likes of which have never been seen since. That night, both Base and Range Streets were lit with torches for as far as the eye could see and the town's only cannon was fired repeatedly in celebration.

During our nation's fight against the invading armies and navies, Madison gave dearly of its sons, and it was once said that a Methodist Circuit Rider traveling throughout the county had not once found a single Loyal Union Man, white or black.

This however did not last long, for soon after the collapse of the Confederate Government, an influx of new residents, mostly northerners, moved into the area. Among the new immigrants were also some who sought refuge from other states where the fighting was much greater, areas where it was unsafe for civilians to remain. Others came because they had learned of the superior farmlands to be had in the county. Some had been stationed in Madison County as occupational troops who liked what they saw and stayed on after being mustered out. Some came as Freedmen, to take advantage of the government's promise of sixty acres and a mule on land that had once belonged to a secessionist; and of course, there were those who had been trained to confiscate these lands and other property. They were commonly known as the dreaded, and severely hated, "Carpetbaggers."

Wall Roberts was not a native of Madison, but he could trace his family back through five generations of Floridians. In fact, his Granny Jemima's father had migrated to Florida when this land still belonged to Spain, and this was a brag few natives could top.

Nate Rugg and his beautiful wife were of a different breed. His ancestor had come as a rich man, as so many had, some one hundred plus years before, and soon became deeply entangled in local and state politics. For almost a century, the Rugg family had always been both envied, and feared. Nate enjoyed the same power his forefathers had. However, his wife was simply known as the beautiful Mrs. Rugg, and accepted as such.

James Hancock had certainly heard of Nate Rugg, everyone within a hundred miles had heard of him, and it was a reasonable assumption he had a wife. James had never seen either of them before that day when he and his little sister were slowly drifting in his coochee boat down the blackwater river, lazily casting for brim and red-bellies.

They stopped at the beach on Ray Swift's property to fry their catch for lunch. When Cindy 'needed to go,' she climbed the high bank and strolled off down the dim road, looking for the perfect spot to squat. Once finished, she heard the sound of an airplane overhead and she watched it through the tree limbs as it came in for a landing.

The curiosity of the young girl couldn't be harnessed and the desire to see more was overwhelming, so she called back to her brother, "James, I'm going to see the airplane." She was sure she had heard him answer. Knowing it would be half an hour or more before the fish would be ready anyway, there really was no need for her to hurry back.

Besides, as much as she loved James, he was not her father, although sometimes he acted like he was, bossing her around. She would be seventeen in a few months and who she dated was none of his business, even though he thought it was. It was one of the few things they ever argued over.

James, though, had not heard her call, and when she did not return in a timely manner, he also climbed the bank in search of her. Following the dim trail to where it split, he heard what sounded like a girl's voice a little off to the east, so he took the road that ran along the side of the river.

He had not traveled far when he saw the big house through the trees and he stopped. He had seen it many times from the river, but never before had he realized its true grandeur and he was caught off guard by the magnitude of it.

There again, he heard the sound of a girl's voice, and he headed towards the back of the house, where the voice, or voices, were coming from. Arriving near the four-foot tall log wall, he suddenly saw the exceptionally tall redheaded woman talking to the shorter girl whose back was to him.

'Now what the hell is she doing over here?' he thought, and he started straight for the pool area.

The four-foot fence surrounding the backyard hid most of the two people near the pool. He could see some of the tall redhead and almost none of the smaller girl she was talking to. All James could see was the back of the girl's head and a small part of her white shirt.

James marched right up to the fence and called out, "Cindy, what are you doing here?"

It wasn't until he actually reached the fence did he realize the redhead was naked, and the shorter girl was not his sister at all, rather a woman who appeared to be a light-skinned Mexican, dressed in a white uniform looking very much like the overshirt his sister had been wearing.

Both women looked surprised at his sudden appearance, but not as surprised as he was. The maid screamed and ran back into the house. The naked woman simply dove into the pool and swam over to the edge, there calling out to him, "I'm not Cindy, and what are you doing here?"

"Oh, I'm so sorry. I thought you were my sister. I mean she was my sister," he stammered. "I was a 'uh, we were fishing, and she went to the bathroom, and I ___, well I came looking for her."

Blue could see he was no threat, and his story, along with his nervousness, made sense. *'If he was a prowler he would have never called out like that,'* she reasoned before saying back "I'm sorry Mister ___?"

"Hancock, James Hancock. I live on the other side of the river, back a ways."

"Well Mr. Hancock, as you see, I am not hiding your sister under my robe, perhaps you need to look elsewhere."

"Yes, Ma'am. I'll do that very thing," James replied, and headed back into the scattered pines the way he had come.

Nate Rugg was just driving up when James cut back through the woods from his property to that belonging to Swift, and Nate got a good look at the lad. *'What's he doing here?'* he wondered.

Instead of driving on around to the garage as he usually did, he stopped in front of his house and walked in the main entrance just as Blue was coming in from the pool. When he saw her approaching, he stepped back near the dark drape that hung from the tall window, and she never saw him.

She had her bikini swung over her shoulder and walked naked over to the bar, poured herself a Rum Cocktail, then headed up the long staircase.

'*So that is the son-of-a-bitch she's screwing,*' he thought, remembering the stains on his bed sheets.

After hearing her bedroom door close, he called out to Famalie, "Si', Senor'?"

"Who was that man with Mrs. Rugg?"

The woman looked out back to the pool and then back to her employer with a worried expression on her face, "I's dun'no."

"You better know."

"I's dun tell you, I's dun'no."

"Well, you had better remember if you want to work here tomorrow," he shouted back, very sternly.

Again, she glanced around, this time as if she was trying to find a place to hide, and finding none, she looked back at him and thought she might lose her bladder. Finally she said, "He a fisherman, he home de udder side of de ribber, I's tink."

"What's his name?"

"Mi dun'no. He tingum. He come, he see Mrs. Rugg. I's terreckly go. I's dun'no."

"Came to see Mrs. Rugg, huh; I'll bet he did," Nate said, before whirring around and going back out to his Allanté and driving away, spinning his wheels on the new pavement. "I'll teach that bitch to bring her studs to my house," he shouted as he slammed his fist on the top of the red steering wheel repeatedly.

Cindy saw the silver convertible speeding away as she was strolling back to the river, but the driver never looked her way, and thus she did not see who he was.

Gainesville Police Chief, Chuck Wilson, had known Mickey Johns since he had been a recruit. In fact, he had been Mickey's first Lieutenant, and not only appreciated the youth's enthusiasm and drive, he saw a little of himself in the 22-year-old man from a poor family. Down deep, Chuck Wilson wanted to see the officer make good, and when the opportunity presented itself, he helped as much as he could.

Only a few months before Wilson was to retire, three new statewide Task Force units were ordered by the Governor's office to fight the increasing concern of drugs becoming too available to schoolchildren. The West Florida Unit would work the area from Tallahassee west to the Alabama State Line. The Central Florida Unit would cover the counties east of Leon to the Atlantic Ocean and down to Tampa including Orange, Osceola, and Polk counties. Finally, the South Florida Unit covered everything else.

These new sub-departments were a collection of officers from the larger agencies all over the state. These officers were given special authority by the state legislature to conduct quasi-undercover work outside their local agency, with arrest and investigation powers throughout the state. They reported to Florida's Department of Law Enforcement's Captain Lutz, who also was the commander of the Task Force units and to him alone.

It was a good move for Law Enforcement and in many ways, it did more to reduce the influence of organized crime than anything else for a long period. Mickey Johns was elated his chief chose him to represent GPD in the Central Florida Unit.

However, during this period where so little direct supervision was applied, Mickey developed a serious infection that would one day, lead to his downfall. He had become infatuated with the TV series Hill Street Blues, and in particular, with Detective Mick Belker. Mickey taped every episode and watched it over and over, especially the scenes where Belker was involved. Soon his favorite adjective for bad guys was Dog Breath.

He even dropped the Mickey from his name and began calling himself simply Mick. It wasn't long before the other officers on the task force began asking not to be assigned with him.

It was during those seven months he truly began to believe that to be a good undercover cop, one had to get down and just as dirty as the bad guys. This, of course, meant smoking a little pot and snorting a little coke along with the suspects. Naturally, he was convinced he would never let himself forget he was a cop first, and never let the stuff get ahead of him.

Finally, after repeated warnings from Captain Lutz that Mick simply let slide off his now very tough back, he was asked to take a pee-test. This he refused and he was immediately sent back to the Gainesville PD.

When Lutz requested a replacement from GPD, he did not give any specific reason to the city manager, other than Johns' cover had been compromised and he needed to be replaced.

Mickey Johns had not started out as a bad cop; on the contrary, he was a good officer for many years until he was sent to Tallahassee as GPD's representative for the Middle Florida Task Force, and his addiction to Mick Belker.

Lutz did warn Wilson to keep a sharp eye on Johns. He even suggested Johns be returned to uniform duty for a cleansing period. "Sometimes these boys just get too deep in their undercover work, and need some time in uniform to bring them back to reality."

Chief Wilson intended to do that very thing, but Mickey convinced him that he had been so very close to making a large bust on a gang who were using the airport at Orange Lake as a point to bring in large loads of pot for Alachua and Marion Counties. So reluctantly, Wilson backed off the transfer for the time being.

This proved to be a good move for Wilson, because within a month, Mickey located a large stash of baled pot being stored in a small garage that belonged to Marjorie Tubman, one of the leading businesswomen in Gainesville.

Marjorie claimed to be a descendant of Harriet Tubman, but when one of the reporters from *The Alachua Sun*, Gainesville's leading newspaper, tried to do genealogy research on her, he was unable to make the connection.

Marjorie was however, a very wealthy woman who owned a multitude of small houses in the black neighborhoods of Gainesville and surrounding communities throughout Alachua County.

She had come south from Rhode Island to attend Bethune-Cookman College several years before and graduated with honors, receiving a BS in African History.

In reality, she was a quadroon, her mother was a mulatto and her father, whom she never knew, was a redheaded Irish longshoreman who worked in Providence.

In the antebellum days, Marjorie would have been called a Yellow Negro, but by the 1980's, she was simply thought of as an exceptionally attractive, light-skinned, African American, and she was so known. This was by her own choice entirely, for neither the color of her skin nor her other features appeared African in anyway, save perhaps a slight inclination of her hair to curl.

By 1985, Tubman was the leading property owner in what had once been referred to as The Quarters, and she enjoyed a very strong position in the circuit of local politics, as well as all Civil Rights activities in Alachua County.

She was twice honored as the leading contributor to her alma mater and highly respected among whites as well as blacks at the University of Florida, where she also was a large contributor to many of their more liberal foundations.

When it was learned that the garage in question was on one of her rental properties, the Chief immediately sent Mickey Johns to her office to explain what had been discovered and ask for her help in locating the culprits.

Mickey did not like this assignment. It required him to appear cleaned up and dressed appropriately, which would involve a bath and trimming his shaggy hair and beard.

"It compromises my effectiveness as an undercover agent and might unknowingly expose me to the very people I am trying to infiltrate," he argued, but he was ordered to do it anyway.

Some of what he said made sense to the Chief. However, Wilson planned to transfer Johns back to the patrol division when this bust was over anyway, and a little cleaning up would just be a step in that direction. Also, he realized sooner or later the ownership of the property would come to light and when it did, he wanted to be able to truthfully say Ms. Tubman was cooperating with the department in its investigation. Tubman just had too much influence in local politics to do otherwise.

Johns was in less than a good mood when he was ushered into Marjorie Tubman's office. However, as soon as he saw her, he was mesmerized and lost all of his previous hostilities.

'*She is beautiful,*' he thought, having never seen her before except on television or from afar.

He was correct in his observation. She indeed was beautiful, tall, slim, and stately.

'*Her movements are almost queenly,*' he thought, and for the first time in many years, he stammered in his speech.

She, on the other hand, found him uncouth and ignorant, but when his reason for being there was realized, she became much more tolerant of his human faults.

"By all means, I will cooperate with the police, in any way I can. I know Mrs. Green, who rents this property. And I assure you, she is in no way aware that the garage there is being used by anyone. You see she is a widow of some sixty-plus years. She has no vehicle, nor has she owned one since her husband was killed some years ago," she assured him.

"Well, I'm sure you are right, and I appreciate your assistance in this manner," Johns replied. Then added a question, "Would it be possible to place a surveillance camera in the house so we can watch the garage and record who comes and goes from there?"

"I think that is a wonderful idea, Sergeant. When will you be able to install it?"

"Detective. I'm a detective, not a sergeant."

"Well, I will say, Chuck Wilson is not using all of the talent he has available to him, if he has not made you a sergeant. I must speak to him on the matter."

"That's kind of you, Ma'am," Mickey said, smiling at her suggestion. "If we could get the permission from Mrs. Green, I will say we could have the camera ready by tonight."

"Oh, so soon? You are very efficient. See, I knew you should be a sergeant," she said, and then buzzed her secretary to enter.

"Miss Johnson, will you assist Detective Johns with anything he needs, and get my car ready. I must personally go and let the poor Widow Green know what has happened; otherwise, she would most surely shoot Detective Johns the moment he steps on her porch. You see, it was a white policeman who killed her husband."

Suddenly Mickey remembered who the Widow Green was and the incident whereby she became such. Eight or nine years before, Johnny Green was caught robbing the 7/11 store on Waldo Road and tried to shoot it out with the arriving squad car. He did get two hits into the cruiser before Officer Fielder sent him to his reward with a blast from the 870 Remington riot-gun he carried.

The old bitch raised hell then, and cried the whole incident had been staged by the racist police to kill her husband. The fact he had served two previous terms in Raiford for armed robbery, and had bonded out of ACDC[14] less than an hour before the robbery on a possession charge, never was reported by the news media. Neither was the fact that it had been a Hispanic cashier who he had just robbed and pistol whipped.

Normally, Johns would not have wanted this many people knowing about surveillance equipment, but considering the circumstances, he replied, "Yes, Ma'am, I would appreciate it if you would do just that."

As soon as she entered the Lincoln, she gave an address to her chauffeur and then closed the privacy window between the driver and passenger compartment. She picked up the phone and dialed. "Tubman here. We need to meet, we have a problem."

Unfortunately, the two weeks of stakeout and surveillance produced nothing except a huge deficit in the Detective

14 ACDC: Alachua County Detention Center, or the County Jail.

Department's overtime budget. They eventually concluded the bad guys somehow got wind of their cache being compromised. So the plug was finally pulled on everything and the PD simply confiscated the bales of pot, which they later burned on the backside of the Gainesville Airport.

This had been Charles Wilson's last real adventure as police chief, and he retired a week after it was over.

Mickey Johns was still a detective with the Gainesville Police Department when Paul Blackbyrd was promoted to Police Chief. Unfortunately for Mickey, unlike Chuck Wilson, Paul never liked him. In fact, he considered him dirty and would have liked few things more than to see him gone. For a couple of years he watched Johns carefully, hoping to either satisfy himself his hunch was wrong, or catch Johns red-handed committing a crime.

Unfortunately for the new chief, Johns was protected by the union, so he couldn't just up and fire him without cause. Paul was never able to get the goods on him, at least not enough to have him let go.

Paul Blackbyrd was not the politician his former boss was. He was a cop who had joined the department straight from his tour in Vietnam, and slowly worked himself up the ladder the hard way. He never rubbed elbows with the wheels downtown, or at the University. He had made chief on his record and he only owed a few, a hardworking and patient wife and some of his fellow officers who knew him. Mickey Johns was not one of them.

Within a month of his promotion, Paul contacted Duke Murrell, who was then heading the investigative branch of Florida Department of Law Enforcement, and asked for a rendezvous.

Paul and Duke had shared a room for a week, many years before at a supervisor's seminar in Tampa, back when Paul had just taken over the Detective Division of GPD and Duke had become Patrol Commander of the New Smyrna Police Department. They remained friends over the years, along with their wives.

Their lunch was to be served in the smaller conference room, near the back of The Brown Derby three weeks after the call. Paul had asked Jon, the manager, for the room personally, and was assured of its use and privacy.

Both Judy Murrell and Sharon Blackbyrd would be there for dinner, but while the girls spent time shopping, the two old friends arrived early for their discussion.

"Duke, I have what I think is a problem. I have an officer, a former task force detective that simply put, has too much cash all of the time. He lives in a rattrap of a house, with a wife who used to be a stripper in Daytona. She now sells Avon. He drives a Mercedes, admittedly an older one, but has a new Corvette for his wife. He was assigned to the Detective Division when I was promoted and I reassigned him back to the Patrol Division. Immediately, he filed a grievance on me for it, but I won that fight. When he was a detective, he had a free hand and Chief Wilson allowed him to work alone as an undercover agent. During that period, he was seen spending a lot of time in the company of a person who has enough political pull to probably get us both fired, a woman, who unofficially leads the civil rights organizations in the area."

"You aren't talking about Marjorie Tubman are you?" his friend interrupted.

"I sure am."

"I was afraid of that," Duke replied, nodding his head.

"I just have a gut feeling, along with what I've told you, he is dirty as it gets. But try as I may, I have not been able to catch him at it."

"You are asking me to set him up."

"No. If I'm wrong, then I want to know it, and I will return him to his beloved Detective Division. But if I'm right, I want him decertified," Paul said strongly.

"Well, in the twenty some years FDLE has been around, we have sent more crooked police chiefs and sheriffs to jail than in the one hundred years of Florida's previous Police history. However, I need to tell you Paul, we seldom find a crooked cop, in the sense most people think. It's usually someone paying back a favor that gets them in trouble, not being on the take. And that is usually the head of a department, or at least someone near the head, not a grunt," Duke told him with a shake of his head.

"I know all that. I also just know in my heart, Mickey Johns is dirty, and I want him gone from Florida Law Enforcement."

"What do you have on him?"

"Here is a file I brought for you," Paul replied, sliding a zipped vinyl folder across the table.

It was at that moment the girls entered the room and Judy said, "Oh, it's so gloomy in here. Let's go out to the lounge where we can hear the band."

"That band is too damn loud," Paul protested.

"If it's too loud, you're too old, Paul Blackbyrd, you ol' fuddy duddy," Judy said, and slapped him on the forearm.

"I'll see what I can do," Duke said, nodding to Paul and took the file before saying, "Paul, will you escort the two best-looking ladies in Gainesville out to the lounge while I check on something in the car?"

"What? Come on, Honey, don't be a party pooper," his wife said to him.

"I'll just be a minute," Duke replied, and then left before she could say any more on the subject.

The next time the two old friends met was seven months later at the Florida/Florida State game in the fall of 1986.

"Here," Duke said, handing back the same zipper folder. "I think this will serve your purpose. I'm not sure we can get him decertified, but I do believe you can get him to resign when you show him what is in there."

That night back in his room, Paul opened the file and took out several photos. Each had from a single note to several notes attached to them, explaining when, where, and for what purpose they were taken. Most simply showed Johns meeting with known criminals. These, Mickey could easily explain he was meeting with them to gather information. Then Paul came to a picture taken from quite a distance, showing two people standing on a balcony and apparently embracing. The note simply said, "Taken in Miami, July 3, 1986."

The next one was of the same clip, only blown up substantially, and in this one, it was very apparent the couple was nude and indeed kissing, but their faces were not visible. The next photo was obviously taken moments after the last, and this time the couple was standing close together looking at each other. The following blow up revealed he had a hand on one of her breasts and she had one hand on his privates. There was no doubt the man was Mickey Johns. However, what truly shocked Paul was the woman was Marjorie Tubman.

"How the hell?" Paul said aloud.

Also in the file were several photos of Johns' Corvette. Some of the photos showed him driving and some with his wife behind the wheel. Each were dated and located. Too, there was a photo of what appeared to be the same car only with an Alabama dealer's plate.

Next was a photo of a wrecked 'Vette that could have been the same car, only Paul knew Mickey's car had not been wrecked since he owned it. He was pretty sure Mickey had bought it new, too.

However, upon reading the note clipped to this photo, he smiled.

The VIN number on this wrecked 'Vette, matches the one on the vehicle Cherry Johns was driving on July 24, 1986. The VIN on the Corvette with the Alabama tag matches the VIN stamped on the vehicle Cherry Johns was driving on August 12, when she had the oil changed at the Standard Oil station in Micanopy.

Then he read the icing on the cake.

This is an incident report from the Hattiesburg Police Department, where the sales manager of Ryan Motors reported a 1984 black and silver Corvette was stolen from their lot. The VIN was the same as what is on Cherry's frame.

"So he bought a wrecked Vette, and switched the VIN plate to a new, stolen Alabama car,' Paul thought. *'Well, I might not be able to prove he knew it was stolen, but I damn sure will take it away and I don't think*

Cherry Johns will like that one bit, especially when I show her the pictures of her husband and a darkey.'

The next day Paul called Mickey into his office and had him close the door. Only Betty Small, the Chief's secretary, was there in the office with them.

Paul could tell the officer was nervous, but he was trying desperately to hide it, "What can I do for you, Chief?"

"You know Mrs. Small, don't you? Her son works for U. S. Customs."

"Yes. I know that. How are you, Ma'am?" he said, nodding to the lady there.

"Mickey, I received some disturbing information recently and I must say it bothers me a great deal. You see, it concerns your conduct, and not wanting to violate your Police Officer's Bill of Rights, I am going to ask Mrs. Small to record this conversation and be a witness to it all. You can have a copy of the tape when we are finished, in case you want to bring a lawsuit later."

Johns moved around in the chair some as he replied, "My conduct, my conduct has always been above board. Where, may I ask, did you get this information?"

Paul nodded his head a couple of times and then said, "That's a fair question. It came to me from FDLE[15]."

This time Mickey really squirmed around noticeably. "FDLE? What kind of information?"

"How long have you been married, Mickey?"

"To Cherry, well about five years now," he said and then added, "You know I was married before."

"Yes, to a nice little girl from Alachua. She gave you two children, if I remember right."

"Yeah, I have two kids, but I don't see what that has to do with anything."

"How long did you know Cherry before you married her?"

"About a year. Listen Chief, this is getting a little personal."

"Yes. I see what you mean, but I need to clarify a couple more things."

"All right."

---

15 FDLE: Florida Department of Law Enforcement.

"Now, when you met Cherry, she was working as a stripper for The Five O'Clock Club, is that right?"

"Yes, but she quit as soon as we got married."

"Does Cherry use drugs?"

Mickey coughed before looking up, "Of course not."

"Really, none at all?"

"Well, she might take some sleeping pills sometimes, but she has a prescription."

"No. I'm talking about smoking pot, shooting coke, or something like that."

"No, not at all. And I would know it if she did."

"That's right. With your background working with the drug task force, you underwent many hours of specialized training just to learn how to detect if someone was using drugs, didn't you?"

"Sure, we all did."

"Did you know she was a prostitute before you were married?"

"What? She never was."

"Well, unfortunately, yes she was," the Chief replied, and he handed over to Mickey a teletype sheet containing several arrest records of one Cherry Carpenter from Orange County.

He read them for a long time, but he did not look back at his boss.

"Mickey, if you will look at the fourth from the bottom record, you will see she was also arrested for shooting a man."

"Well, she was let go on that, it was self-defense."

"Yes, I read the trial transcript. The man she shot was her pimp. It seems she shot him because he had given her a diamond ring, and then took it back, and gave it to another woman. When she found out, she went into a fit. Of course, he was also armed and shot back at her, but considering he had a 38 slug in his gun-arm he missed."

"That ain't the way I heard it. Anyway, what she done back then ain't got nothing to do with me."

"You are right, it's what has happened since you two got married we are concerned with here," Paul agreed.

"Now, on July the second, you called in sick and stayed out for five days. Is that correct?"

"Yeah, I guess so. I had the flu."

"Yes, that is what you said."

"I brung in a doctor's slip to prove it."

"Yes. You did. Here is a copy of it, I believe. From a Doctor Stick it says here."

"Yeah, that's right, he is my doctor."

"I am having trouble with this. You see, I had Mrs. Small call Dr. Stick's office and ask for the original, but they couldn't find it. In fact, they were closed July the second through July the fifth, because of the holiday."

"I don't remember."

"I'm going to show you a photograph that was taken on July the third and ask if you recognize the people in the picture," Paul said, and then he reached across his desk with the first photo.

Mickey was slow in looking up and taking the picture, but when he did look at it, they both could see he was noticeably shaken. Finally, he pitched it back and said, "Naw, it was taken from too far away."

"Didn't you attend that conference last year, put on by FDLE, about surveillance techniques?"

"Yeah, I think I did."

"I know you did. I looked it up. You know one of the things they talked about at the conference was a new camera now available from NASA. It can take a picture from 50,000 feet and be blown up clear enough to see the numbers on a license plate," Paul added. He had to admit to himself that he was enjoying watching Mickey squirm. "Well, this picture was taken with a camera of the same general type and this is what it looks like when it is enlarged."

This time, he dropped the photo on his desk where all three of them could see it - the picture of Marjorie Tubman with her hand around Mickey's cock.

"I think I need to call an attorney," Mickey said.

"You certainly have that right, and being a former detective, you should know when one is needed. However, before you do, let me say this. I have not advised you of your rights yet, so nothing you have said here today can be used against you in a court of law. But if we stop now, I will seek a warrant for your arrest and will see you in court. Now, I will share with you I know a lot more than I have revealed so far and when this is over, I will see you are not only decertified, but also sent to Raiford; and you know the life expectancy of a former cop in there."

Paul stopped a few moments to allow what he had just said sink in, before continuing. "I know about the Corvette, and it will have to go back to Alabama. By the way, if Cherry will shoot her pimp over a $2000 dollar ring, what do you think she is going to do to you when she finds out your actions are losing her that precious Corvette she seems to treasure more that life itself?"

He paused for a few seconds before continuing, "I know about Cherry turning tricks at the last Gator/Seminole game for a party of students from Tallahassee. I know you took her there, and picked her up afterward. I have a sworn statement from the young man you set up the deal with. I know he paid you three hundred dollars for her unlimited performance."

At this point the Chief stopped for a few seconds before he asked, "Did she tell you they were taping the whole thing, including her being injected with something from a hypodermic syringe? Tell me, Mickey, was it speed or coke? Well, whatever was in the vial, it's not in this boy's statement, but it is very clear on the tape, and I'm sure we can find out without too much trouble. You see, he is in school on a rather liberal scholarship and is willing to cooperate fully, so as not to be expelled from his pre-med classes."

Once more Paul stopped for several seconds before asking, "Now Mickey, do you still want an attorney?"

This time the pause was equally long for his opponent, but finally Johns said, "No. I guess not," Johns shook his head back and forth before he said, with tears in his eyes, "I was a good cop."

"Yes, you were; for several years, but you went bad. You picked the wrong heroes. Now, before we do anything more, I want you to go into my bathroom there and give me a urine sample," Paul said, handing him the plastic container.

The defeated man stood, took the bottle, and slowly walked to the private bathroom in the back of the Chief's office. But when he started to close the door, Blackbyrd called out, "Leave the door open, Mickey, you know the routine."

The man slammed the door back against its stop and unzipped his pants. When he returned he handed the half-filled bottle to his boss, and then with slumped shoulders he asked, "What's next?"

"Mrs. Small," Paul said, looking over at the older woman and nodding his head.

For the first time, since Johns had entered the room, she spoke. "This is a letter of resignation. You have eight days annual leave and two days comp on the books. This document is dated effectively May 19, 1987[16], which will be the day your leave runs out, if you sign it now." When she finished her statement, she handed him a pen.

"If you sign this today, I will not turn this file over to the State Attorney. However, if you don't, I will see you in Raiford," Paul said.

"There is one more small price to pay for your freedom. If I ever hear of you attempting to get another job as a certified officer in Florida, or anywhere else, I will see that not only does the State Attorney get a copy of this, but also FDLE's police certification board."

Mickey Johns stood there weaving for several seconds, looking through tearing eyes at the paper. Finally, he reached to his rear where he carried the snub nose Cobra. Paul, seeing this, reached into his lap for the 45 he had ready, just in case Johns broke and did something irrational. Just as the chief was flipping down the thumb safety, Johns came around with a handkerchief, and wiped his eyes

---

16 On May 19 1987 NBC aired the last episode of 'Hill Street Blues'.

before saying grudgingly, "Hell!" and then signed the paper and threw it across the desk to the Chief. He then turned and started out.

"My pen," Mrs. Small said scornfully.

Johns stopped and looked at the pen still in his hand, then turned and tossed it on the desk before he headed for the door.

Immediately, Paul picked up the phone and called the OIC[17]. "Hello, Lieutenant, this is Chief Blackbyrd. Officer Johns just resigned. Please see he doesn't leave the building without turning in his badge and weapon. Yes, thank you."

Setting the receiver back into its cradle, he took a deep breath and turning to his secretary, asked, "What do you think?"

She laid her notebook down, stood to turn off the recorder, and looking down at the photos as she gathered them. She hesitated a moment, staring at the one in her hand at the time. Then she replied to his question, "I think, he has a damn nice cock, for a scum-bag!" With that, she dropped the photos back in the file, turned with it in hand, and went to her desk in the outer room.

Paul shot up against the back of his chair in shock. *'My God, she must be crowding fifty. I never would have expected that out of her!'*

---

17 OIC: Officer In Charge of the Police Station for that day.

Chapter Thirteen
The Key

Hunting season would begin the first Saturday in November, in Georgia, and Wall had been looking forward to it for several months. It wasn't necessarily the thrill of killing a deer that caused a grown man to spend nearly a thousand dollars on guns, ammo, proper clothing, transportation costs, licenses and a world of time. At least, it was not for Wall Roberts.

He had been killing deer since he was a mere boy. In fact, he killed his first when he was only eight-years-old with the help of his father, of course, and that deer, he would readily admit, was truly a thrill. However, since then, there were very few years when he had not taken at least one a season.

No, it was not the thrill of killing that caused him to sit almost totally still for hours on end in a tree stand some twelve to fifteen feet off the frozen ground. It was because Wall loved the outdoors, and he loved the break of day, and there simply were few places on earth where one could enjoy both this well from a tree stand on a fall morning in Dixie.

Florida's deer season would open a week later than Georgia, but he seldom hunted in Florida anymore. A few years back, he had happened on an old man who was in need of a hand repairing a fence a drunk driver had so ungraciously mowed down on the backside of his property. Because of this chance meeting, a long friendship was born between the young man of thirty, and the farmer who was more than twice his age.

Martin Belleville was a descendant of John Belleville, who had first settled the east bank of The Withlacoochee River in Hamilton County. Of the Lincoln assassination conspirators hanged, one of the men was from the village of Belleville. Few know this today. At one time, a century past, this thriving little community known as Belleville was prosperous. Now, however, only a few scattered houses where a large black family live is all that's left, except for Belleville himself.

He had inherited some 1100 acres on either side of the river and had been as successful a farmer as any one-man operation could be, in his younger days. However, when the State Road Department decided to put a bridge across the Withlacoochee River to connect Madison and Hamilton counties in the north, they did not follow the old ferry route. Rather, they cut nearly a mile off the distance between Pinetta and Jennings by angling right through the middle of Martin Belleville's farm. He was paid a fair price for his land, but he resented having to sell it to the state, and ever since, said that it had been the ruination of his farming business. "Cut me slam in two, just ruined me."

The truth of the matter is it was the best thing that ever happened to him financially. The state paid him enough to build a fine brick home on the Madison County side overlooking the river. However, most of all, it gave him a real excuse to retire. Soon, he had sold several ten-acre sites on the Hamilton County side, for big bucks. Later the State of Florida came along and bought most of his land along the river north of 'The Belleville Highway,' as the road between Pinetta and Jennings was now named, and put in a State Park.

This move, however, came to be a thorn in Martin's side, because they then declared it a No Hunting Area, and it had been his best acreage for taking the whitetail and wild hogs, which used the crossing at the shoals. Martin stomped and cursed when his wife was not around, and called every politician he knew, but it was to no avail.

"No Hunting on State Park land," was the statement he received each time he called. Finally, out of desperation, he and his brother, Bragg, went north to Crawford County, and took out a thirty-year hunting rights lease on two thousand acres from Georgia Pacific.

It was a beautiful part of Georgia, with rolling hills of the deepest red clay with the tallest pines one could imagine. It was bordered on the west by the Flint River, right at another deer crossing, along some shoals very much like the ones that had been on his property back in Florida. "Before the State of Floridee' did me out of it," as he would often say.

It was there at Belleville's Hunt Camp, Wall had been invited to pursue whitetails for the last couple of years. He loved every minute of it, even the freezing in the tree stands.

He had used many of his 'comp days'[18] to help Martin and his older brother build their hunt camp along the high bank of the Flint River, and had located, and acquisitioned, an expensive generator to furnish them with electricity until Georgia Power finally put power to the area.

In fact, it had been Wall who came up with the idea to put in a septic tank and trailer pad along the road and let a local deputy move his single wide in there for free.

"This will give us protection from trespassers and poachers, especially night hunters, when we are not here. It will also cause Georgia Power to have to bring electricity to your lease land."

The Belleville brothers agreed, although not without a few squabbles from Bragg.

It was not that Bragg was against the idea. In fact, he saw the merit of the suggestion right away, but the scrawny old man resented Wall, and especially the relationship his younger brother had developed with this young intruder. "He ain't family, he ain't even local. Nothing morn' one of them damn eastern immigrants," Bragg said more than once when discussing Wall and his entry into the family hunting club.

However, in the end, they spent the money for a septic tank, and a concrete pad, and before long, a deputy accepted the offer

18 Comp Days: Compensatory time for working overtime.

to locate a trailer there. It had been a good move and everyone knew it.

Not long after, Wall ran a line from the transformer to the new cabin he and Martin built. Then even on the coldest nights, Martin and Bragg could snuggle under their electric blankets and sleep more warmly.

Yes, Wall was really looking forward to opening day in Georgia, and had put in his vacation request for that whole week almost a year previously. Then, on the day before he was to leave, there appeared in his Post Office box in Pinetta a small puffy envelope. Inside, he discovered a key and a short note printed electronically on a gold outlined invitation card.

'Apartment 2404 Seminole Towers, November the Second, to celebrate my birthday.' It was signed, Mrs. Dunkin.

"Hell fire!" was his only statement. He knew he had to go. There was no way he would do anything to hurt her feelings, and missing her birthday would surely do just that. But oh, how he had longed to be on the Flint River that Saturday morning.

Wall Roberts was not the only one traveling to Tallahassee that first Friday afternoon in November of 1995. Trooper Ben Townsend was also on I-10 following the FHP semi, containing all his belongings. Over a year before, Ben was involved in a serious accident while pursuing a fleeing suspect. He was not expected to live for several days after the crash. However, through some miraculous events that none of the medical 'who's who' could explain, he simply opened his eyes one day while the nurse was changing his bed sheets.

To say he had a full recovery would be stretching one's imagination a bit, but he was pretty much recovered by the time his sick leave ran out. He still walked with a substantial limp, and assigned to the radio room.

Ben was thankful to be alive and glad to be back at work, but he longed for the hard road. Being a dispatcher just was not for him, and he eventually began to push his supervisors to let him back in a patrol car. Lt. Snyder admitted he probably could have done the job, if he didn't have to chase anyone on foot.

Unfortunately, there was another problem Snyder had detected, as well as had Sergeant Howard. Ben Townsend was not fully recovered mentally. Both had observed times when he would go blank, staring off into nowhere, and be very unaware of his immediate surroundings. These episodes usually would only last a few seconds, but they were there and there was no denying them.

That is, except for Ben Townsend. He did not realize they were happening and refused to believe it when told he needed to see his doctor about the problem. Instead, he decided *'It is just Snyder's way of getting rid of me, and that kiss ass Howard hasn't got the balls to back me against him.'*

The more that was said on the subject, the more defiant Ben became, and finally when he was ordered to see the doctor on the matter, he filed a grievance against his supervisor.

Had it been most troopers who found themselves in this situation the Patrol would simply have retired them on a medical separation and that would have been the end of it, but Ben had been a good trooper.

Ben had been with the Patrol since the Thirty-Fifth Recruit class, in January 1969, and had been the first trooper to become a Homicide Investigator in Troop B. Everyone liked him, including his Lieutenant and Sergeant, all the way up to the Colonel himself. No one wanted to see Ben Townsend treated badly.

He was sick and needed to be treated as such, but his illness was too serious to continue allowing him to dispatch. A dispatcher is a trooper's only contact with the outside world when in danger, and it simply would not do for Ben Townsend to be in one of his blank times if a trooper called 10-24[19]. For this reason, the patrol transferred Ben to GHQ in Tallahassee to work in the Statutory Research Division.

---

19 10-24: I need help immediately.

As he followed the semi along at 55 mph, he thought, *'I really hate leaving Gainesville, but at least I am getting away from Snyder and Howard, the bastards. They used to say what good friends we were. I hope the both of them rot in hell.'*

At that moment, he looked over at the white 1963 'Vette as it sped past them. He started to pull out and pursue the car, but at the last moment thought better of it. *'That son-of-a-bitch better be glad I'm not in my patrol car or his ass would be mine.'*

They traveled on until he finally saw the U.S. 90 exit ahead, and was thinking as he followed the trailer off the interstate, *'I will be able to show Colonel Lauderdale there ain't nothing wrong with me, in no time. In fact, I'm requesting a meeting with him first thing Monday morning.'*

Tuesday morning, after a long discussion with Lauderdale, Ben Townsend turned in his retirement papers and left the patrol.

Wall had never been to *The Seminole Towers*, although he had seen them several times. In fact, it was almost impossible to drive into Tallahassee without seeing them soar above all other buildings.

He parked his 'Vette around the block on Eighth Ave, and walked back to The Towers.

Upon entering, he was immediately stopped by a security officer, but when Wall showed him the note and the key, the uniformed man nodded his head, pointed to the elevator, and said, "Twenty-fourth floor sir."

"Twenty-fourth, huh? How many floors are there?"

"Twenty-four, sir," was his only answer.

When he stepped off the elevator, he suddenly realized there were only four doors on the floor. *'Does this mean there are only four apartments on this whole floor?'* he questioned himself.

Wall Roberts was nervous, quite nervous. He felt totally out of place as he pushed the buzzer under the shingle, 2404. However when she opened the door and stood there before him, he melted.

'There is no question, she is the most beautiful woman I have ever seen, and I am so thankful some movie scout did not spot her and swept her off to Hollywood before she married Rugg.'

Unknown to Wall, there had been two movie scouts who had spotted Blue while she was in Vegas, but Willis Cunningham would have nothing to do with their offers, and at the time, she was totally under his control.

Standing there, in a magnificent peach colored gown consisting of several layers of some transparent material he had never heard of, she seemed like a vision from some unreal dream, sent by the gods to torment him. However, when she reached out and drew him to her, he knew it was no dream, and he felt sorry for the fellows who would see the dawn from a tree stand in Middle Georgia.

Later, after she had explained she had left Goldie at the airport, and taken a cab back so he could use one of her parking spots in the underground garage, he went down and moved the 'Vette. On the elevator ride back up, he read the parking ticket he had found slipped under his windshield wiper. *'Son-of-a-bitch!'*

Before he had left her, she had told him to keep the garage gate remote and the key to the apartment. Also sometime during the weekend, she made the statement this was the first time she had ever stayed there, and he suddenly felt very special, and knew they were both falling out of control for each other. *'A forbidden love that can never develop into anything more than clandestine rendezvous, in hidden places. However, the thought of never seeing her again is unimaginable.'*

There had also been another subject that she had brought up during the weekend, Dixie Marie.

"How is the blonde?" she asked as she ran her fingers over his chest.

He was on his back and she lay on her stomach beside him, propped up on one of her elbows.

"What blonde?" he replied, knowing full well who she meant.

"You know, Dixie something or other," she replied, still doing her thing with her long fingers through the dark curly hair there.

"Oh, Dixie Marie. She's fine, I guess," he answered, wondering where this was leading.

"You still banging her?"

"I never banged her. If you will remember I got sidetracked by a redhead."

"Yes, you did," she said, smiling.

"Why do you ask such a question?"

At that point, she took a deep breath and then letting it out she said, "I just want you to know, if you need more than I can give you, I will understand."

"What brought this on?" he questioned, thinking, '*She must have another fellow on the side besides me, and is trying to relieve her conscience.*'

"Oh, I was just thinking the other day that there are so few times when we can be together, and I know you have a strong sex drive and need relief often. I just don't want you to feel you can't have sex with someone else. I mean, if you did, it would not damage our relationship," she added.

She moved over and lay beside him, with her head resting between his arm and shoulder, she took another deep breath. "Wall, if I was free and we were married, I wouldn't want you to ever look at another woman; I'm not though, and as long as Nate is alive, I never will be. So I want to be fair, that's all."

He ingested what she had said, and this time believed her intentions to be just as she had explained. This made him feel good, and he twisted around and kissed her softly on the lips. "You could divorce him, you know."

"No. It's not that simple. You don't know Nate. He would love to be rid of me, but he would never let me go alive. It's far more complicated than a divorce, and it will never happen."

"I don't ___,"

She stopped him by kissing his lips softly.

As much as he enjoyed the time spent with her, and truly, it was time spent with her, because neither left the apartment from the moment he returned from the parking garage until Sunday night. Still when he headed back to Madison, he began to feel the desire to be in the deer camp with the others, and he didn't tell her that he had the rest of the week off. Instead, as soon as he got back to Hanson, he changed clothes and vehicles and drove on to Roberta that night.

Twice he fell asleep on the stand the next morning, and almost fell out the first time, but he was there, where he belonged, and just before dark, he put a 220-grain Krag round through the neck of a big eight-point buck, redeeming himself with Martin Belleville for being late.

What he didn't realize was it was the largest deer ever taken in that part of Georgia. When the Bellville's carried it into town to have it hung in the cooler, a freelance reporter saw it, and after assuring the dressed weight to be just short of four hundred pounds, did a story on it in *The Macon Informer*. The headlines read:

The Largest Whitetail Ever Killed in Georgia

Of course, Wall's tag was attached, so the reporter quickly knew who shot it, and with just a little investigative work, found Wall Roberts was from Madison County, Florida. In no time, he had sold the story to *The Madison Trace*.

The local paper not only ran the story on the front page, they also found a picture of Wall from their files where he had been photographed working on a downed power line.

When Blue saw the paper and realized the date, she sat back and thought hard. *'If he had told me he had more time off we could have spent it together.'*

Two weeks later, when Nate left for Chicago, she drove to Madison and there she used a pay phone to call The Co-op and asked to leave a message for him, but the lady at the switchboard said, "Wall's gone to Georgia hunting again. He won't be back for three days."

Blue then realized the importance her lover placed on this sport. *'My competition is not a Dixie blonde, rather a big-eyed deer.'*

Later that night Blue conceived a way to correct that problem.

When he returned, Ash told him teasingly that a lady had called for him while he was away. She had also told all the other girls in the office.

Wall was sure it had been Blue, but he had no way of getting in touch with her. As a result, he worried something might be wrong and realized the relationship of their affair was becoming a twisted series of pleasure followed by loneliness, followed by worry, and then it began all over again. It was a strain, and had it been any other woman he had ever met, he would have dropped her and moved on to new pastures. But that thought only brought a long spell of heartburn and he skipped his supper that night and ate Tums instead.

A week before Christmas, he received another invitational note on the same stationary at the post office in Pinetta, it simply said, "I'm flying to the Rockies, if you want to see a White Christmas come to 2404 Friday night."

He slowly shook his head. He had already told Belleville he would be on the Flint River over the holidays, but he could not pass up the opportunity to spend the time with her. It had been over a month since he had last seen her and had almost taken up her offer to start something with someone else on the side.

The deer in Georgia would have to get by without him this Christmas, because as soon as he left the parking lot that Friday, he was westbound towards CR 255, which would lead him to Interstate 10, through the town of Lee.

The Withlacoochee Co-Op was located on SR 6 almost to the county line. In fact, the east boundary of their property was the river, and that is where the founding fathers got the idea for the name.

Wall was north of the little crossroads known as Lee, when he saw James Hancock walking ahead on the side of the road. Pulling over and backing up for his old friend, he asked, "You need a lift?"

"I sure do. It's colder than a witch's tit out here."

"That your truck back there?" Wall asked, remembering the old Ford pickup he had passed sitting unattended a mile or two up the road.

"Yeah, she just started spitting and a' spatting, and then quit running. I couldn't get her to start up again and finally I ran the battery down."

"Sounds like you got water in the gas."

"Yeah that's just what it acted like, only it ain't been out in the rain. I was over to Brice Meal's for a while. Maybe some of them little brats that live down the road from him put some in it."

"You want to go back to his house?"

"Naw, he's gone to pick up his girl. Supposed to meet them later at Debbie's. Just take me to Lee."

"Yep. Found on the Road Dead, is what my Pa always called Fords."

"I almost want to agree with you this evening," James replied, as he held his hands up closer to the heater vent.

"Tell me about that big ass deer you shot," James asked. Wall gave him the details, leaving out the reason he had been late in getting to the hunt camp. Finally as a means to change the subject he asked, "Been diving lately?"

"Hell no! It's too blame cold, even with a wet suit."

"Now that don't sound like the Old Navy Seal talking to me," Wall teased him.

"Navy Seal, ha. That was a long time ago. Maybe back in those days."

"You never mentioned why you left the navy, is it personal?"

"No. Not really. It's just that Draft Dodger Clinton cut the navy budget so much there just wasn't enough money to go around. Our training was cut way back, and as a result, one of my friends lost his life. It just pissed me off so much I quit. Probably shouldn't have, but that's spilled beer now."

Leaning his head back, he looked up at the roof of the car for a few moments, and then said, "Yeah, I was crazy enough back then, but these days, I know better. Just you wait until spring comes. I know where there is a cavern that has catfish big enough to eat a man. White as a ghost, they are, too"

"You're crazy."

"Hell no, I ain't. Right here on the Withlacoochee. You just wait, when this cold snap is over, I'll take you down there and you can see for yourself."

"That's alright. I ain't much for cave diving," Wall said. "By the way, how's your Mom and Dad?"

"Gee, I'm not sure. They have taken to fighting a lot lately. I don't know. Pop, is always accusing her of running around on him, and she yells back he's always too drunk to know it if she did or not."

"That's too bad. I know he loves her very much. I can see it in his eyes when he looks at her."

"Yeah. Well, she's right about his being drunk most of the time, but I ain't sure he's wrong about her either. There's this fellow, some Italian guy, who has taken to hanging around *The Crossroads* a lot the last few weeks, and I seen her look at him myself. Pop seen it too, and that is what started this whole argument, I reckon.

"Funny thing is, he ain't much to look at, but he seems to have unlimited funds," James replied and then added, "Claims he has a home business on the computer, but when I tried the address he talked about, I couldn't get it to come up.

"The other night, he was in with some creepy looking little shrimp. They were both overdressed for *The Crossroads*, and even I could tell their expensive outfits came from K-Mart or som'ers like that. Only thing is, Mom seems to like this guy. Well, anyway, she sure is flirting with him, and it makes Pop mad-earn' hell. Kind a' scares me on account of what Pop might do."

"I'll bet she's just flirting with him to make your Dad jealous."

"Maybe. I hope so, but Mom's up in her forties now and you know what they say about mid-life crisis, and all."

"Your Mom is still an attractive lady. I doubt she needs to prove anything to herself or anyone else," Wall said back, trying to encourage his friend.

"I hope you're right," James replied, just as they arrived at the blinking light in Lee. Stopping there Wall asked, "Where can I drop you, James?"

"Oh, here's good. I'll go over to Archie's and call my girl to come get me.

"We were going out tonight anyway, and I'll just surprise her and buy her supper, too. Hey, why don't you join us, Dorsey has a seafood buffet on Friday nights, and then you can meet Sissy. Man she has legs that run all the way up to her ass. We are planning on having a few beers at Debbie's later, they do Karaoke there, and Sissy can naturally sing some country, I want to tell ya. You'd think Patsy Cline's done up and been reincarnated. They got some pool tables, too."

"Gee, I'd like to, but I got a date myself."

"Hell, bring her along."

"No. She's in Tallahassee."

"Oh, well don't strain a nut," James said smiling. Just before he closed the door, he said, "Merry Christmas, Wall," he paused and with a slight grin he added, "And thanks."

Wall waited until James had crossed U.S. 90 before he pulled away from the stop sign. He tooted his horn as a good-bye gesture just as his friend was going into the old service station, turned restaurant. He saw the arm go up in reply, but the boy never turned around.

Wall used his new car phone to call the apartment as soon as he got off the interstate and she told him she would be in the garage. "I have the Lear waiting for us, but I want to drive to the airport in Goldie, just in case Nate's had someone follow me here."

"Okay. I'll be there in twenty minutes if this traffic will let me," he replied and then turned off his phone.

True to her word, when he opened the garage gate he saw her Olds back from the parking place and he pulled into it. It only took him a couple of seconds to grab his bag and hop in beside her, and then the dark windows hid them from any nosy outsiders.

"Damn, you look good," he said.

"You don't look so bad yourself, cowboy," she said back and then smiled.

Again, they had a long sexual encounter on the jet, but after landing, Wall noticed they were not at the new Denver International Airport, and looking around, he had no idea where they were. The terminal was much smaller than at Denver, and the area was not nearly as well lit. "Where are we?"

"Our home away from home," she replied, with a twinkle in her eye.

He knew better than to question her when she was being mysterious, so he just followed her to the baggage pick up.

"Will you get our luggage while I secure a cab?" she asked, almost as a statement rather than a question.

He nodded his head, "Sure, just don't run off and leave me. I'm lost."

"Don't you worry, cowboy, I'm never going to let you get away from me," she replied before turning.

"Coliseum Motors," she said to the driver, when they were both seated in the back of the cab.

"Si' Ma'am," the dark skinned driver replied and Wall wondered how long he had been in this country.

When they arrived at the big Chrysler dealership, she paid the driver, and gave him a ten-dollar tip. Wall knew she had more money than God, but he never understood overpaying for anything, and a ten-dollar tip for a ten-minute ride, was ridiculous in his mind.

Wall could only see two or three people still at the dealership when they arrived, and they appeared to be cleaning people. He did notice a green Ford pickup with white doors, and a red light bar on top, was parked around the side. The exhaust smoke told the tale the deputy who had left it there was most likely nearby.

She tried the large glass door, but it was locked, and then she knocked on it a couple of times, but her gloved hand was not making enough noise to be heard over the tile polisher a fat Mexican woman was using on the showroom floor.

Wall balled up his fist and pounded on the door a couple of times hard, with the base of his hand. Immediately a deputy's head shot out from one of the offices. He was a huge man, well over six feet, maybe as much as six-feet six-inches, and Wall would guess near two hundred and fifty pounds, perhaps more.

Seeing them, he looked back into the office, and a young lady quickly came rushing out to unlock the door, letting them in. "Oh my, Mrs. Dunkin. I am sorry. I never thought you would get here so soon, the roads being like they are."

"The cab driver was quick," Blue replied, as they walked inside, and clear of the howling wind.

Wall could not help but notice the deputy giving Blue the once over, and for just a moment he felt a streak of jealously. But then realized, he would have done the same, and in fact did, to the smaller woman who was now leading them into her office.

"This is Sergeant Sanders. He will make sure you don't get stuck going up the mountain. We had a bad drift there earlier today, but the road is supposed to be open now," the sales lady said, and then she offered two chairs for them to sit in.

Wall was completely confused. He had seen two or three car rental booths in the airport terminal and had no idea why she would come here to rent a car when she could have had one waiting for her at the airport.

Looking at the deputy's shoulder patch as he shook hands with the big man, he read, Natrona County, Wyoming. He lifted his eyebrows slightly, '*So that is where we are.*'

"Nice to meet you," the deputy said.

At that moment he heard Blue say to the sales lady, "I want this vehicle in my husband's name only," then she turned and looked up at him. "Darling, do you want just Wall or Wallace on the title?"

"What?" he replied, looking around at her quickly.

"Oh, just put Wallace Roberts."

"Roberts?" Sterling Gilman questioned.

"Yes. You see I have retained my maiden name, for business purposes, but his is Roberts," Blue explained.

"Oh, I see. Well, this will need to be corrected. I did not know."

"That's okay. We'll stop back in, a couple of days from now, to pick up the papers. Now, where do we sign?"

"Well, I guess you do not need to sign anywhere, if your name is not going to be on the title."

She then passed the document to him, "If you will sign here, and here, Mr. Roberts," indicating lines next to red X's.

When he finished signing, the lady took the papers and placed them in a filing basket, then rose. "Now, if you will follow me, I have your new Grand Cherokee in the back, so it would not be too cold for you."

"I need to make a call first, if I may," Blue said to her.

"Certainly, you may use the phone here in my office."

She reached for the phone but then seeing him standing there, she said as she flipped her fingers at him, "Go ahead, Darling, I won't be but just a moment."

There was something he found distasteful in the way she had dismissed him, not that he thought she couldn't make a private phone call without his overhearing, but there was just something.

Wall reached for his bags, but the deputy beat him to them, "I'll carry them for you, sir," he said, easily lifting the three bags with one hand. The short, dark-haired sales woman led the way with Wall following and the deputy bringing up the rear. They walked back into an unheated garage area, to a black jeep with a trailer attached to the rear bumper. On the trailer was a snowmobile.

Wall did not notice the Deputy leave; he was too interested in looking over the new Jeep.

"Yes, Mr. Bowin? This is Miss Duncan. I would like you to start the fire now. We are on our way up," Blue paused and then said, "Yes, thank you," and then she returned the receiver to its cradle before leaving the small office.

Blue saw the large deputy standing by a door. "This way, Ma'am," he said, and opened it for her. "I hope you will be pleased with the snow machine," Nick Sanders said. "I got the one I would buy, if I was getting a new one this year. It's a Polaris XCR 600. The best money can buy."

"I'm sure it will be just perfect," Blue said back to him, and then handed him an envelope before she added, "We will need to leave Monday morning. I do hope you can see that the Mountain Road is not closed."

Feeling the thickness of the envelope he replied, "It will be open Mrs. Duncan, if I have to shovel it out myself."

"Well, let's hope that is not the case," Blue replied, and then she walked into the open garage where she took the keys from Miss Gilman and handed them to Wall. Then giving him a soft kiss on the cheek, she said, "Merry Christmas, Darling."

Next, she walked around to the passenger's side, where the lady opened the door for her. At that time, she handed an envelope to her and said, "I do appreciate you staying so late, and I hope you have a Merry Christmas as well."

The sales lady motioned for Sanders to pull on the chain that opened the big door, and Wall drove out onto the ice-covered parking lot.

"Damn this thing sure smells new."

"It is new. Do you like it? I wasn't sure about the color, I remembered you said you had a jeep that your father gave you, and your Corvette is white. I wasn't sure about black." Then she quickly added, "If you don't like it, they have a white one on order. It will be here in a few days. We could trade."

"Hell, I love it, but I don't understand any of this."

"I'll tell you all about it later," she said and slid over close to him and hugged his right arm. "It arrived with those awful bucket seats, but I had them replace them with this one so I could sit next to you." Then she squeezed his arm tight.

"How much did she give you?" he asked her.

"A thousand dollars."

"The same for me," Nick said back, and picked up the small woman. He held her high over his head before adding, "Tonight honey, we are going to have us a ball."

"Not until you get back from escorting them up the mountain."

"That won't take long," he said. "I'll drop off this pickup at the SO and get my truck and come by for you. Be ready."

"I'm already ready, big boy. You hurry back," Sterling said.

At the next light, Wall noticed the Sheriff's pickup was beside them, and when the light changed the Deputy pulled in front of his new Jeep and Wall was satisfied just to follow him.

Driving on ice-covered roads was something new to him and twice, he almost slid into the pickup before he began to give himself plenty of room. Finally outside of town, the Deputy pulled off on a side road and Wall saw his arm wave at them as they passed headed up the mountain.

Blue directed him at the two cutoffs.

It was obvious someone had recently cut a road through the white blanket, for the sides of the driveway were at least six feet high, of blown snow. At last, they came to a log structure.

The trail in the plowed powder led to the rear of the cabin, and it ended there against a ten-foot high wall of hard-packed snow and ice, and it was there he had to stop.

"Come on, I want to show you your new cabin," she said, as she opened the door allowing a rush of sub-zero air to enter the Cherokee. '*I reckon I have no choice,*' he thought, and soon followed her around the rear of the Jeep and trailer, where she was plowing a narrow trail through the powder between two cabins, one small and the other larger, with her strong legs. On the west side, he saw her stop at a door and begin fumbling with the keys to unlock it.

A thin column of smoke was rising from the chimney. It was one of the most picturesque scenes he had ever witnessed, with the moon shining on the blanket of whiteness that covered everything as far as the eye could see, save this little cabin nestled among some pine and aspen trees.

"Here, give me the keys," he said, and taking them from her gloved hands, he opened the hardwood door and let her in. Inside, the cabin was lit by small hidden lamps high overhead near the tall ceiling and they bathed its all-wooden interior with a warm glow.

To his left as he stood in the doorway, was a large rock fireplace with a single huge flat rock secured into the structure and serving as the hearth. Above it, hanging on the wall, was a fishing rod. In front of it on the floor, was a black rug made from a very large bear's furry hide. To his right, was an open kitchen and behind it were two doors.

"Come on in, you're letting in a lot of very cold air," she said, throwing her silver fox shawl over the long beige couch before turning around and lifting her arms out wide, as one would think an angel might do. Then she said, "Well, Mr. Roberts, what do you think of your new hunt camp?"

The fireplace as Wall first saw it.

"I don't know what to say," he honestly replied.

"Here, I want to show you something," she said excitedly, pulling him over to the bar separating the kitchen from the great room.

"See," she said, pointing to several identification cards laying there alongside a legal size document.

"Here are your new ID cards, officially making you a resident of the State of Wyoming. A Wyoming drivers' license, a Natrona County voter's registration card, a photo ID, an AT&T calling card on your Wyoming phone number. And this, My Darling Man, is the deed to your new cabin," she now held up the document sheet for him to read.

Wall just stood there slowly shaking his head, before saying, "I just don't understand."

"What's to understand? Merry Christmas!"

"But, I ____."

She stopped him mid-sentence, "Now, in that red refrigerator over there," she turned him by the shoulders pointing into the kitchen, "is a bowl of large prawns. If you would be so good to get them out and run some water over them, while I change. I will be back in a jiffy and prepare for you the most scrumptious shrimp salad you have ever eaten.

"Oh yes, there are a few bottles of champagne in there, too. Open one, please." Then she quickly disappeared through a door on the right side of the kitchen, without giving him much of a chance to respond one way or the other.

Wall noticed there were three inside doors, one on either side of the kitchen, and another off to his left, he opened it and looked in. *'Ah, a bathroom.'*

Turning back and looking in the freezer door, he removed the large bowl of shrimp, placed them under the faucet, and began running cold water over them. *'Damn, I don't know about this girl,'* he thought. *'I can't keep up with her.'*

"Wall, will you put some more wood on the fire?" the voice called out from the other room.

"Sure," he replied, and walked over to the well-stocked wood box. From the box, he retrieved three pieces of split poplar. He turned, pulling back the dark mesh screen before gently placing them over the single remaining flickering log.

There was considerable ash under the grate, and he could see faint embers still glowing from it. He knew the fire had been burning for some time before they arrived.

He was just standing when the door opened and she came out, and again he had to catch his breath. Never had he seen a more beautiful woman.

This time she was in a long, white, flowing gown reaching almost to the floor. He was sure it was meant to do that very thing, and it would have on most women, but she was so tall, it allowed him to see her ankles, and the sparking diamond bracelet she wore around one.

There was just a hint of color where he knew her well-trimmed bush was hiding, and he could see ever so slightly her large areola, through the material. He immediately felt his manhood begin to move about in his jeans. Her fiery hair was the perfect contrast to the white gown, and the sight of her standing there on display for only him to view, was something to behold.

"You like?" she asked.

"My God, you're beautiful."

"Being with you makes me want to be beautiful," she said back, and then looked over to the sink where the water was still running over the shrimp. Turning off the faucet, she shook the colander to allow the water and small pieces of ice to fall away. "Are you hungry, Wall? I'm famished."

"I'm hungry for you."

His statement pleased her. Of course, she knew she was exceptionally attractive, the fact she stood six-foot and one-inch in her bare feet in itself, was enough to attract attention to her, by both men and woman. She also realized she had been blessed with a voluptuous figure to complement her height, and any heterosexual man would have desired her, but she was no longer attracted to any heterosexual man. She was attracted to only one man, and it was this man who had just said those wonderful words to her, "Oh, you silly man, you just had me not two hours ago," she replied to him, as if the statement he had made was of no real importance to her.

"Yeah, well like the Democrats are always saying, that was then and this is now."

"Soon, my man, soon, but not before I eat something; you don't want me to get too skinny do you?"

"No," he admitted. "I don't want you to ever change one little bit."

This also pleased her, but she didn't tell him. Instead, she asked, "Will you pour us some champagne while I throw this together?"

Pulling the chef's knife from the large wooden castle sitting above the stove, she began to chop celery sticks.

When he held the goblet in front of her, she stopped, laid down the Cutco and reached for the glass.

"To the prettiest woman I know," he said, lightly tapping his glass to hers.

"To my man, among men," she replied, and re-tapped his glass before she took a sip.

"Wall, will you peel the shrimp for me? I don't want to get my gown all stained."

He hated peeling shrimp, but he would never let her know it. "Sure," he said, reaching for one of the crustaceans. "Where did you find such large shrimp in the middle of the desert?"

"Oh, there is a really wonderful fish market over in Vancouver. I was there a couple of years ago with Nate. There is this most delightful little old lady who runs it. I think her sons do the fishing. Anyway, I called her and had them flown in last Friday when I was here. Aren't they nice and big? I think she said they went 14 to a pound."

"You were here last week?"

"Sure. I had to come out and finish the paperwork on purchasing the cabin, and also make certain they would have your new Jeep ready when we arrived. There were a lot of details that had to be taken care of. Didn't I do a good job? I'm a good lover, don't you think so?"

"You are a Cracker-Jack all right," he admitted, "but all of this, it is so much."

"Not for someone who can curl my toes the way you do," she said and winked at him before she half-filled a large pot with water and placed it on the burner.

"By the way," she began, more as a means to change the subject than for information, "they say water is very scarce up here, and we should be quite conservative with it, or the well will lose its prime."

Wall looked around and then asked again, "Just where are we anyway?"

"We are on Casper Mountain. I think they said, eighty-three hundred feet above sea level, in Natrona County Wyoming, at the cabin of Master Wallace Roberts. Anything else you want to know?"

He really didn't know what to say. This whole trip was such a surprise, he was truly caught off his feet. Finally, he replied, "Why Wyoming, I thought you were from Colorado?"

"I am, and that is exactly where Nate's spies will be looking for me. Now, no more questions. I'll explain it all later after we have eaten and done certain other chores," she said, pointing to the shrimp that needed peeling.

"I can't believe you had these flown in just for this meal."

"Well I did, and I also had these onions flown in from Vidalia, Georgia, so there," she said, as she made a very thin cut into the bulb, then held up the remainder of the onion for him to see before she chopped up the slice into tiny cubes and placed them over the cut celery.

The only table was small and near the window. On it sat a glass pitcher and four glasses beneath an overhead light, hanging from the ceiling.

"Wall, will you remove those things and turn off the light?"

Once he had, she brought a tall candle that she placed in the center of the table, and then a couple of large plates filled with the salad. These she set on either side of the tall candle. When she lit it and turned off the kitchen lights, he had to admit she had created a most romantic atmosphere. The candle offered just enough illumination for the table area and the light from the flickering flames in the stone fireplace bathed the interior of the log cabin softly.

Wall's table as he first saw it.

Wall looked about and ingested it all before nodding his head.

"You approve?" she asked seeing his gesture.

"I approve," he replied as he turned back and looked into her sparking emerald eyes.

"I tried to get a Christmas tree. I even have all the lights and everything, but the man I hired to cut and deliver it had a serious accident and wasn't able to do it for me. I hope you are not disappointed for not having one."

"Silly girl; Trix are for kids, and so are Christmas trees."

"Well, this kid likes Christmas trees and Trix for that matter," she said, with her head lowered. She began slowly raising it until he could see her eyes staring straight at him, big beautiful emerald eyes.

After eating, they took their goblets to the great room and she dropped to the floor on the bearskin rug and began gazing into the fireplace.

He sat down beside her, and then leaned over and kissed her strongly and passionately on her lips. She immediately felt her juices begin to flow and responded equally with his embrace.

Feeling him fumbling with the tie belt at the small of her back that secured her gown, she stopped him, "Let me do it."

Standing, she slowly removed it, letting it inch down until the upper portion of her breasts were visible and he could see a hint of her nipple area. There she stopped for a few seconds, and then slowly she lowered it some more, revealing the fact she had inserted small silver badges over them. A hole just large enough for her nipple to protrude through was cut in the center of each badge, and through these, were tiny silver pins with an emerald on each end.

This was something new for him. He did not know she had her nipples pierced. She had nothing in them on the airplane, and he did not notice the small punctures. He now remembered, she seemed unusually sensitive, and stopped him when he wanted to suck on them. Now here they were, right before his eyes, with the obviously expensive jewelry, and he immediately became even more aroused than he had been before.

"When did you have that done?"

"I was over in Daytona a few days ago, and decided to give it a try. Do you like?"

"Very much. Very much indeed."

Being satisfied her new additions had accomplished her intended goal, she continued lowering her gown until she reached her naval and there, he saw a fair size emerald. On down came the white gown until her triangle was visible.

The first time they had been together, she had her hair trimmed into a two-inch wide skid-strip and he had commented about liking it. Since that time, only the night at Ray's hanger had she not had it trimmed in that manner, and he was pleased to see this was not such a time.

Finally, she stepped from the garment, which now lay in a highly expensive pile of material on the floor, and lifted her arms to her sides, with bent elbows she opened her hands and held her palms up as if to say, "How do I look?"

"Come here," was his answer.

"No," she replied, and then turning, she walked away dressed only in a pair of green spiked heels. When she reached the heavy drapes to the right of the fireplace, she stopped and pulled the cord.

Immediately they opened to reveal a pair of glass sliding doors. Opening one, she looked back and asked, "Are you coming?"

At first, he thought she wanted them to have sex in the snow, and he wasn't sure his man-thing would go for that. However, he knew he had no choice and got up and followed her.

When he reached the glass door, he realized it opened into a small room, which was logged up about three feet, and then roofed with a glass dome. In the center was a large wooden hot tub and she was just stepping into it.

'Damn, I didn't realize this was even here. Hell, I didn't even realize there was a door behind those curtains.'

"Wall, pull the drapes, too, please. I want to look at the stars."

Later, they each had a huge orgasm on the bearskin rug in front of the fireplace, the third of the night for him, and something over the twentieth for her.

The next morning broke bright and sunny, and even though he had only gotten to bed three hours before, he was up to view its rising. However, she had only stirred a little when he rose.

First, looking at the near empty bottle of wine he found on the table, he filled a goblet and swallowed the warm liquid in a large gulp. Then he gathered the dirty dishes and placed them in the sink.

He picked up her discarded gown, and folded it as well as a man can, and laid it on the leather couch before stepping out into the Jacuzzi room.

There he picked up his jeans and shirt, located her heels, and brought them back inside. He was just starting to put on his pants, when he thought better of it. He went to the bathroom before returning to the bed where he slipped in beside her, to give his body a little time to regain some of its strength.

It was nearly three o'clock when he felt her getting out of bed and soon after, he heard the toilet flush.

"Wall," she called out softly and alluringly and he thought, *'My God she is ready for some more.'*

"Yes?" he replied.

"I'm hungry. Do you know how to fry bacon?"

"Do I know how to fry bacon? I am not just a bachelor, I am a bachelor supreme. Not just a cook, but a chef," he bragged, and throwing off the electric blanket, sprang from the bed and started out to meet her.

Neither dressed that entire day, but the day was not spent in each other's arms every minute.

She explained why she had put everything in his name, and why it was important that no one knew where this hideout was located. "I know someone will eventually learn you have been in Wyoming, but I want the exact location a mystery. Nate has so many spies and he could," she paused and then changed her statement, "Would use this information to hurt you. So let it just be our little secret piece of heaven. And then someday when you tire of me, it will still be yours, for as long as you wish to remember the times we shared here."

"I will never tire of you," he said very positively.

Taking a deep breath, she looked deeply into his eyes before she spoke, "I hope not, but I want you to remember there are no strings. If and when you want to pull the plug on this, you are free to do so."

"Never happen," he said, and kissed her, drawing her to him. She felt his manhood moving against her leg and reluctantly, she had to push him back. "Not just yet. I have some more things to tell you, important things."

"What could be more important than this?" he asked, reaching down and running his fingers softly over her privates.

"Stop that," she scolded, and slapped his hand before pulling away. "I need to tell you about your identity here."

"Yeah, I was wondering how you got me a driver's license without my knowledge."

"How is not important. It is a driver's license, and it is real, only you must not renew your Florida License. These people out here are nuts about dual residency."

"But how? It even has my signature on it?"

"My dearest Darlin', I realize you are not knowledgeable in these things, and Lord knows I hope you never become so, but believe me when I say, enough money placed in the right hands will get you anything you want."

"I suppose you are right, but you are spending a lot of your money on me____." She stopped him. "It's not my money. My money is where no one can touch it. What I spend is Nate's money, and all of it I spend, is money well spent, especially when it's on you. Just remember not to renew your license in Florida, and don't vote down there either. In reality your true residency is where you vote."

"What difference does that make?"

"I will show you why," she said, and rising from the sofa she walked over to a wooden cabinet and opened the top drawer and removed a file. From this, she retrieved another identification looking card. "This is your 1996 Wyoming hunting license," she said holding it out to him.

He took it and looked at the folded paper.

"Of course hunting season is over for this year, but by having this, you will be able to get a resident license next year, and then get all the permits you want without going through all that damn lottery gimmicks out-of-state-residents must comply with. This will prove you have been a resident for over a year."

"How did ____,"

Again, she interrupted him and simply said. "Money in the right hands, in Cheyenne, nothing to it."

Wall just shook his head as he looked at the license.

"Darlin', I saw the newspaper article about you and the big deer in Georgia, and I was sad I had not been with you when you shot him. I wanted so to share a hunt with you, but knew that could never be, at least down there.

"I remembered going hunting with my dad and the great times we had together, and wanted so to share times like that with you. Then this idea came upon me, and this is what has become of it, so far," she explained, as she hurried over and kissed him softly on the lips. Then stepping back, before he could begin touching her she added, "This year when you killed the biggest whitetail in Georgia, I was not with you. But next year when you kill the biggest Muley in Wyoming, I will be at your side."

"You are something else," he said, not believing his good luck to have passed her broke down Olds on I-10.

The next morning he awoke and looking out, he gazed upon a wonderful snow scene, as far as he could see.

Soon after breakfast, they headed out to the new Polaris and for the rest of the day they played in the snow. He was trying to learn about a snowmobile, and she was trying to teach him. Actually, they spent more time digging the stuck machine out of drifts in the deep powder than riding. Regardless, it was an experience he loved and he was hooked for life. On the flight back to Dixie, he told her he believed snowmobiling was real close to flying in his heart. "I'm not sure which I love the most."

She felt a warm glow in her chest when he said it.

Christmas morning was as she promised, white. Wall was up first, as always, and after brewing coffee, he walked over to the heavy dark drapes that hid the jacuzzi room and pulled them open. As far as he could see was a blanket of white, dotted here and there with evergreens. Directly in front of the dome was a small ponderosa in the early years of its life. Beside it were two white barked aspen.

He suddenly had an idea and went back and began rummaging in all the drawers, until he found them. Before she was up and moving, he was finished.

When she came out, she was nude, and the sight of her was once again breathtaking, even with her hair in disarray, and her eyes puffy, and without makeup.

"Damn, its cold in here," she said, "You didn't build a fire. We need to turn up the electric heaters." She walked over to the wall thermostat and adjusted it. Satisfied with her work, she turned back to him and asked, "Is there enough of that for me?"

He came over to her and kissed her gently on the lips and said, "Good morning, Blue." Then he poured her a cup of coffee, but before handing it to her, he opened the door to the refrigerator and brought out the sweetly spiced cream she liked, but this time, she stopped him. "No, this morning I want it black, just like you drink it."

This surprised him, for he hadn't realized she was here living her own fantasy. Blue remembered her father and mother never drank their coffee any other way than black, and that's the way she wanted hers.

Had Wall used cream or sugar in his coffee, he would have fallen short of her expectations of a man. Something thus far, he had not done in any manner.

"I want to show you something," he said pulling on her hand.

"Wait, I'll only be a moment," she said, before turning back to the bedroom. When she returned, she was wearing the red and black plaid shirt she had worn the day they arrived, nothing more, just the shirt.

"Until it warms up in here, okay?"

Looking at her long legs and seeing a hint of her lips, he smiled, and nodded his approval, and then said again, "Come on, I want to show you something," and taking her hand, he led her over to the heavy drapes.

This time he didn't open them, only pulled them back so they could step out. The Jacuzzi room was not heated, save what escaped from the warm water, and she was glad she had insisted on the shirt.

"Look." he said pointing out.

She looked and saw nothing, "What?"

"There, the little pine between the aspen."

It was then she caught a twinkle of red and then green. The sun high overhead in the cloudless sky shining on the snow, had been so bright she had not seen them at first.

When he saw the smile slowly develop on her face, he said, "See, you have your Christmas tree, only it's outside."

There was no way he could have known, but she remembered when she was a small child, her mother telling of their honeymoon in the old cabin high in the Colorado Rockies, and about how her father had decorated a tree with red and green ribbon for her. More than once Dottie Belle told the story and always ending by saying, "That was the most beautiful Christmas Tree I have ever seen."

'God, how I love this man. If he only knew. If only we could live here for the rest of our lives,' Blue thought, slowly shaking her head, as she gazed at the lights that were wrapped around the short pine.

Wall had his hands on her shoulders and he used them to turn her around. To his surprise, he saw she was crying. A tear was making a rapid run down her cheek and he reached up and stopped it. "Did I do something wrong?" he questioned, suddenly thinking perhaps she had some sort of bad memory about a decorated outside tree, or something.

"No. That's what makes me cry, you never do any wrong. You always do everything right, everything perfect for me. It is as if _____,"

She never finished her sentence. Instead, she grabbed him tightly and hugged him, drawing his body as tight to her as she could. She wanted to tell him how much she loved him, but she was afraid to. Afraid he might somehow feel threatened, maybe smothered, or trapped, and then want to leave her. She wasn't sure she could go on living without him, but she dared not tell him so.

Finally, she said, "I want so to see my tree after dark. Do you think it possible you might miss a day of work?"

In his entire life Wall Roberts had never called in sick when he was not so. In fact, when he had worked for Florida Power in Volusia County, he had only missed three days sick in seven years. On these days he had reported for work, only to be sent home because his laryngitis was so severe, they could not understand what he was saying over the radio. Wall detested men who, *Called in Sorry*, as he thought of it, but he also knew he was going to do as she asked.

At that moment, Wall realized he would do anything this woman asked of him, and this caused a cold chill to run up his spine.

"Sure, why not?" was all he said as he watched her head back inside, where the cabin offered more warmth. The shirttail being too short, when she walked a tiny bit of each cheek could be seen and he felt his blood rushing downward.

"I'll have to call Deputy Sanders, and tell him not to worry about the road, and Mississippi Aviation, but it will be worth it."

Frank Alvarez and Ken Martinelli were already over Kansas when they got the call to return to Meridian.

The night before, she suggested they open their presents because they both thought they would spend Christmas aboard the Lear, headed back south. There, too, was the fact she had always opened her presents on Christmas Eve when she was a little girl. Doggy and Dottie wanted their children to be able to distinguish the presents they received from each other, from those Santa Claus brought, back when he still came to the Belle home. It had become a tradition with her before she moved east, and she never liked the big shindig the Rugg family put on each Christmas Morning.

'There will be no family Christmas in the Rugg house this year,' she thought, and tightened her eyes very thin as she thought of her husband.

Wall had been at a loss as to what to get for her. 'Just what do you buy a woman who has everything?' he wondered, and it had become no small problem for him. Finally, he saw a magazine advertisement from the Franklin Mint Collection. It displayed their Cinderella Set, which consisted of a pair of earrings and a necklace on a silver chain, featuring an exceptionally well-cut glass slipper. It was quite expensive, at least for his budget; however, he fully realized she often left tips for waiters that exceeded what the gift cost him.

When she opened it, she just stared at it for a long time without saying anything. "I didn't know what to get you," he tried to explain. "I know it's not expensive, like all your other jewelry, but I ___,"

"Oh, hush up you silly boy. I love it. You know, you really are my Prince who rescues me from mean and horrible relatives. What more could a girl dream of?"

Wall wasn't sure if she really meant it or not, but what she said, and the way she said it, made him feel good, and he was not so frightened about her being disappointed anymore. He quickly followed up with another small gift. "Here, this may be something you can use more often," he said handing her the flat package.

She ran her fingers over it and shook it, just as she had done as a little girl when she was trying to guess what was inside a wrapped gift. Finally unable to figure out what mystery hid inside, she tore open the paper and began to laugh, looking at the month's supply of birth control pills.

"You nut. I get a shot," she said, slapping him on the forearm.

"A shot?" he replied somewhat confused.

"Yes, a shot. A birth control shot. It's good for two years."

"Oh, I didn't know such existed," he replied honestly.

She was still chuckling when she stood and walked through the right door, into the guest bedroom. When she returned, she had a long box, which was covered in Santa Claus paper.

He could see she was having some difficulty in carrying it, due to its size. "Let me help you," he said, rising, but she stopped him.

"No. I can manage. You just wait where you are."

He did just that.

Handing him the present, she dropped down in front of him to her knees and sat on her heels, as she waited anxiously for him to open it. Twice, she bit her lower lip while he was fumbling around removing the paper carefully so as not to tear it. Finally, she could stand it no longer and she reached over and ripped a large piece from it, so there would be no point in trying to save the paper.

"Hey," he said at her intrusion.

"Hurry up. We can afford to buy more wrapping paper."

Although she didn't realize what she had just said, it did not pass him by, and he suddenly felt warm deep inside, *'She said WE can. Almost as if she thought of us as one, a pair, a couple,'* and he smiled slightly at this thought.

Finally, he had the paper off, and saw it was a gun case covered in glove leather. The corners were tooled in a maple leaf pattern, and in the middle, in a large, egg-shaped oval was tooled, **Wall Roberts** and he almost gasped at the thought.

He had never seen such a gun case, and he suspected the case alone cost more than all the guns he owned. Opening it carefully, he noticed she was moving around nervously again, and he realized she was into this as much, or even perhaps more, than he.

Finally, he fully opened the case revealing a rifle, stocked in the most beautifully figured walnut he had ever seen. The checkering was not of the usual diamond pattern, rather hand carved tiny maple leaves matching the décor on the leather case.

She immediately began, "I didn't know what kind of rifle you liked. I can get a different one if you don't like it.

"You silly thing, I love it," he said, rubbing his hands over the highly polished stock. "I have never seen anything like it."

Picking it up, he turned it so he could read the markings on the barrel, *Winslow Deluxe Cal 270 WM.*

"I didn't know what caliber to get you. I remembered my father once said he would like to have a 270 if he ever replaced his saddle-gun, so I had this done in 270 Weatherby Magnum. If you don't like it, I can get you a different one. The man at the gun shop said I could even have a new barrel put on this one if you didn't like this caliber."

"Just stop it. I wouldn't trade it for anything in the world," he said, and then lifted it to his shoulder and took aim through the scope.

"The scope is a Shepherd, I think. It has those little lines inside so you can judge the distance. He said it was the best scope made. The military use it for their sniper guns."

"I have read about them, but I have never before seen one," Wall admitted, and he carefully laid it back in its case and reached for her.

She knew what was about to happen and she stopped him. "I have more gifts for you. Over there in the corner, that's a gun safe, and it's secured to the floor, so no one can steal your rifle when you are not here, and_____,"

"The only gift I want is you, sitting on top of me, screaming your lungs out."

"Wait," she said standing quickly. "I'll be right back I have to go to the bathroom first."

This stopped him and he nodded his head. There was no stopping a woman when she said she needed to go, and he knew it, so he consoled his passion while she hurried off.

When she returned she was wearing her heels and a highly transparent red gown. She pushed him back on the bearskin, and tugged at the buckle of his jeans. Finally opening them, she pulled them from his legs until he was nude from the waist down, and he then removed his shirt. She reached down and caressed his manhood until it stood at full attention, and then she very slowly sat down on him, moving her arms out so the material of the gown did not get in the way.

Their passion was not the long experience they both had expected. Rather quickly, she realized she needed him badly, and soon they were at it, as fast as they could, and he received the present he had asked for.

During the last couple of minutes of her passion, she kept her head and neck bent backward so far against her shoulders and back that she slowed the blood flow to her brain causing her to almost pass out, and thus she collapsed on him. Although he almost lost it when she gave her finale scream, he was able to hold back and wait. Sometime, after she caught her breath, and her head cleared, she realized he was still erect and still inside her.

"My God, I can't believe you are still hard," she said, looking down at him in amazement.

"I didn't want to end it before I had a chance to play with your beautiful breasts," he replied smiling.

Immediately she pulled the red garment over her head and tossed it aside. It was then he saw the small clear shoe in the valley between his targets, dancing about on its silver chain, and from each nipple hung it's companions, which had been designed to be worn from the ears. When he reached up and touched them, she said, "Now aren't you glad I got my nips pierced?"

He then took the palms of his hands and placed them under her heavy melons, lifted each, then gently squeezed them, before he let them go. Reaching around her back, he pulled her down where he could touch her nipples with his tongue, first one and then the other, very softly, over and over again until she could stand it no longer. Suddenly, she sat back straight and began again riding him to another screaming climax. It was the most sexual night he had ever enjoyed in his life, and would remain so in his memory forever.

The next night while they sat in the hot tub and looked out at the lights sparkling brightly on the snow-draped limbs of her Christmas tree, she said, "Wall, I'm so happy when I'm with you."

"I know, honey. I feel the same way," he replied softly.

"Do you? Do you really?" she asked, almost pleading for his statement to be the truth.

"Can't you tell?"

"I can tell you like banging me, and you like it when others look at us, and envy you. I know you enjoy showing me off to other men, but do you really___?" She stopped and then rephrased her question, "Are you really happy when you are with me?"

"I have never been more happy in my life. I just wish it would never stop. That I would never have to go back to being a lineman for the Co-Op, and you did not have to go back to once again being Mrs. Nathan Rugg."

She wanted to say something back, but she didn't know what to say. She had no doubts Nate would have Wall killed if he ever found out about him. Even if she divorced him, it would make no difference. Nate was a man who truly had no scruples. Anyone who, in his mind did him wrong, especially someone who took something he considered his, must die. It was as simple as that.

'Perhaps it started with his school friend, and then he even sent his own sister to the insane asylum, her husband, and sons all died mysteriously. Even his mother. So many have died because he felt in some small way they wronged him. No question if he found out, Nate would see that an unexplained accident would befall Wall Roberts and when that happened, I will surely kill Nate.'

Instead of replying to his statement, she moved her back closer to Wall's chest, and pulled his arms tightly around her, while realizing the web of torment she had woven for herself, and she wept silently inside.

At the same time, Wall was watching the tiny flakes of snow, which had just begun to fall.

**View from Wall's new cabin
looking to the west from the entrance.**

Chapter Fourteen
The Murder

As soon as Wall reported to work on Tuesday, he had to go into the office and fill out a sick leave slip. The first to ask was Ash, "What do you think about James Hancock?"

"What about him?" he asked, looking over at her.

"Where have you been? It's all anyone in Madison County has talked about since they found his body."

"His body!" Wall turned suddenly, starring at the young girl.

"Yes, his body. He drowned last Friday night."

Wall narrowed his eyes at her. *'There is no way James Hancock drowned. He could swim from here to Jacksonville.'* "Are you sure it was James Hancock, from Lowndes County?"

"I ought to know. If you will remember, I dated him in high school," she said back harshly.

"No. I didn't know," he replied and walked away towards the breakroom where the blank forms were kept in an open cabinet, much like mailboxes, attached to the wall.

'What did he say? He was going to Debbie's for a few beers, and what was his new girlfriend's name? Cindy, Sandy or something like that'?' Wall tried to remember, but couldn't at the moment.

When James Hancock had left Wall that night, he did as he had said, and called his girl.

Sissy Joyce was twenty-seven years old, and despite her accent and command of the local jargon, she was originally from Peoria, Illinois. James never knew that, any more than he didn't know Joyce was not her real name. In fact, James did not know anything at all about her, other than she was tall and slim and very pretty, and she liked to give head, and he liked the way she gave it.

He had met her via an accident. That is, they had run into each other in the Wal-Mart store on St. Augustine Highway in Valdosta. It was true, they had literally run into each other. At least their shopping carts had. He was coming down the aisle looking for a jar of Reese's Peanut Butter and she came around the corner and plowed her basket head-on into his. When they recovered from the surprise, they both laughed and began a conversation that continued into the parking lot.

"Say, you aren't married are you?"

"No. You?"

"Not a chance," he replied smiling. "Look, there is a lounge in the rear of Jax's Package Store, just up the street yonder; you want to get a drink or something?"

She looked back at the lanky man with dark unkempt hair and nodded her head slightly. "Yeah, I guess so, but I can't stay long. I am supposed to be meeting someone at eight o'clock."

"Great," he replied, and soon, while helping her load the few grocery items from the offending cart into her trunk, he was pleased to see that she had not bought anything that would soon need refrigeration.

Near midnight and several beers later, he said with slurred speech, "I think you are late for your meeting."

"That's okay. I like you better than him anyway," Sissy replied, and smiled before she looked around as if to make sure no one was listening, and she whispered to him. "Do you live around here someplace."

"Naw. I live down south, a long ways," he said, gazing into her blue eyes.

"Well, I live just around the corner in the Norman Apartments. Do you think maybe we should go to my place and finish our drinking there?"

"You betchum, Red Ryder," he replied, and stood on unsure feet.

Half an hour later, he was learning of her special talent!

The night he died, while they were eating at Archie's, an old enemy approached their table and without invitation sat down beside James and started a conversation. "Where's that beat up old truck of yours?"

"Up the road a piece, waiting on me," James answered, but thinking, *'If it's any of your business.'*

"Waiting on you? Broke down is more like it."

James never had a lot of use for Seth; he had played defensive tackle for the Madison Cowboys the same time James played quarterback for the Trojans in Valdosta and they had met many times on the field.

James always thought Seth had taken great pleasure in sacking him long after he had released the ball and apparently one of the referees thought so, too, because Seth was thrown out of the game their senior year for that very offense. James limped off the field with two broken ribs and Seth just smiled and raised his arms to the cheering Madison fans, as he headed to his bench.

James had always felt his not being in there for the last quarter was what cost them the game. A lot of others thought so, too.

"Who is this pretty lady?"

"Sissy Joyce, Seth Coe," was all he said.

"Sissy, I like that. What's a pretty girl like you doing with a skinny runt like him?" Seth said, and snickered. Then nudged James in the ribs and added, "Just kidding, ol' buddy."

Sissy could see James' dislike for the bigger man, and to put him in his place, she replied, "I'm with him because he can screw my eyeballs out, which is something a chubby guy like you could never do."

"Well, listen at that, will you," Seth said, standing and twisting his mouth and nodding his head, "I think she likes you James, better hang on to her."

Neither replied and finally Seth slapped James on the shoulder and said, just before he turned away, "Be seeing you ol' buddy."

After finishing their meal, while walking to her car, she said, "James, would you mind if we skip Debbie's tonight? I had rather go up to my place and have you all to myself. Besides, it is Christmas weekend."

James had been looking forward to being at the little bar for several days. He really enjoyed her singing, and also the way the men were always ogling at her. Once Beady Perrey had ask him if she could screw as good as she could sing. He would have taken it as an insult had not Beady been quite drunk. Besides, it made him feel kind a' proud of being able to have others wonder about their private life. So instead of punching Beady's lights out, he leaned over and whispered, "She had rather give head than eat fried chicken."

Beady just roared out in laughter and slapped him on the back, but after that, Beady never took his eyes off Sissy the rest of the night.

However, this night, James also knew what having him all to herself meant and he wasn't about to refuse that. "Sure," he replied, "but on the way, let's stop by my truck and get my spare keys out of the glove compartment. I forgot to get them when I started walking."

Arriving, she pulled over in front of his truck. James had spotted the other car sitting behind his pickup with the lights off. The smoke rising from the tail pipe revealed the engine was still running.

"Stay here and stay alert," he said, as he got out and headed straight for the passenger's side of his vehicle. Looking in he could see the glove box door open and it was obvious it had been ransacked.

He turned and looked back at the two men sitting in the black Crown Victoria and reached to the small of his back and drew the Colt Pony he carried there in a reversed holster. Holding it close beside his leg so they wouldn't see it in the darkness, he walked forward. When he arrived at the front of the new Ford, the doors suddenly opened and they both stepped out.

It was Vinnie who spoke. "Hey, it is you, boy. See Estes, I told you that was James' truck."

"Watch out! He has a gun," came the voice behind him.

James turned back and looked at her. She was no longer behind the wheel of her car. Instead, she was standing there beside his truck. *'Why did you say that?'* he wondered.

He then looked back at the men and saw both were holding large revolvers pointed at him. He might get a shot at one of them. Might even get lucky, but if he tried, he would surely die where he stood. There was no way he could hit them both, before they shot him. He tried to think of any way of escaping, but nothing feasible came to mind.

At that moment a car turned onto the Lee Road from SR 6, some three hundred yards away, and they all knew something had to give and very soon. Vinnie finally said, "Lay your gun on the hood and come up here."

He shook his head slowly, but then knowing better, he laid the Colt down and walked towards the open door of the sedan.

"Chrissie, get his gun," the shorter man said.

This caused James to turn back and look at Sissy.

She hurried forward and grabbed the little automatic, slipping it into her purse. Then she said, "I have to go. I'm expecting a call."

"Go ahead," the short man said. "We'll get in touch with you later, when you're needed."

Vinnie pushed James into the backseat and then climbed in beside him. Worm quickly made a U-turn. Switching on the headlights, they sped towards the approaching car with her blue Mustang following close behind.

When they reached the crossroads in Pinetta, she turned north towards Valdosta, but the Crown Vickie crossed the Colon Kelly Highway, and stopped at the rear of the post office.

Wall was very distraught over his friend's death and all day, he kept trying to remember anything James had said that would somehow bring something, anything, to light. Finally, after work, he stopped in at the county jail, and asked to see the officer who had worked the case.

"Sergeant Mendoza is not on duty. Do you want to leave a message?" the desk officer asked.

Wall just shook his head and walked out thinking about the deputy he had just spoken to, *'That guy is as queer as a three-dollar bill; never thought I would see such on the Sheriff's Department in North Florida.'*

After leaving, he drove up to Georgia and into the little road that led to Betsy's Crossroads. The bar was closed, and there was a large wreath hanging on the door. However, he could see someone inside and when he knocked, she came to the door. "Oh, Wall," Cindy said, and burst out crying, falling against his chest.

"Who is it, Cindy?" he heard her father call out, in a gruff voice. "Ain't people got no respect? There's a wreath on the door, for God's sake."

"It's me Mr. Hancock, Wall Roberts."

The older man stopped and looked through squinted eyes and then said back, "Oh, Wall, I didn't know it wus' you. Come in, come in."

Cader Hancock looked a lot older than Wall remembered him, old, strained, and bent.

"I just came by to pay my respects, not to bother. Maybe I should go."

"Nonsense, Wall, you come right on in. You is one of____, well, was one of James' best friends. You will always be welcome here. Can I get you a drink?"

"No. That's okay. I just wanted to pay my respects."

"Here, boy, you sit right here and I'll get us a beer. It's Bud you drink, I remember. I'll draw us one."

Cindy let go of Wall and sat down in a chair beside him, before looking down at the table.

"How is Mrs. Hancock taking it?"

Cader set the two mugs down and then followed himself, before replying. "Not good. Not good at all. She's down at the river house. Barry is there with her. Somehow she is blaming herself for it."

"Why, that's silly. Why on earth would she do that?"

"Well, she and James got into it t'other day about som'ting or the other, and he lit out of here and ain't been back. Don't know where he's been staying the last couple of weeks."

"He's been staying with his girlfriend in Valdosta."

"Girlfriend?" Cindy looked up. "He never told me about no girlfriend."

"Me, neither," Mr. Hancock added.

"Well, I know he was, because he told me so, last Friday night."

"Friday night? That's the night he drowned," Cader said, looking strongly at Wall.

"Yeah, that's what I heard. I picked him up on 255 and took him to Archie's in Lee. His truck broke down and he needed a ride."

"His truck was found by the pond where he drowned, there out'a Pinetta, Saturday morning," the older man said, shaking his head back and forth a couple of times, "Nothing wrong with it. Barry drove it home. It are yonder at the river house right now."

"That don't make sense. He said it just quit on him, and he was walking towards Lee when I picked him up. His truck was there on the side of 255, just south of SR 6 almost to the William's home. I seen it myself when I passed it."

"William's home? There are two Williams who live on 255."

"The truck was a little south of SR 6. He was walking just past the south one, you know, the old Drigger's farm. He said he tried to call from there but neither Dale nor Mel were home."

"Yeah, it don't make no sense. 'Cause there weren't nothing wrong with it when me an' Barry went to get it."

"Maybe he got it fixed," Cindy offered.

"Maybe," Wall replied, but he still didn't believe it. *'Things just don't add up.'*

Suddenly it hit him, "What did you say?"

"I said his truck____."

"No. About a pond."

"Yeah, that there pond there near the Mt. Horeb Church, that's where he drowned."

"Hell, you couldn't drown a rabbit in that damn pond. It's nearly dry."

"Well, that's where they found him drowned dead," Cader said, as he emptied the last drops from his mug, then got up and drew himself another.

After Wall left, Cindy was taken aback by his words. She tried to get her father to think about what Wall had said, but his brain was too filled with grief and alcohol to think clearly on anything.

Later when she was home, she shared Wall's thought with Barry and they both agreed to press their father, when he was sober, to do some checking into the possibility that James had not simply drowned, as the Sheriff's initial investigation reported.

Later, she cried herself to sleep, but at least with the satisfaction they would do something for James.

The next day, not long after the ten o'clock hour, the dispatcher called Wall, "Mr. Miller wants to see you."

"Hellfire. What is it this time," he said, before he keyed the mike. Then he replied, "10-4."

Gritting his teeth, and twisting his head, he yelled out to Dave and Huff, "I got a' head back to the yard, Miller wants to see me."

"Don't be doing no ass-kissing while you're in there," Dave said, and snickered at the big man beside him who was pulling wire.

Wall didn't think the comment rated an answer, so he simply climbed in the pickup and slammed the door before cranking it up.

"Don't forget to wear your seat belt," he heard Dave call, as he turned the truck around and headed towards the east end of the county.

'That damn Kerr, if he had bat-shit for brains, he'd be dangerous,' Wall thought, speeding away.

Walking past Ash's desk, she rolled her eyes and said, "You must have done something bad, a law-dawg is here for you."

Wall just gave her a dirty look, and walked on past, towards Miller's office.

"Come in, Roberts. This is Deputy Mendoza," Miller said.

"Sergeant," the uniformed man quickly corrected.

"Oh yes, Sergeant Mendoza. He wants to ask you some questions."

"Sure," Wall answered, and stretched forth his hand.

"I understand you were at the jail last night looking for me, something about that drunk boy drowning."

"Yes. I did come to see you, and I thank you for looking me up."

"Well, were you there when he drowned?"

"No, and I don't think he drowned."

"Oh really, and just what do you think happened?"

"I don't know, but when I talked to him Friday night, he made the statement it was too damn cold to be swimming. Besides, he was much too fine a swimmer to have drowned anywhere, let alone that damn pond off the Mt. Horeb Road."

"Really? You say you were with him Friday night."

"That's right. I gave him a ride to Lee. His truck broke down."

"His truck broke down? He drove his truck to the pond, where he and his girlfriend went skinny-dipping, and he drowned."

"Skinny dipping in this kind of weather? My God!" Wall almost shouted.

"Mr. Roberts, I suggest you control yourself. I don't take kindly to your questioning my investigation."

Turning around Wall looked at Miller, and then back at the Deputy, "Is there anything else you want from me?"

"Not right now," Mendoza replied, emphasizing every word as strongly to Wall as he had spoken to the deputy.

"Mr. Miller," Wall said as a departing remark to his boss, and then left the office without further comment.

When he passed Ash's desk, she intended to ask him about what the lawman had wanted, but he never slowed down in his dash for the parking lot.

A week later there was a small write-up on the second page of the local paper about the coroner's autopsy, confirming the cause of death of James Hancock was suffocation by drowning. There was also a comment about large amounts of alcohol found in his stomach, and nothing more.

"That's bull," Wall remarked, when he read it and threw the paper down.

Chapter Fifteen
Prominent Families

This had been the first time Worm had let Vinnie participate directly in any of his hits, but he decided it would be good insurance to have something on his friend. *'Just in case the pigs ever got too close.'*

He liked Vinnie a lot. They had camaraderie from being in Nam at the same time and from the hospital at Clark Field. However, he also realized Vinnie was not strong, like he was, and would surely break if he were ever really put to the test.

That night as he sat with his fourth Scotch and water in hand and watched his friend lose a game of pool to a not-so-beautiful dark haired wench Vinnie was pursuing with hopeful lust, he thought, *'Now he will not dare break our trust. Not since it actually was Vinnie who had popped the kid in the brain stem with the ball-peen hammer down in Florida. It, too, was Vinnie, who held him under the water long enough for him to die. Now he is really more under my control than Uncle Uberto.'*

Worm had cautioned him about just how hard to make the blow, so as not to leave a large swelling, as well as how to grasp gently while he held his head under. "Don't hold him by the neck; that will leave bruises. Hold him by the shoulders, remember not his neck."

"Oh, that's good thinking, Worm," Vinnie replied, as he swung the naked and unconscious man over his shoulder and walked slowly into the water until he was near the center of the pond.

Vinnie didn't much like it when the man's cock slapped against his upper chest *'But there are always things one didn't like when doing a job,'* he thought.

Vinnie also thought about being thankful this little pond was not too deep, because he really didn't want to let his balls hit the icy water. "This far enough, Worm?"

"Yeah, I guess so. Just hold him under, like I showed you."

"Sure, Worm. I'll do it, just like you showed me."

There, too, had been the woman. Worm did not approve of using her at all. In fact, he did not like her, nor liked being told to work with her. Nonetheless, it had been a part of the contract, and he fully realized his future would always hinge on his ability to keep Chicago well pleased. Only for this reason had he not refused to work with Christina Voorhies.

There was another reason Worm did not like Voorhies. The first night they had been together to work out the details of *The Accident*, he had drank just a little too much and his judgment was just a little off center, and he had made a pass at the very attractive Christina. Before he could breathe, she had rammed a PPK in his crotch and cocked it. Worm quickly backed away, but burned the incident in the get-even portion of his brain.

The payoff to Worm was $5,000 plus expenses for *The Accident*. However, unknown to him, Christina Voorhies' pay off would be ten times that much. Her money included the task of meeting the law and explaining the drowning, as well as being available later, should any inquest be held.

Uberto Spindetto had used her before and was always well pleased with her results. It was he who had insisted that she be a part of *The Accident*.

Had it been a simple hit, there would have been no need for the girl. However, Uberto's friend had been very precise on the whole affair appearing to be an accident. That required more than what Vinnie's proficient, though disgusting, little comrade could provide.

Retrieving the truck had been a simple matter of pouring two cans of Heet into the gas to disperse the water they had put in the gas tank earlier. Then, with the help of a set of jumper cables, the old Ford cranked right up, spit and sputtered a few times, but was running fine by the time they reached Mount Horeb Church, where she was waiting.

Worm remembered well, Christina standing beside the old Ford truck, silhouetted by its headlights as Vinnie carried the boy out and drowned him. He also remembered well the nakedness of her slim body, when she stripped and waded out to where he had left the body. To make the skinny-dipping story believable, she needed to be found wet under her blouse and pants when the law arrived and to that end, was the only reason she had walked into the 38-degree water.

The sight of her blouse clinging to her wet tits had been forever singed into his brain, even more so than when she had been completely naked. *'I will have her one day and then kill the bitch, or maybe I'll just kill her and be done with it.'*

The fact that Estes would see her nude body and realize he would never get to enjoy its pleasures gave Christina an inner feeling of satisfaction, for she detested the little man even more so than did Mr. Spindetto.

Christina made the call from the pay phone outside of the Pinetta Post Office and then drove James' pickup back to the pond to await the Deputy.

Her two accomplices were across the state line when Deputy Sanford arrived at the scene. After pulling the nude man from the water, and confirming he was indeed dead, Sanford called his supervisor, Sergeant Mendoza.

It all would have ended just as they planned it, had it not been for the bulldog determination of Wallace Roberts.

The morning after the coroner's report appeared in the paper, a very sober Cader Hancock was in Madison at the Sheriff's Office, asking for an interview with Sergeant Mendoza.

When he did not find the cooperation he searched for there, he began a campaign to get the case looked into as a possible murder.

He had several of James' friends write letters to the editor of *The Madison Trace*, commenting on James' ability to swim, and also his being a former Navy Seal, and the likelihood of him drowning in a pond one could wade across, was quite ridiculous.

The 'Letter to the Editor' Wall Roberts sent in read:

The one weak point in the planning of this 'Accident' is, none of the people involved could have been locals. If they were, they would have surely known of James' Navy background and picked another method to murder him. This is a point any competent investigator would have quickly concluded.

A week after this appeared in the paper, Cader Hancock was called to the Sheriff's Office.

"Cader, I fully realize you have lost a great treasure in your son," Sheriff Coons began. "However, you must remember there was a witness. The woman he was dating was there and she said he was so drunk he just passed out while they were having sex in the pond and he was too heavy for her to pull out before he drowned. You must also realize some of the things a full-scale investigation might turn up could taint the memory of James.

"We all are aware that James was not lily white. His name has appeared several times on spread sheets in the local narcotic investigations and even though he had never been arrested, we know of his connections with those who import drugs into Madison County."

Cader started to interrupt, protesting these remarks, but he could tell there was something the Sheriff was not telling him, and he wanted to see if he would slip and let it out.

Cader Hancock lived in Georgia, not Florida, and even though his home was only some seventeen miles from this very courthouse, he had no obligations to Sheriff Coons or to the former Sheriff either. *'If this man slips and tells me something I can use against him. I will send the information to FDLE. They will get to the bottom of this.'*

The Sheriff continued with the same line of talk, never leaving the idea that if in fact, the death of James was not an accident, it most surely had been the result of his involvement in drugs, a fact Cader Hancock considered bull.

Cader would never have said James had not ever done any drugs. Almost every boy or girl in his age bracket had, to some extent, experimented with some form of drugs. In any event, James was very proud of his service record and Cader was positive he would have never done anything that would have tainted that.

'No. James might have not been the perfect child, but he had never done anything to keep his father from being proud of him. You Sheriff Coons are way off key on this matter.'

It was at that very moment the Sheriff said something that took Cader by surprise, "Another thing you should consider, Mr. Hancock; you have a family, other children. If a full-scale investigation was to be turned loose, there might be others in the community that would suffer. Maybe some very prominent families; I for one would guess they would go to extremes to protect their loved ones," here the Sheriff stopped for a couple of seconds.

When he began again, his words were, "To protect your loved ones, I would think it would be wise if you did not pursue this campaign any further." He stopped once more and let what he had just said sink in. "I remember a case I read about. I believe it occurred in Texas. There, a man found himself in somewhat the same position you are in, and he just couldn't let sleeping dogs lie. He began to drag the good names of a few old time local families in the mud, and the next thing you know, his other son was found dead, and then several Mexicans broke into his home one night, and repeatedly raped his wife, and lovely daughter. It was just a shame, an awful shame, because these wetbacks were back over the border before anyone knew about the incident. Of course, nothing was ever done about it. Nothing could be done." Once more, the High Sheriff paused, and finally ended his statement with, "You get my drift, Mr. Hancock?"

Cader knew if he went to FDLE with what had just been told him, they would surely investigate the Madison County Sheriff's Office. *'And if I could prove that the Sheriff had really told me these things, most likely Coons would be out of a job.'* Cader looked down at the floor. *'Of course, I can't prove he said these things.'* Then slowly he nodded his head, "I get your drift, Coons."

On the way home, he thought hard on the experiences of the morning with a clearer mind than he had in years.

It was during this thirty-minute drive, Cader Hancock made a decision to do three things. One, he would not endanger his family, and he would ask all his friends to stop the campaign against Sergeant Mendoza and the drowning investigation. Two, he would sell 'Betsy's Crossroads' and move to Madison County and re-enter his old profession as a machinist - that way somehow, he might find out who had killed his son; and three, he would never touch alcohol again. Cader Hancock was a man of conviction and he did just that.

Wall respected the family of his dead friend. Although Cader did not explain his reversed attitude, Wall suspected it had something to do with his meeting with Sheriff Coons and Wall did not feel it was his place to question him. Thus, he also stopped his open campaign to get to the bottom of the so-called accident. But in his heart, he was convinced James had not drowned. He would continue working to prove that very thing, only in a clandestine mode of operation.

Hancock remembered over-hearing Wall say something about seeing the big airplane landing at Sampala Lake late in the evening, and he knew that Sam Price owned most of the land around the lake. *'It doesn't take a rocket scientist to figure out who the Prominent Family running drugs in Madison County is,'* he thought. *'I'll somehow get to know Mr. Prominent Price, and get in on his property.'*

The previous Labor Day, while enroute to Tallahassee, Nate Rugg had pulled from the stop sign at CR 150 onto US 90, and headed west. Suddenly, an older Toyota slammed into the rear of his vehicle.

Neither his Allanté nor the Toyota had received a great deal of damage, but the two black women in the Toyota both were screaming of back and neck pain.

The investigating Trooper said he was not going to write a ticket, but would charge him with the accident, citing his failure to yield the right of way as his offense. Nate had first tried to point out that she had been so far away when he pulled out, he could not have seen her, and pointed to the long skid marks to prove his point. When this did not immediately sway the Trooper, he then began to make it well known just who he was and the political pull he had in Madison County. This move only strengthened the position of the accident investigator, who considered it a great sin for anyone to attempt to intimidate a State Trooper.

Nate left the scene quite aggravated. Two months later when he received a notice he was being sued personally by the women in the accident, he became furious.

Finally, after calming down, he called the office of Johns and Townsend. "Your card reads, 'Private Investigations and Accident Recreation Supreme.'

"That is correct. There are none better in the State of Florida," Ben Townsend assured him.

"If this is true, I have need for your services."

During the first day of the civil trial, Investigator Townsend proved the Toyota had to have been traveling ninety-one miles an hour to leave so many feet of skid marks, had it stopped before it struck the Cadillac.

"And of course, it did strike the Cadillac. Therefore, the complainant had to have been driving at a speed greater than ninety-one miles per hour. Good people of Madison County, remember this occurred on a two-lane highway. Also it is important to remember this speed was far greater than one could have been traveling and not realize they were speeding."

He further produced pictures of a Toyota identical to the one driven by the black lady in the accident, positioned at the precise location on the highway where the skid marks began, east of the intersection of CR 150 and US 90.

It was very plain to everyone, the vehicle was so far away no prudent driver could have realized the approaching car was traveling at such a high rate of speed.

"Therefore, Mr. Rugg was well within his right to enter US 90, and did not violate anyone's right of way," he told the jury.

Next, Mr. Johns was placed on the stand as the defendant's second witness, and qualified as an Expert Witness in the field of criminal investigation. Johns brought forth several court records from St. Louis, San Francisco, Santa Fe, and Santa Barbara.

"At these cities, these same two women, have brought almost identical suits against others, always claiming the same injuries, along with the doctor's reports confirming the injuries."

This information was quite damaging, as both had previously sworn to the court, they had never been injured or received treatment for neck or back injuries.

Immediately, the attorney for the plaintiffs requested a short recess and after speaking to his clients, he asked the court to drop all charges against Mr. Rugg. Judge Carter honored the motion to dismiss the charges, but not until he gave the women a stiff bawling out, and reminding them of the penalties for lying under oath. He also informed them he would make available all court records, should Mr. Rugg wish to file a countersuit for his defamation of character. He ended his comments with, "Of course, if you two no longer lived in the State of Florida, he would not be able to take you to Civil Court."

Nate Rugg was well-pleased with the service he had gotten from *Johns and Townsend Investigations* and, on the very day he saw the thin man slip from the wooded area behind his home, it was to them he turned for help, in proving his wife had a lover.

In less than a week, they had a file on James Hancock, which they turned over to Rugg.

However, Mickey Johns was not satisfied, and he continued working on exactly what he had been hired to do.

He had never been convinced a woman of Blue Rugg's caliber would lay with a lowly tramp as James Hancock.

The flaw in his theory was that Mickey had forgotten, if he had ever known, that true love knows no social class boundaries.

There was one other problem, which was Mickey Johns was not the investigator he envisioned himself to be.

Upon receiving the report from Johns and Townsend, Nate had simply called his old friend and said, "Uberto, there is this local man who is harassing my wife. His name is James Hancock and he lives, just across the river from my home, over in Lowndes County, Georgia. I would sure like to be rid of him, but only if an accident was to occur."

This was all that needed to be said. Unfortunately for James Hancock, Nate had not waited until Mickey Johns had made a more complete investigation.

Mickey was quick to catch the relationship between James and Sissy Joyce, and it did not take him too long to find out this was not her real name, or that she did not work at Moody Air Force Base as James thought she did.

In fact, she had no local job; still, she possessed a substantial checking account at the Sun Bank in the Valdosta Mall. She drove a leased Mustang, spent hours at the salon weekly, and had a nice apartment on Norman Drive, although she wore very down-to-earth outfits.

When she was not with Hancock, she ate at only the best restaurants in the area, and twice he sat a few seats behind her on a plane bound for Atlanta, and once for New Orleans. Each incident surprised him, for she never met anyone as he had suspected, rather only indulged herself in expensive pleasures.

Johns stayed confused about this woman, but he did not give up.

Chapter Sixteen
High Rock

Before he began, Ken Martinelli had been told that his one run to pay off his gambling indebtedness would wipe the slate clean and he would not be bothered again. However, after viewing the video, he knew he would never be free of them, and his assumption was very correct.

In fact, his required service had become so great, he missed just too many scheduled flights with *Mississippi Aviation* and Greg Winn fired him. Ken realized this was a deathblow to his dream of landing a job with one of the big carriers, but at least he was still flying, even though many of his flights could not be logged.

Ken had to admit not all was gloom. He was surely bringing home substantially more money than he had seen with *Mississippi Aviation*. Once, after an exceptionally good payoff from such a flight, he located a Murphy Rebel outfitted with amphibious floats. The man and wife team who had constructed the homebuilt two-seater had a reputation of producing a finished product better than any aircraft factory of the day. After careful inspection of the little green plane, he paid them cash and flew it out of their Suwannee River Field.

One night, while sitting in the terminal lounge at *Charlotte International Airport,* Ken met a rather attractive lady in her early forties. They hit it off right away and soon, after learning she had just seen her husband off on an American flight to Detroit, they strolled out together.

Cullen Teague spent far too much time attending to his speedway interests, and far too little time attending to his interests at home, a chore Ken was more than happy to assist him with, even if Mr. Teague didn't know anything about the assistance.

Soon after he began his relationship with the attractive blonde, Ken was able to acquire a T-hanger at Wilgrove, and it was there he based the Rebel.

With the little plane, he and Lucinda Teague could be at the cabin she owned on High Rock Lake, in less than an hour.

As soon as he had another windfall, he upgraded the electronics on the Rebel until it was fully IFR[20] equipped, including an autopilot slaved to the Apollo SL 60 GPS.

There was no seaplane base at High Rock, but he had entered the Lat/Longs for five hundred feet in front of her cottage, and could make power on landings there in the worst of conditions.

At first, she was a little reluctant to fly in the *Tiny Little Green Thing*, as she described the Rebel, but after a couple of hops she found the *Tiny Little Green Thing* stirred her juices almost as much as its pilot.

Lucy Teague had met her husband some twenty years before, when he owned his first racecar, and she was a race fan groupie. That was back in the days when NASCAR was truly a stock car racing organization. His car had won, or at least placed high often enough in those early days, for his name to become well known in the echelon of NASCAR, and she was totally infatuated with the man.

In the first three years, she went with him to every race, and he seemed so pleased with her, always buying her new outfits and other rather nice gifts, proudly showing off his pretty blonde to all his friends and non-friends in the business.

Then in the fourth year of their relationship, they married, and very soon thereafter, everything seemed to change. She got pregnant, and had a bad time with it. She no longer was able to

---

20 IFR: An FAA term meaning flying under Instrument Flight Rules.

go tromping around from one track to another, and when their child was stillborn, it seemed to be a blow to the relationship from which neither ever fully recovered.

He was convinced the death of the baby was caused by her drinking while carrying it and she felt he turned away from her at the moment she needed him most.

At first, she suffered a terrible depression, which led to her turning to food and scotch for relief from her pain. She tried to eat and drink her sorrow away, until she was tipping the scales at just over two hundred pounds.

Having a frame built to carry one hundred and twenty pounds made her look like a five-foot four-inch Miss Piggy in a wig, and he stopped taking her anywhere. In fact, he even suggested a divorce. However, his attorney reminded him he had not insisted on a prenuptial and she could take him for enough he would have to get out of racing and find a job that paid better. Suddenly, he totally readjusted his thinking about divorce. Instead, he encouraged her to attend a local spa, which she agreed to do.

It was at the spa Lucy found Mary Evans, which was a very lucky break for her. Lucy met Mary at one of the NASCAR dinners a couple of years before, although she didn't recognize her at first. She just couldn't believe the Mary of 1996 was the same Mary of 1994. The lady had lost over two hundred pounds, and simply looked wonderful and Lucy had to find out how she did it.

"Well, it's no secret. The spa here is in a joint venture with *The Amos Toole Physical Fitness Gym* next door and I took advantage of their plan."

"You mean you lost all that weight by going to a gym?"

"That's right, Honey, and you can, too. Just wait until you find out what the reward is for meeting your goal," Mary teased.

"Tell me," Lucy asked.

"Not a chance, Honey. If you make it, you will find out. If not, I will not be the one to break the secret," Mary said, slapping Lucy's chubby little hand.

Eight months, and eighty-five pounds later, Lucy learned the secret and that night with Amos Toole, she experienced her first extra-marital affair.

For a while after, she once more felt good about herself. Cullen had taken her to a few of the NASCAR events and many of her old acquaintances seemed pleased to see her again.

However, the old spark was just not there anymore and she eventually stopped going with him. She was not really surprised when he seemed relieved he didn't have to ask her.

Cullen became more involved with his race team. He now owned and/or sponsored three cars with NASCAR, and another with ARCA[21]. It was a good team and some began to compare *Teague Racing* with *The Wood Brothers*, of ten years before.

One thing that did surprise Lucy was she had no guilt feelings letting Amos sexually devour her. It had been a night that no woman would, or could, ever forget.

First, he had taken her to dinner at one of the most famous restaurants in Charlotte, and then they returned to the gym for her reward.

There, he prepared her a drink he said was the only alcoholic beverage he approved of. She loved its peachy flavor and forever after, believed it contained some sort of narcotic, for almost immediately after drinking it, she began to drift off into a dream-like world. When he began to undress her, she made no protest. He took her to the reclining bench in the gym and there he tied her.

Lucy experienced no real comprehension of time, but before she knew what was happening, two or three of the other trainers who worked at the gym were standing before her and touching her, each ever so gently, and all at the same time.

It seemed every sensuous point on her body was being touched at the identical moment, and she had never in her life become so hot with desire.

Finally, after some period of time during this wonderful torment, Amos was there and she was no longer tied. When he entered her,

---

21 ARCA: Automobile Racing Club of America.

she burst into the most intense orgasm she had ever experienced, and was soon meeting every Thrush of his powerful body.

Later, she seemed to remember the other men watching, but she was sure it had only been Amos who actually had sex with her. *'So this was what Mary Evens had kept secret. No wonder. I will never tell either.'*

Although Lucy, of course, was no virgin when she met Cullen, she had never strayed in all the years they had been together, until that night with Amos. After that wonderful evening, she enjoyed several lovers during the next five years, and not once had she regretted a single time.

The same was with Ken Martinelli. However, all the others had been playthings, excitement that her husband no longer expected from her, nor gave to her. However, with Ken, it was different.

She soon began to realize, and admit, she really liked this new lover, above all the others. He did not come around too often, as some had, and when he did, he always wanted to take her out dancing, or to dinner, or to some new place, rather than just bedding her, smoking a cigarette, and then leaving.

Ken was truly different, and she liked that. She was even surprised how much she had come to love flying, particularly in the little Rebel, and especially when they would fly off to some new lake, or reservoir to have lunch at a marina, or a nearby restaurant, before heading back to High Rock for dessert.

She also enjoyed the energy a man twelve years younger than she possessed.

At times, a flashback would come of Cullen when he was in his early thirties. A pleasant memory of their young love, but these only lasted for a moment or two, and she would race back to Ken and reality.

It had been this extra interest that had encouraged her to take Ken to the lake cottage to begin with. He was the only lover she had ever taken there. This very cottage had been where Cullen had taken her for their honeymoon, and she loved it so much, he bought it a year later. It had always been a special place to her, but when the specialness of their marriage had slipped away, neither she nor Cullen had gone there for a long time, and it showed.

She spent three full days cleaning the cottage and getting everything in perfect order, before she suggested to Ken that they fly up to High Rock Lake and dine at *The Big Bass,* a local restaurant there at *The West Bank Marina.*

It wasn't until after their dinner did she show him where to taxi the Rebel and tie it down to the long dock Cullen had built years before.

Ken Martinelli had become rather pleased with the older woman, who seemed to enjoy his company in Charlotte. Now that he was making one or two runs a month to North Carolina, the whole affair was working out very nicely.

Ken, though, was never one to keep his accomplishments to himself, and he just had to brag about Lucy Teague to others.

In fact, one of the men, an A&P[22], who had been a round engine mechanic for Pratt & Whitney back in the glory days of the big radials, was now heading up the engine team for *The Company.*

Paul Deckle was not only one of the best round engine men still alive, he was also one of the biggest NASCAR fans in the south.

He not only knew much about *The Teague Racing Team,* he also knew Cullen Teague and his wife. Not that he knew them personally, rather he knew of them, as all fans everywhere know about the heroes of their favorite sport.

Paul had every magazine ever printed on NASCAR, and was never one to throw anything away that he might use or enjoy later. So when this young punk began to brag about banging Mrs. Teague, Paul Deckle had but one thing to say, "Bull Shit with a capital B and S."

The brags in front of the other lowly mechanics had been just a little too much for Paul to stand for and he was determined to make Martinelli eat his words, and he told Ken just that.

The next time Martinelli was in North Carolina, he had gone to the cottage alone and installed two hidden cameras, one video,

---

22 A&P: Airplane mechanic who is licensed to work on the airframe and power plants.

which was focused straight at the bed, and the other a single reflex 35 MM that he could control remotely with a small electronic transmitter he kept in his pocket.

The video camera was not of the highest quality, and due to its size, did not provide the clearest of images. However, the 35 was a top of the line Nikon and would produce unquestionable pictures. All he had to do is get her in the right place in the right outfit, and naked was the outfit he had in mind.

Lucy's forty-third birthday was coming up during the second week in September and she had hinted she would like to have Ken around sometime near her special day.

Since Ken had not been contacted about a flight by late August, he dropped the word here and there around the Gulfport FBO; he was taking off for a few days to the mountains, but nothing more. If the *The Company* should try to reach him, they would find out he was gone, but not exactly where he had gone. Although he might get a chewing out for not checking in before he left, he would not be in too much trouble. *'Besides I am not the only pilot checked out in the PV-1.'*

He did not have to fly a lot; in fact, he seldom made more than one or two flights a month. Very often, these were simple hops to the Caribbean to transport some big shot and his woman for a weekend of hidden pleasure, or at times, the planes would be leased out.

The university dive team had contracted to have their students taken downrange[23] twice a month for several days of clear water diving during the summer.

Also, a rather large flower company leased the Lockheed to make one or two flights a month to Costa Rica to bring back huge loads of tropical plants. These they would then distribute to various florists throughout Mississippi, and even as far away as DC. All of these runs were drug free and they were made to legitimize the planes *The Company* owned with customs. Although any agent

---

23 Down Range: Somewhere in the Caribbean.

might assume a DC-3 could haul more cargo at a third the cost of the PV-1, still it was a legitimate contract and the PV-1 was the sole aircraft used for transporting the tropical plants.

Ken could not wait to get back to Alligator Town[24] where *The Company* had bought the old Buster Brown Shoe factory at the abandoned airfield north of Lake City. During the war, the army and navy had built some seventy plus training fields in Florida. Usually those built for the army were a triangle affair, with three hard-surfaced runways 5000 feet long. The navy added a fourth runway that crossed the triangle. In this layout there would always be one runway aligned with the wind, no matter which point on the compass the wind might want to come from on any particular day. Alligator Town Airfield had been named for the Seminole Chief who located his village there some one hundred years before the army requisitioned the land for their training base, located on the southwestern tip of the Okefenokee Swamp.

In the sixties, a local hot rod club had leased one of the runways as a drag strip. Eventually the surface pavement deteriorated to the point Columbia County, who at the time was in control of the old airfield, requested permission from the FAA to close that runway.

When *The Jimerson Company* bought the abandoned Buster Brown plant, the Alligator Town Airport had only a small, one-man operation going. This little outfit offered flying lessons in a single Cessna 150 and rented space in the rear of a small building for a skydiving club to operate on the weekends.

The coming and going of Jimerson's larger aircraft brought new life, and new blood, to the old field, and most everyone in Lake City was happy to see it happen. Of course, only a hand full of Columbia County residents knew the true business of *The Jimerson Company*, and they had good reason to remain silent about it.

It was in the big hanger which had once produced Buster Brown brogans for schoolchildren, and paratrooper boots for the army, that Ken Martinelli was showing off his photographs. One of which was especially good. It clearly showed Lucy Teague's face, as well

---

24 Alligator Town: Early name for Lake City, Florida.

as her slim nude body, as she leaned over to accept a light from the arm that extended from a chair.

This photograph did not reveal who was sitting in the chair, but the expression on her face was one of excitement and everyone there had their eyes glued to the pear-sized breasts that obviously were quite firm on her body.

At forty-three, Lucy was an exceptionally attractive woman and most of the mechanics gazed lustfully at the picture. "Well, this is a picture of a fine piece of ass all right," Buck Higdon said. "But how do we know you took it, and who the hell that arm belongs to?"

Ken was ready for this question and the next picture he handed out, showed him standing next to her, also nude, with his fingers pinching her taut nipples. There was no question, but it was Martinelli in the photograph.

He then said spitefully, "If Deckle knows as much about NASCAR as he claims, then he can identify this gorgeous babe I banged just before this picture was taken."

All eyes suddenly turned to the master mechanic for his comment. Paul took the photograph and studied it for a while, and when satisfied Martinelli had not faked it, he nodded his head, "It looks like Lucinda Teague," he reluctantly agreed, and tossed it back on the opened Snap-On toolbox.

Ken then turned to Buck, "If you still question my rendezvous with Mrs. Teague, I have here a video that I will show in the lounge later. It will erase all your doubts," he bragged, holding up a VCR tape.

"All right," was the loud reply, made by one of the younger mechanics.

After work that day while the tape was being shown, Paul Deckle was cleaning his hand tools and carefully placing them in their correct resting place in his tall red toolbox. The whole affair just welded the growing hatred, and contempt, he had for the bragging Martinelli. *'A man shouldn't go around showing off pictures of another man's wife like that.'*

When the group finally came out of the office whooping and hollering, showing their pleasure with what they had just witnessed, Paul watched them walk off to their cars. When Martinelli went to his brand new Beamer, Paul saw him drop a manila envelope behind the seat before stepping in. The wise old man stayed back near his toolbox in a darker side of the big building and none of the men even knew he was still there.

The next morning when Ken came down to take advantage of the breakfast buffet at Shoney's, he found the driver's window had been busted in during the night and his car had been ransacked. The only things missing were the Smith & Wesson Chief Special he had in the glove box, and the envelope containing the tape and photographs. The loss of the pictures did not bother him much, he still had the negatives, but he had failed to copy the tape and he hated losing it.

'I can reinstall the camera I guess, and make a new one sometime,' he thought, but he never did.

Murphy Rebel on Amphibious Floats

Chapter Seventeen
Yellow Is Beautiful

B lue had not gone anywhere with Nate for over a year. In fact, she would not have gone with him on this trip had not Hilton James, her attorney, advised her to do so. "It will be in your best interest to go, Blue," he had said. "You never know what Nate is up to and when he is summoned to Washington by the government, I think you should be nearby, just in case."

"I don't see why," she replied, obviously in disagreement with him. Then again, she knew he had always provided her with the best legal advice and she also knew she would make this trip with her husband.

From VAL to IAD was only a little over an hour hop in the Citation, but over South Carolina they received notice that Dulles was closed due to an alert from the White House. Nate elected to lay over in Charlotte instead of returning and waiting for the temporary restriction to be lifted.

Nate had been pleased when he learned Blue would accompany him on this trip. He always liked to show her off to his acquaintances in Washington. Even though their battle lines were drawn and the trenches dug, he had not lost his desire for her and hoped that perhaps among so many influential people, she might once again realize his true importance in society, in and around the nation's capital, and call a ceasefire. Even if it only was for the three days they would be there. Actually, it was the three nights he was hoping for.

'Now that her lover is dead, she surely might be getting horny enough to be friendly at least one night,' he reasoned.

He reasoned wrong.

"Will you call and have a limo awaiting us from the Sheraton Hotel," he said to the pilot, over the intercom phone. It had been delivered as a request, but Courtney Busk knew it was a command. "Yes sir," he replied.

Immediately afterwards, he heard her voice come over the line, "And reserve two suites for us, Mr. Busk."

Nate was not surprised, even a little pleased, in that she had not requested, they not be connecting suites. That was something unusual. *'Maybe,'* he thought.

That night, while Nate was having his dinner in the Atrium Lounge, Blue was dining in Oscar's Restaurant. Two hours later when he staggered up to his room, he found the connecting door securely bolted from her side.

The moment she entered the doors of Oscar's, he spotted her. There was no one who possibly could have missed the six-foot one-inch redhead, dressed to kill. Especially one who had seen her before, as Ken had.

He had only been in the Sheraton once previously, and that was all business. This time, Mrs. Teague made the reservations the week before when she found on her answering machine one expression, "331MR0517P."

She immediately knew Ken would be in town on May 17, sometime after noon. The N numbers of the Rebel were November 331 Mike Romero and the 0517P represented the date and time he would arrive.

She also assumed he would stay for two or more nights, as he usually did, when he came to Charlotte. Since Cullen already said he would be taking a flight to Indy on that very night, it all presented a lovely opportunity for Ken and her to enjoy their pleasures in the luxury of Charlotte's finest hotel.

Too, it was only a short drive from there to the smaller airport where he hangared their little plane. If they wanted to go somewhere on Saturday, it would all be so convenient.

Ken would have missed seeing her had he not stopped to pick up a couple boxes of Marlboros before he went up to the room. *'I wonder what Ms. Dunkin is doing here?'* he thought, as he gazed at the beautiful redhead.

The next morning as he was leaving with Lucy, he again saw her, only this time, she was with an older man who was much shorter than she. Lucy also saw her. However, the reason she looked at Blue was because she had seen her lover staring intensely at something, and she wanted to know just what had so captured his attention.

When she saw Blue, she just said softly to the man by her side, "Pull your tongue back in Honey, she is way out of your class."

"I don't know. She might like what I could offer her," he replied, remembering the many times he had watched the tape of Ms. Dunkin and her lover in the rear of the Lear enroute to Colorado.

"I'm afraid not, she could buy and sell us both, and probably NASCAR to boot."

"You know Ms. Dunkin?"

"Ms. Dunkin?" she said, looking questionably at him before adding, "That, Honey, is the multi-millionaire Nathan Rugg, and the lady is his wife."

"Rugg?" he replied.

Of course, he had heard of Nate Rugg. Everyone in aviation had heard of how the man with a few dollars bought some derelict bombers and flew them straight into one of the most successful businesses in the field. However, he had never seen him before, except in a few smaller pictures, once when *Professional Pilot Magazine* had printed a feature article on him, several years back.

'Son-of-a-bitch,' he thought.

Nate had been both pleased, and disappointed with Blue, on the trip. She had been the perfect wife at all their public appearances, but the door between their suites remained bolted at all times. He returned home without enjoying her pleasures, and in a bad mood.

This fact gave her the most pleasure of their whole trip and as soon as she detected his changing mood, she decided to make a trip of her own, to the Rockies, at her first opportunity.

Ken Martinelli had made a big mistake at the tables in Biloxi in early June. He was up almost five thousand in a game of stud in one of the backrooms when he saw the cards begin to fall his way. Face-down was a queen and the next three cards dropped were her sisters. It was time to bet and he pushed his whole winnings forward. But the dealer met his challenge and raised him another five thousand. Ken was out of cash. However, he had a winning hand and this pot would pay off all his debts.

After he had become employed by *The Jimerson Company*, his credit had always been good here, so he wrote an IOU for the extra five thousand. When his last card fell, it was a king, and he smiled. The dealer had a seven low flush running, but the chances of him having the missing nine, was almost impossible. Almost, but not impossible, as Ken soon found out, when the dark man with a single gold tooth smiled before turning over the last card; a nine of diamonds.

A straight flush beats, four of a kind, and that beats the over-confident, every time.

Suddenly, Ken needed five thousand dollars, and he needed it badly and quickly.

He also remembered well the last time he had been visited because he was late on paying his gambling debts, and he did not want to dance to that tune a second time. In fact, he was not sure if they would even let him dance. They had been pretty straight forward as to his outcome should he fail to pay on time again.

Never had he requested to make a flight for *The Company*. He waited and they contacted him. However, they did not call him and he needed money now. Finally, he went back to Florida and tried to see some of the big shots who came in and out of the airport from time to time, but was not successful in this endeavor.

In desperation, he asked Peter Pitre, who was the top dog there at Alligator Town, but he was told they were not moving anything right then and it was best he did not ask again. "You will be contacted when needed, as always."

His note in Biloxi was due in four days and he was becoming more and more desperate.

Finally, he remembered the tape of the Rugg woman and the man. *'My tape was stolen. Why couldn't that tape of Mrs. Rugg turn up stolen?'*

He immediately drove back to Mississippi, arriving in Meridian only a couple hours before dawn. Parking half a block from the apartment complex he waited.

Just after seven, he spotted Frank Alvarez come out and drive away. Ken followed at a distance until satisfied Frank was truly headed to the airport before he turned back.

His big hope now was that Frank had not changed the locks on the rear door to his apartment. Finding he had not, in a matter of minutes, Ken had located several tapes he coded with L24. He now only had to find the one the Rugg woman was on.

He started to take them all, but knew Frank would notice if all were missing and eventually figure out where they had gone. No, he must confine his theft to the Rugg tape only. After some time he located it, and returned the others to the case before slipping out through the backdoor, and the neighborhood.

Ken found it was not an easy thing to speak to a man like Nate Rugg, and he was beginning to think he would run out of time before he did. However, finally with less than twenty hours to go, he had Rugg on the phone. "Mr. Rugg, I have a tape I think you will be interested in seeing."

"Who is this?"

"That's not important. What is important is the man on this tape has offered me five thousand dollars for it, and since it is your wife with him, I thought you might want to buy it."

There was a long pause before the rough voice replied, "I think you are somewhat late with your sale. My wife's lover is dead."

"Wrong. I spoke to him only today," Ken lied. Then he paused a moment before adding, "Perhaps she has a new lover."

Again, there was silence on the line and he felt sure Nate Rugg was having the call traced, but it would do him no good. Ken had tapped into a line box along the side of an Alabama highway to make this call and he knew no one could connect it to him.

After quite a long time without a reply, Ken said, "I suppose I was mistaken, Mr. Rugg. Maybe you don't want to see it after all. I can understand a husband not wanting to see his lovely wife screaming her head off while she rides someone else's cock. Sorry I bothered you."

"No, wait!" Rugg said. "Just how much do you want for it?"

"Well, like I said, the other man is willing to give five thousand for it_____," he let it drop and waited for his opponent to counter.

"Alright, if it's legitimate, I will pay six thousand."

"Oh it's legitimate, alright. I need the money today."

"Where will the exchange be?"

"At a rest area on I-10," Ken replied, thinking that it would be a public place with plenty of witnesses should Rugg try something.

"There is a rest area east of Tallahassee. I will have my man meet you there in an hour."

"No. That's too soon. I'll be there at two this afternoon. I will be wearing a Panama hat, white blazer and dark pants," Ken added, and then at the last moment, he remembered to say, "The westbound rest area."

"My man will be there with your six thousand. We will need to verify who is on the tape, you understand."

"It must be done at the rest area. I ain't going nowhere with him."

"That will be satisfactory," Nate Rugg replied and then pressed the button on his phone, then immediately dialed Johns and Townsend, and explained the situation to Mickey Johns.

"I'll meet him Mr. Rugg. That will be no problem. I'll draw the cash out of our account here and mark all the bills. Did he ask for any certain domination? Mickey asked.

"No. Just six thousand."

"Good. I'll have 60 Franklins, all marked and ready."

"You have seen my wife."

"Yes. I have seen pictures of her. I will know if it is truly her, before I pay for the tape."

"Good, Mickey, and I want to know who this man we are dealing with is."

"That should be no problem either," Johns replied, and then he hung up.

At precisely 2 p.m., Ken Martinelli walked from the bathroom at the rest area and sat on a table under the shade of a tall pine. Almost immediately, he saw the short man head his way carrying a rather thick attaché case. When he was close enough to be heard, without attracting attention, he said, "That is a nice Panama you have there, did Nate buy it for you?"

Ken reached inside his blazer and retrieved the envelope, which contained the VCR tape, and laid it on the concrete table beside him. Mickey sat down across from him on top of the table and placing the case there also, opened it. Inside the brown leather case, Ken saw the stack of bills with a thick rubber band around them and a feeling of relief came to him for the first time since that damn nine of diamonds was turned over.

Also, inside the case was a video camera, which the man removed. He opened the envelope, placed the tape in the camera and then pressed the play button.

Ken already had the tape set so Blue Rugg's face was plainly visible as she sat atop some man's lap bouncing up and down wildly.

Mickey was convinced it was her all right. It would be nearly impossible to find another woman, her size, to try to fake such a scene. He nodded his head and slid the case over.

Ken quickly released his grip on the pistol in his pocket, and counted the one hundred dollar bills. Satisfied they were all there, he nodded back, closed the case, and sat it down on the concrete bench beside his feet and there he waited.

"Mr. Rugg never pays twice for anything," was all Mickey said, before he stepped away from the table and walked over to his car. He placed the camera in the trunk and then drove off.

Ken waited for a long time before he rose and walked over and stood beside the Neon he had rented at the Tallahassee airport on his way to this rendezvous. When he was satisfied the man was gone, he opened the door and got in, and soon was headed back to Tallahassee where he turned in the Plymouth. All the way, he kept remembering the stern words the short man had said, "Mr. Rugg never pays twice for anything."

Ken had in fact, delivered a copy of the tape and kept the original as insurance, just in case something had gone wrong today. Of course, he thought if the man would pay $6000 for it sight unseen, he might want to buy the original for much more after he had viewed it. However, now he decided he would keep it for his own pleasure and nothing more. In fact, he finally decided he would slip it back into Frank's collection.

When Mickey left the rest area, he headed west to the Monticello exit then north into Georgia until he reached SR 84. There, he turned east toward the Valdosta airport. He had arranged with Mr. Rugg to deliver the merchandise there.

Rugg took the camera, removed the tape and handed the Canon back to the detective. Then he placed it in the player in his hangar office and turned it on. Immediately, he recognized two things; it was indeed his wife and it was taken in an airplane. It was at that point he stopped the film, turned to Mickey, and said, "I want to know who he is."

"The man who I dealt with or the man in the video?"

Nate hesitated only a couple of seconds before replying, "Both." Then he looked out of the window and watched a military C-130 make a practice missed approached before climbing out and leaving four tracks of dark smoke trailing behind. Nate's eyes did not leave the trails until the smoke finally twisted into oblivion by the wing tip vortices of the big plane. Only then did he say without turning back, "This will be quite a game we are about to enter Mr. Johns, quite a game."

"Yes, sir. I will need a copy of that tape to find as much as I can from it."

Nate didn't like the idea of others watching a triple X movie where his wife was in the starring role; however, he did realize the detective would need the tape to analyze. "I'll have a copy sent to your office tomorrow," he replied.

"No, offense sir, but I will be able to learn a lot more from the original."

"Tomorrow," was all Rugg said in reply.

Ben Townsend stayed in his old Econoline van parked among the semi-trucks the whole time his partner and the mark negotiated the deal. Then from a reasonable distance, Ben followed him back to Tallahassee.

Upon realizing his destination, he was concerned because he would not be able to get a seat on the same flight the man was taking, however, once he saw him head out of the terminal towards the Short Term Parking Lot, he smiled.

When the blue-gray Beamer waited at the stop sign before turning north on Capital Circle Drive, Ben stopped directly behind him. He was recording not only his tag number, but also a nice picture of the car from his own hidden camera in the grill of the old Ford.

That night, while he and Mickey made their calls and did the other research the information they had in hand afforded them, Nate Rugg was watching his newly purchased skin flick for the third time, while he downed more and more bourbon there in his office. Finally, he reached down and relieved himself. It had been the first time he had needed to do so since the night they had returned from Washington. It would be the last time he did so without a woman.

Two weeks later, Nate received a call from Tallahassee. "Mr. Rugg, this is Mickey Johns. I have some information you might like to know about. Should I come to Valdosta?"

"No. I will be in Tallahassee tomorrow. I will come by your office around eleven."

The tape had been delivered via overnight mail to his office. In the same envelope was a check for ten thousand dollars. A note attached to the check simply read, "Working Capital."

Mickey smiled and thanked his lucky stars for that stupid black bitch who had tried her scam on the rich whitey in the Cadillac. However, when he viewed the tape he found much to his disappointment, Rugg had copied only a small portion that showed only Mrs. Rugg's lover's face.

"This is a photograph of the man who sold me the tape," Mickey said as he handed Rugg the picture. It was obviously taken at the rest area where the exchange had taken place. "And here is a copy of his driver's license."

"He is Kenneth Keith Martinelli. He lives in Gulfport, Mississippi. He is a pilot for *The Jimerson Company* and flies out of their base here in Lake City, Florida. It's at the old military field north of town, not the main Lake City airport.

"So far, all I have been able to find out about them is they haul freight out of Central America and a few passenger contracts, back and forth in the Caribbean. I will have more on them the next time I get in touch with you.

"Martinelli used to fly for *Mississippi Aviation*, who is out of Meridian, but he was fired about a year back. They run a small-time charter business to and from the islands, also in and out of the gambling towns along the gulf coast.

"Mostly they use Piper Chieftains, but they also have a Cessna Citation and a Lear. I think the video was shot in one of these. If you will notice the seat arrangement and the leather upholstery, I would say most likely the Lear.

"I don't think your wife was aware the movie was being shot. It is almost impossible for a non-professional not to at some time, glance at a known camera, and at no time does she even look in that direction, neither does the man.

"And, that brings us to him. He is Wallace Roberts. He works for one of the local Electrical Suppliers in Madison County, *The Withlacoochee Co-Op*. Here is a copy of his Florida driver's license, but for some reason he recently turned it in for a Wyoming License. I will check into that further for you." Johns stopped to give his client time to digest all he had presented him with, before he continued. "It is this Roberts that was pushing so hard to have the death of James Hancock investigated as a murder. That has quieted down a lot, but he still is working silently on the case."

Once more Johns paused and then he said, "Mr. Rugg, I believe Roberts is the only lover your wife has had. At least he is the only one we have been able to turn up anything on."

Nate looked up sharply at him when he heard this. "What about that Hancock boy?"

"No sir. I don't believe so."

"Hum," Nate replied, as he thought on that for a moment.

Nate had used Johns to identify Hancock but nothing more on the man. However, when Mickey heard of Hancock's drowning, and the subsequent stir questioning it being an accident, he suspected Nate Rugg had something to do with the man's death. *'Had he asked us to find out for him, that mistake would not have been made,'* Johns thought.

"I want to know all you can get on this Roberts fellow," he said, as he was thinking, *'If he works for the Co-Op I will see he is fired before noon tomorrow.'*

"Yes, sir. That is in the works at this time," Mickey Johns replied.

On his way back to Tallahassee, he thought, *'If I can do this well enough, I should receive a swell bonus, maybe even enough to get Cherry back.'*

Blue had gone to Wyoming for a week shortly after her trip to Washington, but Wall could not get the time off.

While in Natrona County, Deputy Sanders approached her with news, "I have learned a T-Hangar, here at Casper International will soon be available, and I wondered if you and your husband would be interested in sharing the expense with me. It would give you a good secure place to store the Jeep Cherokee when you are away, and also give me a place to keep my snow machine and boat out of the weather."

She did think it was a good idea, and after looking at the size of the hangar, she made this agreement with Nick. "I will lease the hangar alone, and you may store your things in it in exchange for a personal assurance that our cabin is not molested while we are away. Also, should anyone make inquiries about either of us with your agency, you learn as much about them as you can, and keep me informed."

Nick looked at her questioningly.

"Sergeant, I am a very wealthy woman. There are people who simply can't stand that fact. There is always at least one, and at times more, who are trying to acquire information about us to use as material in a blackmail scheme.

"Even though we do nothing here that they could use in that capacity, if we know who they are and what they are seeking, it may help us either to stay clear of them, or perhaps even trap them in their conspiracies. Am I making myself clear?"

This time he nodded his head, "Yes, Ma'am, I will do as you ask, as long as it doesn't require me to violate my oath of office."

"I assure you, Sergeant, I, and especially my husband, would never ask you to do that, his loyalty to the law is unbelievably strong"

"Well then, I will be glad to help in any way I can."

"Good, and I want you to help me with something else also."

"Yes, Ma'am?" he answered a little uneasy.

"Sometime in the next week or ten days an airplane, a Piper Cub will be delivered here. It is a birthday gift for my husband. I would like to give the pilot your name as the person to contact when he arrives. Will you see it is placed in the hangar and that he makes his flight back to Yakama?"

"That should be no problem, if you will just let me know when he will be arriving."

"Should I have him contact you through the Sheriff's Office or_____?"

Nick hesitated for a moment. "Please don't let this get out," he requested, and then gave her his personal phone number.

"I assure you it will not," Blue answered.

When she turned and walked away, Nick had to admire her shape. *'Man, that is one hell of a woman. I wonder if she is as red on the bottom as she is on the top.'*

Wall was able to get Friday the 24th off so he would have a long Memorial Day weekend. Once again, he found himself on a private jet bound for Wyoming. It was the first time they had been able to be together in two months and the wheels had barely cleared the ground before they each were tearing away at the other's clothes.

When they deplaned at Casper, he found his Cherokee sitting in front of the terminal parked in a space reserved for Police Only.

"What is this?" he inquired looking over at her.

"Just one of those little perks that come to the privileged few," she answered, and walked to the passenger's door and waited.

Wall liked that. He had been raised to respect a lady and opening a door for her was just one small way to display his upbringing. An upbringing he was proud of.

One of the things that had always been a sour spot with him was the first time he met Ash. On the day he interviewed for his job, he had attempted to hold the door open for her as she entered the CO-OP. Immediately, she told him quite harshly she was perfectly capable of opening her own doors. Later, after he went to work there, she began to come on to him, but the bitter taste had already stained her image in his mind. Blue, on the other hand, was not a feminist. She was her own woman for sure, but above and beyond that, she was a lady, and she appreciated a gentleman.

'It is quite impossible for one to do the acts of a gentleman, unless the woman is enough a lady to permit him to do so.'

He, of course, had never met Doggy Belle, but he would bet his new blue jeans her father had been a gentleman, and her mother a lady. Blue was just too down to earth for them to have been otherwise. Even with all her wealth and refinement, had she not been a lady, he would have escaped this relationship long ago.

Casper Mountain in late May is a mixture of snow, slush, and an almighty lot of mud. He had to engage the front third member after they left the pavement and turned onto the dirt road, which ended at the tall television tower some three quarters of a mile beyond their cabin. It was the same when they left the confines of the Jeep and walked to the porch, mud caking heavily on their boots. "Damn, this stuff is as bad as middle-Georgia," he said.

"They tell me it is only like this for a few weeks," she said, almost apologetically.

Realizing her tone, he replied, "You know, Blue, I'd wade through hell to spend a few hours with you."

"I hope you never have to do that," she said, unlocking the door and then stepping aside for him to push it open.

When he entered, his attention was immediately drawn to the high wall above the stone fireplace. Where once hung a fishing rod, now was a very different décor. There in a sunburst, were Winchester rifles, one at every degree of the clock, and in the center were two revolvers. "My God!" he exclaimed looking at them.

"Do you like them? I just knew you would. They were my father's collection. One of every model of the old lever Winchesters, and the two pistols are both 44-40's. One an 1873 Colt and the other an 1875 Remington," she explained with so much glee, he just shook his head in disbelief.

"They are yours now," she added.

"Oh no. I couldn't, they were your father's."

"Now they are yours. Wall, please say you will accept them. I still have his 25-35 down in Florida," she added, as if it would change anything.

"I just don't know what to say."

"Say you are happy. That's all I want to hear."

"I'm very happy. Very happy to have found you."

The next morning she awoke earlier than usual and it surprised him. "Come on, get dressed cowboy. I want to go to town."

"What? And not get to look at your beautiful body for hours?"

"Listen, I need to buy something, and I want to show you something, so come on," she said, and slapped him hard on the chest.

"Ouch!" he exclaimed.

Doggy's Winchesters over the Fireplace

"First, I want to stop at a store, a clothing store. I think there is one on Second Street," she said, pointing to the overhead sign as they approached the intersection. "Look there, there it is," she again pointed.

Wall pulled into a parking space just a little past *Lou Taubert's Western Wear,* and she jumped out of the Jeep the moment he got it stopped. "Come on," she said excitedly, and motioned for him to hurry to her side.

"What's in here?"

"A new pair of boots for me and a hat for you."

"The wind blows too much out here. I don't think I can keep a hat on," he said looking over at her, but then realizing if she wanted him to wear a hat, he would try.

"That's because you never had a real Ka'boy hat before. They come with a good latigo stampede string that either goes under your chin, or my dad usually wore them behind his head."

They looked at several hats and finally both agreed on a 10X Stetson in silver belly. "Now get rid of that redneck ball cap," she said to him, and then turning she spoke to the saleslady, "I want to see your boots, and I read an advertisement in the paper that you had bras for full-figured ladies."

Immediately Wall cut his eyes around at her. "I know, Darlin', but sometimes these things really hurt my back, and I need to wear one."

To him it seemed like such a waste. Her breasts, even though quite large, did not sag in the least and her nipples pointed ahead, if not slightly upward. He hated to think of them being jailed in a bra.

"What size are we looking for?"

"Forty-two Triple D," Blue replied.

"Oh my. I'm not sure we have anything pretty that comes in a size that large."

"Let me see what you have," Blue said and the two women headed off leaving him there.

It was all right, he really didn't want to go anyway. The very thought was a disappointment. Instead, he wandered over to the boot section and strolled around looking at first one and then another. He knew they would come here sooner or later anyway, because she wanted new boots. *'I don't see why she wants new boots, the ones she brought with her look new, at least to me.'*

It was a full-half hour before he saw the two ladies coming towards the boot department. He was immediately disappointed because it was obvious she was not bouncing around like she normally did, which meant she had found a bra that fit.

"Now let me see," the saleslady said, "You did say a 9A didn't you?"

"That's right. A, or sometimes a B, depending on the manufacturer."

"A western boot with a flat heel."

"Yes," Blue agreed.

Eventually, after she tried several pair, each time asking his opinion, finally settling on the first ones she had put on.

When they left, it was obvious he was a tiny bit miffed and she knew why, so she tried to tease him. "You have your bottom lip stuck out like a school boy who has just had his cap-pistol taken away."

Wall gave her a cut of his eyes and instead of giving her a reply he asked, "Where else do you want to go?"

"The airport," she quickly replied.

"The airport?"

"Yes, the airport. Don't you think it's a nice day for flying?"

"Not in a Lear Jet."

"Now, you don't like Lear Jets?"

"I like little planes, you know, like Cubs and Champs and such. Like the ones I used to fly over your house."

They rode on for a short time and he asked, "Why the flat heels? Your legs really look good when you wear high heels."

"Because the man I'm mad about is an inch shorter than I am, and I don't want him to feel inferior," she shot back.

"Oh," he replied, and then thought a moment and added, "I don't feel inferior."

"Good, because you are not. Neither do I want others to see him as a shorter man. I married a short man, and I love to look down on him, and to have others snicker about that. I don't want that to happen with us," she explained, and then said, "The boots are not what you are miffed about, it's the bra."

"Well, you have the greatest boobs in the world. I just hate to think of them being all cramped up in that thing."

"Okay, I'll take it off as soon as we get in the airplane."

'Oh great. That won't be for another three days,' he thought, but he didn't say anything.

When he turned into the long driveway leading to the terminal, she said, "Just before you get to the main circle, turn right and head down to that big hangar there."

He looked at her questioningly.

"There is a museum in there, Airplane Museum. I think you will like it."

He parked in the graveled lot and they walked in. Immediately, he was glad they had stopped. It was filled with several old warplanes and a few newer types that he recognized as used in the Reno Air Races.

In less than a minute, a short, older man came out and smiled, "Mrs. Dunkin, nice to see you again."

"Mr. Good, I want you to meet my husband Wall Roberts."

"Wall?" he asked, making sure he had heard it correctly.

Wall was glad he had the courtesy not to question the different last names. She seemed to have no problem with the deception, but he found it hard to lie, even under these circumstances. "Yes, Wall is short for Wallace."

"It's Jim, short for Jim Good," the man replied, extending his hand.

They were standing next to a Mig fighter and Wall said, "This is some place you have here. Are all these yours?"

"Mostly. I do have a few investors, but mostly they are mine."

Good looked over at the tall woman, but she quickly shook her head. Understanding, he nodded his in reply.

They walked around for over half an hour and then she said, "Well, Mr. Good, we have a couple of more things to do this morning, so we had better be getting on."

"Yes, the winds will be up soon, and you will want to be inside when they arrive," he suggested.

They made their goodbyes and walking to the parking lot Wall said, "He is one hell of a nice guy."

"I'm glad you like him. I do, too," she said, and then pointed north. "There is something out there I want to look at before we go. Let's drive out there towards those little buildings."

"Those little buildings are called hangars," he explained.

"Oh, okay, those little hangar buildings," she said mocking him.

There was another vehicle stopped directly in front of them when they arrived at the electronic gate and when the driver punched in the correct numbers, the bar rose, and Blue said, "Hurry and we can drive in on him, then we won't have to walk."

Wall hugged in close behind the Blazer and they both entered before the bar came back down. He saw the driver of the Chevrolet looking at them in his rear-view mirror and Wall felt a little guilty.

"Turn there," she said, pointing down a row of larger than average T-Hangars. When they had almost reached the north end of this row she said, "Stop in front of number 27."

Wall was beginning to wonder what she was up to, but before he could question her, she offered, "Come on, Deputy Sanders keeps his boat in here and I want you to look at it."

He shook his head a little, as he put the Jeep in park. "I ain't much on fishing and boats, except maybe a Jon Boat."

"Come on," she urged rushing over to the walk-through door and opened the padlock. Before he got to the door, she had stepped through it and Wall followed.

Once inside the dark hangar, he saw it truly did house a boat and a snowmobile on a trailer, but also there was a bright yellow Super Cub.

Wall walked right past the boat and raising the clamshell, peered inside the Cub. "Damn, this one is almost brand new."

"Yes, it is. One of the last ones they made," she replied as if she was an authority on Super Cubs.

"Oh, is that so, and just who told you that?" he questioned, but he did not look at her, he was too interested in the little Piper.

"Mr. Paul Davidson, that's who."

"Yeah? And who is he?" Wall asked, not really interested in her conversation, but not wanting her to think he was not.

"He is the man who flew it home from the factory when it was brand new."

"He's a lucky man. I'd give my right nut for a new Super Cub."

"Well, let's not go too far. I have some claim to your nuts," she answered, leaning over him so her boobs were pressing against his back, a distraction he appreciated.

"But you are right," she said, "He is a lucky man. He bought two new ones. He said he was convinced these would be the last Piper would ever make and he wanted one for himself and another just as an investment."

"Must have money, too," Wall replied, once again looking inside and running his fingers over the soft leather of the front seat. "Damn, this is nice. I didn't know these new ones had such a nice seat."

"I think that is an addition from Cub Crafters," she offered.

Wall was amazed, he stood back and turning to look at her, he asked, "When did you find out all this about Cubs?"

"In the last month. I really like them, don't you?"

"Hell yes, as they say, Yellow is Beautiful."

"I'm glad you like it, and I hope you are not too mad at me about the bra."

"I'm not mad. I just like to see you bounce around, that's all," he said and kissed her gently on the lips.

"Well, I did say I would take it off when we got to the airplane."

"No, what you said was, *'when we got in the airplane,'* and that won't be for another three days."

"What if we were to get in this one?"

"I wouldn't dare," Wall replied, shaking his head. "I don't know about this Paul David, but if this was mine, I damn sure wouldn't want anybody climbing around on or in it."

"Davidson," she corrected. "His name is Davidson, not David, and he is just that way. In fact, he told me other than the fellow who went with him to Vero Beach to pick it up new, and his flight instructor, no one has ever been in the back seat."

"I can understand that," Wall said back, once again looking inside, this time at the radio package mounted in the panel.

"You really do like it, don't you?" she said, smiling broadly.

"You bet I do," he replied, still not looking at her.

"Well, it's your birthday present."

At first he didn't notice what she had said, but after a few seconds it began to sink in. Suddenly when her statement hit home, his head shot straight up and he banged it on the overhead cross bar. "What?"

"I said it is your birthday present," she smiled, and then added, "I done good, didn't I?"

It was something she remembered her father saying once, when he had brought home a beautiful Pinto for her mother's birthday.

Dottie and Patches

"I just don't believe you are real," he said back to her.

"Well, take a look at these and you might just change your mind," she said, and began unbuttoning her blouse. When all the tiny blue buttons were undone, she pulled it loose from her pants, then released the front hooks of her bra and opened the large white vice, allowing her breasts to burst forward, free at last. When they did, he saw them - two yellow Cubs dangling from her pierced nipples.

"I had to get a bra, or you would have seen them under my blouse," she said, explaining the whole affair.

He just stood there and looked at her and shook his head.

"Now, do you think you can get this thing out of here, so we can go flying?"

"I think I might," he replied, nodding his head, "but not before I do this," and then he reached for her and pulled her close to him and kissed her for a long time.

When they finally broke, she said, "We had better go flying or I will want to have you right here."

"That sounds like a good idea," he agreed, but she rushed away from him and pushed a button that activated an electric motor, and the big overhead door began to slowly rise.

"Jim said the wind would be up before long, and we need to get going."

When it was fully opened, she rushed around to a strut and began to push. "I have an electric *Taildragger Dragger* ordered, but it hasn't arrived yet."

When they had the little yellow plane clear of the hangar, she jumped in the jeep, drove it inside and started the door back down.

"You had better button up or someone will get a gander at those melons." She looked down at her breasts, seeing they were still exposed. Suddenly she stripped her blouse and bra off and pitched them into the back seat and then said, "Told you I would take it off when we got in the airplane." Then she climbed in the rear seat. "Let 'em see them. I want everybody to envy you, because if they see them, they will want to play with them, but only you get to do that, these days."

He smiled and climbed in the front seat and reached for the starter.

Ground Control in the tower instructed them to taxi to runway 03 and hold for a landing heavy. This caused them to pass the control tower and the main terminal. Both were too far away for anyone to see them, however, a controller in the tower was admiring the bright yellow Cub and he reached for his binoculars to look her over good. "Son-of-a-Bitch, that gal in the back of the Super Cub is topless, and man-o-man, does she have a set of jugs."

N41577 flying into the sunset.
One of the last Super Cubs built by Piper.

Chapter Eighteen
The Arrest

'*I*
am well pleased with the results I have received from 'Johns and Townsend Investigations'. Ben Townsend has more than proven his skill as an accident investigator and Mickey Johns is turning out to be the best private detective I have ever used,' Nate was thinking when the voice of his pilot came over the intercom, "Mr. Rugg, we are letting down for Meigs Field, sir."

"Thank you, Courtney."

Nate really disliked Chicago. He couldn't remember a single day he had ever spent there when one could see a blue sky. It had always been cloudy and gloomy, as it was this day.

"John, I will most likely stay overnight and return tomorrow, but just in case I need you, have the Citation ready for immediate departure."

"Yes sir," John Nesmith answered, while he was thinking, '*Hell fire, now we will have to stay here at the FBO all night.*'

The long black Lincoln was waiting for him and the chauffeur opened his door as soon as he approached.

"Uberto," he began, as he looked from the fortieth floor window of *The Sprint Building* at the gray waters of Lake Michigan, "I might have made a mistake on that boy in Florida. Ah, the Hancock boy," he paused and turned with his drink in hand. "I have new information. Much better detailed information, and now have a plan that will not only serve my needs, but will hurt the bitch at the same time."

The older man only nodded his head and let Nate continue.

"This Voorhies woman, is she anything to you?"

"She is a mechanic, nothing more."

"I was thinking, just how far will she go for the right money?"

"I suspect, for enough money, she would do most anything," Spindetto said, nodding his head.

"I want to talk to her," Nate said, then turned and again looked out of the window once more. "Can that be arranged?"

The wise old man cleared his throat and moved his lips in and out over his teeth a couple of times, "I will say only one thing in caution, my friend, I never," he paused and remembered the boat rescue in The Virgin Islands, "Well, almost never, make personal contact with the people I employ. I think it is better if they do not know for sure who pays them. I would suggest you do the same. But if you insist on speaking directly with this woman, I can arrange it."

"What I want her to do is somewhat different than her normal work. I don't want any foul ups this time."

"As you wish," Uberto replied, and then he picked up the phone and made a call. "I will have an answer for you within the hour," he said to Nate and then added, "Now let us talk about the Costa Rica business."

Christina Voorhies listened quietly as Nate explained his plan. When he finished, he added, "This is worth a quarter of a million dollars to me." He paused, and tightened his eyes looking for a sign in her expression, when he saw nothing favorable, he added, "Plus expenses of course."

Christina killed her first man for The Company when she was still in high school. It was a simple thing; dress the part, stand on the corner where she had been told he made his pickups, and at the next stoplight shoot him twice, step out and walk away from the car. The older man immediately spotted the young hooker standing there and beckoned her over to his car. She opened the door, slid over next to him, and raised her skirt revealing she was wearing nothing under it.

At the next red light, he started running his fingers in the curls of her bush and she placed the 22 Magnum revolver at the base of his skull and pulled the trigger. The car suddenly started slowly moving forward, and she laid the Charter Arms in her lap and placed the car in park. She knew the second shot was not needed, but she had been told to shoot him twice, so she placed the second round in his right ear. It went exactly as planned.

Once the realization she had been so successful swept over her, Chrissie was surprised at the warm feeling that suddenly rushed through her loins.

Very calmly, she stepped from the white Buick and walked to the curb, then up the street and into an alley where her boyfriend was waiting.

The next day, he gave her ten one hundred dollar bills. At that moment, Chrissie knew she had found her profession for life.

After high school, she left Peoria to attend Westwood College in Woodridge, to major in journalism and minor in foreign languages.

Each year she had done at least one hit, and in her senior year, she was contacted three times.

During those early years, she spent her earnings almost as fast as it came, but as she approached thirty, she began to realize the days were coming when work would not come as often as in the past. Too many of her marks would not have been so easy, had she not been a youthful and innocent looking girl. *'These contracts will soon go to someone younger.'*

Wisely, she began to set aside one third of her earnings on every contract. This quarter of a million would bring her Zurich account to five million US, the exact sum she had set as a goal for retirement from this business.

Their meeting location had been at his penthouse in Atlanta and when she looked around at the money this placed oozed of, she began to like the idea even more.

'This man who is asking me to expose myself to the court system is not handsome at all. He is at least my father's age, maybe older. His hair does

not show any sign of gray, but I'm sure it is colored. He is fifty pounds overweight, and no taller than me, but he has money, and I saw the lust in his eyes the moment I walked in. Perhaps I could put up with a boar hog, if he is as rich as he seems.'

"The sum seems sufficient for the job, but it will almost surely end my career, and then what will I do?" she said, looking at his round face and blinking her big blue eyes.

"I think I might find something for you to do, to keep you off the streets," Nate replied. Using her question as an open opportunity, he reached for her and pulled her to him. When she didn't resist he kissed her violently, before leading her into his bedroom.

One of Dorsey Bigelow's forefathers and namesake had settled on a piece of land west of San Pedro Mission only a year after Florida became a United States Territory. He had sold his holdings in North Carolina before moving his family and twenty slaves south to build one of the most productive plantations in Middle Florida. By 1850, he laid claim to four thousand acres and had full intention of making *Albemarle Plantation* the home place of Florida's future governor. Unfortunately, the coming of war clouds put a halt to his plans. Four years later with the loss of his labor force and the title of Secessionist hung on him by the appointees who arrived to take over after the fall of the Confederacy, his political dreams came to a crashing end.

Dorsey Bigelow gave up the ghost before he saw the end of the infamous Reconstruction Period and his wooden marker slowly rotted away. It was not until his great-great grandson had made a successful career as an attorney did the family have sufficient monies, or inclination, to place the large marble headstone above old Dorsey's grave. At least, that was the grave they had been told was his, there in the old *Plantation Cemetery*.

Dorsey the Second was in his fourth term as State Attorney for Madison County and was well respected, respected as an attorney that is.

Albemarle of 1997 was only a shadow of what it had been in 1857; however, Dorsey had bought back as much of the old place as he could. Today, he had a deed for just over six hundred acres, most of which was good, dry land. There, he had restored the main house, and a few of the slave shacks, which now served as out buildings.

He neither had the time, nor the interest in farming, but did appreciate seeing red cows meandering about in his fields, munching away on the rich grass that grew naturally there.

When he was called by Nate for a meeting, he hesitated for a moment, trying to think of a way out of it, but finally realized he could not. They set up a rendezvous for lunch at *The Country Kitchen* just north of the Lee exit on Interstate 10.

When he walked in, Dorsey's attention was immediately drawn to the young girl sitting at the table across from Nate Rugg. *'I know her from somewhere,'* he thought, but simply couldn't remember.

"Ah, Dorsey," Nate said, when the attorney approached. "Good of you to make it."

"Nate," he replied, nodding his head.

"Dorsey Bigelow, may I introduce Miss Joyce."

The attorney noticed Rugg did not bother to stand for the introduction. *'Too good for mere manners, huh, Nate,'* he thought. Then turning, said, "Miss Joyce, so nice to meet you," offering a limp hand to the girl.

"I'm glad you were able to come here to meet with us, Dorsey. Miss Joyce made a rather disturbing confession to one of my employees and he came to me for advice. After talking with her and confirming several facts, I thought it best we meet with you privately, before the police and the papers find out about it."

Dorsey didn't trust Nate Rugg any more than Rugg trusted him; in fact, neither had much use for the other, but both knew their importance in the county and neither would show anything but pleasantries to the other. "Just what is it you want me to know, Miss Joyce?"

She turned to Nate and looked questioningly, but the older man said, as he took her hand and patted it, "You go ahead and tell him the truth. It will be all right. I'll see to that."

It was the last part of his statement that caught Dorsey's attention.

"Well, okay, if you say so, Mr. Rugg," she replied, and then looking slowly back to the State Attorney, she licked her lips and began.

"I have lied to the police about something and I want to come clean."

Dorsey started to stop her right then, but he looked over at Nate and saw the expression on Rugg's face. Nate Rugg was the one man alive who had something on him that could really hurt him, and although he had never once ever made mention of it, Dorsey knew, it was not he who held the trump card in this game.

"Last year my boyfriend was killed, and I told the police it was an accident," she paused and again wet her lips and stared down at the silver set on the table. "The truth is, it was not an accident."

Dorsey raised his hand just above the table, but Nate spoke before he could. "Let her tell the truth while she is in the mood to do so. You may not get this opportunity to so easily uncover a well-planned murder again."

The attorney lowered his hand allowing her to continue. "I know who killed him, and how he did it," she said, and then paused and looked at Nate.

"I assured her, you would give her full immunity, if she told the truth, and delivered the murderer to you," Rugg said strongly. Dorsey took a deep breath, and wondered just what he was getting into, but finally spoke, "Yes, I can guarantee that."

"Well, you see, I went with James for several months, and then I met another guy. After a while, I stopped seeing James as much as I was. You know, being involved with my new man, but James became suspicious and started following me until he caught us together one time, and they really had a bad fight about it."

"Just who is this new lover you were seeing?"

"His name is Wallace Roberts. He works for the electric company. At least that is what he does for a front, the truth is, he is a big drug dealer here, and that's what the big trouble was all about."

She stopped and took a deep breath. "You see, the place James caught us at, is the old airstrip down on the Suwannee River. A big airplane came in and unloaded a large haul and Wallace was there to make sure his Coolies, that's what he calls his Mexican helpers, unloaded and divided the coke as they were supposed to.

"James was watching, and when we started out of there, he ran his truck in front of us and blocked the road.

"Later on, he called Wallace and said that he was going to turn him in if he didn't stop seeing me.

"They had a big fight about it, up at James' father's bar in Lowndes County, and that was when Wallace started planning to kill him.

"He's pure crazy. I wanted nothing to do with it, but he said I already knew too much, and if I didn't help him, he would get rid of us both. I was just so scared I agreed to lie about the murder to keep him from killing me, too."

She was now weeping and although her story was a little shaky, Dorsey believed her. At least, he thought he believed her.

At this time, Nate stood, excused himself, and went to the bathroom.

When he saw Rugg step from the men's room door, he got up from his booth in the other room and walked over to where they were seated. Dorsey looked up as the big man stopped beside him. At that moment, Madison Horry nodded his head to them.

Dorsey never liked Madison. He knew the county was not named for him, it had been named for the President. The town was not named for him either, it had been named for Madison Livingston, an early settler here, but Madison Horry had most surely been named for the town, or the county, or both. It really didn't matter, Dorsey didn't like him.

"Dorsey, I have retained Madison as Miss Joyce's attorney. He will handle everything from here on, on her behalf," Nate said.

'Hell fire!' Dorsey thought, *'I've been had.'*

"Hello, Dorsey."

"Madison."

"Will there be anything more you need from my client at this time?"

"I guess not. I will arrange for her to make a full statement to the Sheriff. Probably tomorrow," Dorsey added.

"Let me know and I will have her there," Horry said, and then placing his hand under her arm, he guided her from the chair.

"By the way, Dorsey," Nate said, as he also rose, "I don't want my name to come up in this in anyway."

Dorsey understood it was an order and not a request. He knew he would abide by it, but he had to ask, "I want to know something, Nate. Just what is your interest in this whole affair anyway?"

"I have known the Hancocks for many years and really liked James. I gave him money for school and even helped him get in the Navy. Didn't you know?" Nate said back.

Shaking his head and picking up his small recorder, the State Attorney replied, "No, as a matter of fact, I did not know."

It was just past noon the next day when Wall got the call on his radio to report back to the yard. When he got there, he was told Miller wanted to see him and he gritted his teeth at the thought, but he went on in and was surprised to find the deputy there.

"Roberts, Sergeant Mendoza wants to talk to you some more," Miller said, and then left the room.

Mendoza explained he was indeed re-opening the case on James Hancock's death and wanted him to come down to the County Jail where they could talk in private.

Wall was so happy about the fact his friend's death was finally being looked into, he didn't hesitate a minute agreeing when the officer explained he had to advise all potential witnesses of their rights.

Wall followed the dark Crown Vic west bound into Madison, and parked his old Ramcharger in front of the jail and walked in.

An hour later, he was being finger printed and booked for the murder of James Hancock.

Nate could not help but glow when he read the headlines in The Madison Trace:

LOCAL MAN CHARGED
WITH PREMEDITATED MURDER

Nate dismissed Famalie for the remainder of the week. After he was confident the Bahamian was gone, he opened the paper and laid it on the breakfast bar where there would be no question Blue would see it. He wanted to be there when she did, but he thought better of it, and left for Atlanta before she returned home.

"Hilton, have you seen the paper?" she spoke into the phone.

"You mean about the murder?"

"Yes," she confirmed.

Hilton James could tell she was crying when she spoke.

"What is it, Blue?"

"I need to meet with you right away," she said.

"Okay," he agreed. "Come on in to the office."

"No, I want you to come out here," she replied.

"Blue, I have other appointments this morning and I'm supposed to speak at the Elk's Luncheon today."

"Hilton, it's urgent," she said, and he could tell she was desperate.

"Okay, I'll be there in half an hour."

"Thank you so much," she said, and he could hear her sobbing before the receiver was replaced.

"Jackie, cancel all my appointments for the remainder of the day, and contact Jim Sales and tell him I won't be able to be at the luncheon today. Give him my apologies and all, but an emergency has come up, and I must go out of town immediately."

"Yes, sir," she replied thinking *'It must really be something. I have never seen him cancel an appointment since his last baby was born.'*

Hilton James had known Blue for several years, having first met her when Nate brought her home as a new bride. However, it wasn't until a few years later when she sought legal advice about how to protect herself, had he really come to know her.

He had been pleased when she said to him, "I thought of doing this alone and have carefully considered all the other attorneys I know. I finally came to the conclusion you were the only honest man in the field. At least, you are the only honest one I have ever met."

It had been Hilton James who drew up the insurance policy they delivered to ten of his colleagues, in ten other states. Personal friends of his, with instructions to deliver the contents to the appropriate Federal, State, and local Law Enforcement Agencies, as well as the national news, upon her death. These instructions were very specific about this being done upon her death, not just death due to unusual circumstances.

She was too suspicious of the accidental deaths of people who had crossed Nate, and Hilton understood that.

When he arrived, there was no answer to his rings so he opened the door and looked in. She was sitting at the bar drinking her third Bloody Mary for breakfast. She was still dressed only in the heavy silk gown she had worn down the stairs when she came seeking Famalie, an hour and a half earlier.

Looking up at him revealed she had been crying heavily, but at this time, she was under control. "Look what I have done," she said, pitching the paper over to him.

"I don't understand."

"Nate. Nate is behind this. He has drummed up this whole affair to get back at me."

Hilton looked at her and asked, knowing full well the answer before he did, "What is this Wallace Roberts to you?"

She took a deep breath and quickly shook her head slightly a couple of times, "He is the only man I have ever been in love with in my whole life," she said, before taking a long swallow of the deep red liquid.

"There, I have finally said it. I have known it for a long time, but I would never say the words. I love him. I love him more than life itself, and I have ruined him."

It was his time to take a deep breath and then he spoke, "Just what do you want me to do?" Again, knowing full well the answer.

"I want you to represent him. I want you to clear his name."

"I will, under these circumstances."

"Yes, anything," she replied, looking back at him surprised he would say such a thing.

"You must tell me all, and you must be totally truthful with me."

She was silent for a few moments and then she finished the drink and said, "That's the last alcohol I will consume until he is a free man, and, yes, I will tell you all, and truthfully."

It was over an hour before he closed his notebook and looked up at her.

"Can you get him out? I will put up the bail."

"No. You stay totally out of this. You must not in any way contact him, or otherwise do anything to let them know you even know this man. I will handle what needs to be done, but I must warn you. There is no guarantee of bail in a murder case. It's totally up to the judge."

"Oh, Hilton, I just can't bear the thought of him sitting in jail because of me. He hates to be inside, it will drive him crazy."

"There is hope, Judge Blair is a very honest man, and above that, he has more horse sense than any other judge I know. I might be able to convince him to release Roberts in my custody."

"An honest judge? I didn't think there were two honest Attorneys in all the world."

"You may be right; Wetzel Blair is not an attorney, he is the last judge in the State of Florida who is not."

Then he looked at her and added, "And it just burns the Bar to no end that he keeps being elected. See Blue, there is a God."

"Stay close in touch, Hilton," she implored, and he winked at her in reply.

Chapter Nineteen
The Parting of the Waters

He turned to the man in uniform, and in just short of a shout said, "This damn idiot has just diverted eleven billion from our budget to the damn Commies, over at First and Forty-Sixth, for some idiot World Peace plan.

"If we don't get him out of Washington in the next election, there won't be a whore left that doesn't hold a government job, or an American soldier left in uniform in the whole damn country. Hell, that idiot has closed more military bases than the Russians ever had, and now he wants to give our top secrets to China, for God's sake."

The General did not look pleased and reluctantly opened his file. "There's something else I think you need to know about, sir," he said, and reaching in, he withdrew a sheet of paper and handed it to the outraged man.

"What the hell is this?"

"Nothing confirmed yet, but there is scuttlebutt that the New York Times is working on a story about Nathan Rugg and his relationship with the Pentagon."

"I thought we severed ties with him?"

"Well, we did, until last year when we needed the expertise he was able to provide, and we used him just once more."

"Why do I have such a bad feeling you are about to tell something I don't want to know?"

"Yes, sir. Well, Rugg has definitely been connected with the mob, and this story, so I have been told, tries to link us to them also, through him. It doesn't look good, sir. You know the Boss wanted him eliminated years ago."

"Maybe we should accommodate the whore-mongering bastard on this one."

Christina Voorhies had an answering service to take messages for her. Only one person had the number, but she was expected to check it often, just in case she was needed. This was something she neglected to do during the two weeks she was aboard *The Savanna Witch* with Nate Rugg. Finally, when they were in St Croix, she made the call. There was a message. It was not a fresh message.

"I must say, I am somewhat disappointed with you, Christina. I needed you and had to get someone else to fulfill my commitment," the old man said.

"I am sorry, sir, but I was at sea, and the batteries in my satellite phone went dead, and I had forgotten to bring my charger."

He knew quite well where she was and he also knew *The Savanna Witch* was fully equipped with all the latest communication equipment.

"I hope this doesn't happen again, Christina."

"No, sir. I assure you it will not."

The following week they flew back to the states so she could make her subpoenaed date to testify before the Grand Jury.

While there, she stayed in Valdosta, but Nate returned home and acted as if nothing had happened.

It pleased him immensely to see the hate and contempt showing in Blue's eyes when he walked in unannounced after being away since the day Wall was arrested.

"Hello, My Dear. I hope all is well in your world," he said.

"You bastard, if you hurt Wall Roberts I'll kill you."

"Who's Wall Roberts?" he said back smiling.

"I'm going to tell you something, you are going to one day wish you never met me," she said back with a fury that would have frightened most people.

"I already do that, My Dear," he replied smugly, then turned to the bar and pored himself a double Hirsch Reserve[25] on the rocks.

Blue went upstairs, changed her clothes, and then left the house. After backing away from the garage, she stomped the accelerator to the floorboards and the 300 hp Northstar immediately began squealing the tires of her red Eldorado for some distance down the paved driveway.

Uberto Spindetto was a businessman first. He had certain loyalties to the people he served, as well as to the people who he referred to as friends. These loyalties also were extended to those he considered as loyal employees. However, he felt no loyalty greater than what he owed the business and when someone became a burden to the business he had to, by conviction, sever ties with that person. The failure of Christina Voorhies to make contact when called was a breach of his trust, but not quite a burden. He would give her another chance, because of her long years of nothing short of perfect work performance. *'Yes, another chance for the lovely Christina, one more chance.'*

Hilton James had requested, and been supplied with, the prosecution's case as required by Florida Law. In reviewing it with Blue, they knew immediately it was a fabrication.

On the night in which Elvira 'Sissy' Joyce stated she assisted luring James Hancock to the lake where Wall Roberts could murder him, he was on a Lear Jet bound for Colorado, and there were two pilots who could swear to that fact.

The only problem with this evidence was Dorsey Bigelow would surely require them to explain how a forty thousand dollar a year man could afford to fly around the country in a jet that cost ten thousand dollars a trip.

---

25 Hirsch Reserve: Very expensive Bourbon.

If Hilton were to bring to court his trump cards, he would have to expose Blue's affair with Wall. This she was quite willing to do, but he was not so sure the jury would be sympathetic with an adulteress wife, and a family busting man.

"This is after all, Middle Florida, and if you are not a Methodist, you had better be a Baptist, or have enough financial standing to spend plenty of your money with these Christian businessmen."

She knew Wall Roberts was none of the above. His God did not give credence to man's additions to the Holy Scriptures, and he often said he attended *The Church of The Withlacoochee*.

Wall's parents had been religious people and there was seldom a Sunday morning, or Wednesday night, that he did not sit on a hard pew in the little concrete building in Bunnell.

However, Wallace Senior, being a former Viet Nam Marine sniper, did like a drink of whiskey of an evening, and he didn't like fat preachers, or gossiping sisters, condemning him for it. Many was the time, after sitting through a hell-fired sermon with a message of condemnation on those who indulged in the devil's brew, and a warning it was a sure fire way to everlasting damnation, Wallace Senior would mumble all the way back to Rayonier.

"These self-righteous hypocrites take certain precautions to avoid speaking on gluttons, and extortionists, or gossipers.

"Hell no. You will never find a preacher with the guts to tell Elder King, who just happens to own the True Value Hardware Store down there next to Moody's Drugs, that to overcharge poor folk is the very thing Paul was condemning and calling extortion.

"No. Nor will they speak about that busybody, Deacon Ivan's wife, who spreads more harm and destruction with her wicked tongue than all the legions of Rome. And, and who could be more of a hypocrite than a gluttonous preacher, condemning a man for taking a drink? Not a drunk mind you, just one little drink, but never once have I heard him speaking about his hundred pounds of excess fat.

"You know, Jerry Enfield walked past me today. While he was passing the communion plates and I near chocked on the tobacco stink that reeked from him. Another blasted hypocrite."

Wall's mother would say, "Now Wallace, judge not."

Which would just fire him some more. "That's exactly what I'm talking about, them judging me and you. They pass judgment on us because we are poor, not because we do wrong. You know how much money Lawyer Tennille has? Nobody ever speaks about his sinning. He'd better start learning about them camels and the eyes of a needle, before he starts a shaking the hand at this sinner."

By the time they drove the five miles back to their little house, Wallace would be in a steamer of a fit and Wall, even at a young age, realized there was a lot of truth in what his father was saying. Thus, much to his mother's disappointment, after he was grown, he steered clear of church services, a habit that would come to haunt him when self-proclaimed Christians filled the jury box.

Judge Blair had indeed agreed that Wall Roberts need not be incarcerated awaiting his trial. He had never been arrested for anything before, and there was no evidence indicating he was a likely candidate to become a fugitive. Hilton James posted the fifty thousand dollar cash bail, and again warned Blue, and Wall, not to see one another until the trial was over.

Wall understood, but Blue took this hard. She desperately wanted to tell him how sorry she was about him being used so cruelly just to hurt her.

The trial was set to begin the third day in November, just one day after Blue's thirty-fourth birthday. The first week was mostly attorney maneuvering and the selection of a jury.

Hilton James had worked hard during this process. He gladly accepted black women, but was able to dismiss every black man. He also had no objection to two jurors who obviously had strong Mexican blood, a man and a woman, but he fought vigorously against Cory Tuttle, who owned a Creamery in town, knowing full well the Tuttle family was well established in old Madison, to which Wall Roberts was not.

There was also the fact that Tuttle had been the one who offered Rugg's name to become a member of the local Elks Club, and was well acquainted with Nate.

Of course, Hilton hoped he would not have to bring out the name Rugg at all in his defense, but this was an ace in the hole, should it come to that. Mainly, he did not want anyone who might have fear of Nate Rugg on the jury.

Friday afternoon near the two o'clock hour, the judge recessed until Monday morning and cautioned the jurors not to discuss the trial in any way until then. It was a statement closely resembling a warning to trail-weary cowboys to sit quietly in the lobby of a whorehouse on nickel-night and not indulge in the pleasures that surrounded them.

Monday brought the first of the prosecution's witnesses and that being Colson Lively, who frequented *Betsy's Crossroads*.

"Mr. Lively," Dorsey began, "Please tell us about the fight you witnessed at the home of James Hancock."

"Well, I was there at Betsy's and I seen him, the deceased, ah, fighting with him yonder."

"Let the record show Mr. Lively is pointing at the defendant, Wallace Roberts."

"Mr. Lively, can you tell us when this fight took place?"

"I ain't exactly sure of the date, but it were sometime about a year ago. October, I think. We was watching a football game on the big TV there."

"Now Mr. Lively, are you sure it was that man sitting there you saw fighting with James Hancock?'

"Yes, sir, I am."

"No further questions."

At this point in the trial, a trait few people in Madison County knew of, was about to show itself. Hilton James was a quiet, good-natured lawyer who mostly handled wills, property legalities, and other civil cases. He was well-liked by most who knew him, but also considered meek, for criminal work. Blue knew better, she had conducted an extensive background investigation on several attorneys in Madison as well as other counties, before she chose him to handle her insurance policy against her husband.

What Blue knew the others did not, was in 1972 when Dorsey Bigelow was marching among the other war protestors during the University of Florida riots; Major Hilton James was shooting down his forth Mig over the skies of South East Asia.

Hilton had first gone to Vietnam sitting in the bombardier's seat of a B-52, but later was able to go back in an F-4D Phantom and everyone who flew with him knew of his gut instinct and flying ability. They, too, were sure, had the war not ended when it did, he would most certainly have added that last Mig to his kill list and his name would have been forever recorded among *The Few* who can call themselves *American Aces*. It was with the mind of a fighter pilot Hilton James flew into the offense.

"Mr. Lively," the six-foot four-inch attorney began, "Do you know Wallace Roberts?"

"I've seen him a couple of times. Like I said, I seen him and the deceased fighting that time."

"That time, and one other time, is that correct?"

"Yeah, I guess so. Yeah."

"Could that other time have been the night you ran your car into the side of his truck, while you were exiting *The Yum-Yum Tree* parking lot in Valdosta?"

It was obvious to all James had hit a nerve and Lively looked around like he wanted to find an escape route but could not. "I don't remember nothing about that," he finally said.

"That's strange. I have here a certified copy of the Georgia accident report which not only identifies you as the driver, but also clearly states you were cited as the cause of the accident, and arrested for driving under the influence."

Hilton paused a few moments to let everything sink in. Then he added, "It also shows Wallace Roberts was the driver of the other vehicle of that accident on Hill Street."

"Well, maybe he was. I don't remember."

"You do remember a Mr. Jones. Wilber Jones, who was riding with you that night, don't you?"

"Yeah, I remember him," Cole admitted.

"Yes, I would think so. He was injured that night. Stayed in the hospital for over a week, according to the hospital records."

"Yeah."

"The hospital records also show he lives at 211 South Adel Road. Isn't that the same address where you live?"

"No, I live on Gordon."

"Well, you must have lived at 211 Adel Road at some time or another, because that is the address you gave to the Georgia Department of Drivers' License, isn't it?"

"Well, maybe I lived there a while."

"I have also an arrest record from the Valdosta Police Department where a Wilber Jones was charged, back in 1982, with sexual assault on a minor, a seventeen year old boy by the name of James Gray. I believe Mr. Jones was only eighteen at the time and as a result, received probation. Did you know about that?"

"No."

"I understand *The Yum-Yum Tree* is a gay bar. Are you a homosexual, Mr. Lively?"

"I object, the witness' sexual preferences have nothing to do in this trial."

"Sustained," the Judge agreed.

"I withdraw the question, and apologize to the court," Hilton James said, before turning back to the witness. "You said, you were watching a football game on television at the time of the argument between Mr. Roberts and James Hancock, is that not correct?"

"Yeah, that's what I said."

"Could that have been the Florida/Georgia game?"

"Yeah, it was at that," Lively nodded his head.

"I'm sure it was, too, since everyone else who was there remembers it as being that game. I'm glad we agree on something, Mr. Lively.

"Let's see, that would have made this so called fight you have testified to, as damaging evidence against Mr. Roberts, to have taken place on November 2 when we beat the Dawgs 47-7."

"Yeah, I guess so. That's about when I seen them at each other."

"Yes, I have the date of that game right here to introduce as evidence, should the need be," Hilton said.

"Now, I wonder about something. This fight you witnessed, was it a fist fight?"

"Well, I can't remember if they came to blows or not, but I was sure scared they would."

"Do you know who owns Betsy's Crossroads, Mr. Lively?"

"Betsy, I guess," he said back, smiling at his cleverness and looking around the courtroom.

"That's almost right, but do you know Betsy's last name?"

"No. Don't guess I ever heard it said."

"Have you ever seen her?"

"Yeah, I seen her, there behind the counter. She is the barmaid."

"Well, I'll tell you. Her last name is Hancock. She is James Hancock's mother," Hilton said, and then turned and looked at the jury.

"As you testified a few moments ago, she was there that same day, and so was her husband, and so was her daughter, and so was her younger son.

"I would think they, being James' family, would surely have put a stop to a fight such as you have led the jury to believe took place, there, that day, between Mr. Roberts and James Hancock."

Once more James stopped and looked at the jury before he added, "Being the family of the dead man, they surely, above all, would want to see his murderer put away. Don't you agree?"

"I don't know, maybe," Lively said, looking at the back wall of the courtroom.

"Well then, why would each of them come here today, ready to give sworn testimony, that no such fight ever took place? They will testify under oath that James and Wall Roberts were having a friendly argument over a drag race that had taken place between

232 - *Murder in Madison County*

those two friends years before, a subject they each teased the other about many times."

"I don't know nothing about that."

"That's right, you *'don't know anything about that.'* If you had, you would not have come here spitting out this distortion of the truth. And speaking of the truth, Mr. Lively, the truth is you are here because you have a grudge against Mr. Roberts.

"The truth is, you have always hated him because he was the driver of the other car in your accident, the accident in which your lover, Wilber Jones, was seriously injured, and in which you lost your drivers' license for a year. Yes, I have that record too.

"By the way, did you drive here today, or did someone else drive you?"

"I drove myself. I got my license back," Lively spat out, forgetting entirely to deny he and Jones were ever lovers.

"I'm finished with your witness," James said, turning to Dorsey.

"I have no further questions," the prosecutor said.

"You are dismissed Mr. Lively," the Judge said, and slapped his gavel on the bench before adding, "Recessed until after lunch."

When they reconvened, Bigelow called Seth Coe to the stand, but before he could begin, one of the jurors became sick and the trial was postponed until the following morning at nine o'clock.

That night, as they went over the day's court action, Blue said, "Well, you hit them a good lick today."

"I can knock every one of their witnesses down, except the woman. I don't know about her. She is so pretty and so innocent looking. I just don't know if I will be able to discredit her without bringing in the pilots."

Blue took his hand in hers and squeezed it as she said, "I know you will, Hilton. I have total faith in you."

Dorsey Bigelow and Madison Horry were likewise together, discussing the effects of Lively's testimony. "Well, he sure shot the hell out of that great witness you had today. I do hope you can do better tomorrow," Horry said harshly.

"Tomorrow, I will put on Seth Coe. He can positively place James Hancock in Roberts' Corvette the night of the murder."

"What dark secrets does Hilton James know about Coe that we don't?"

"None, none that can hurt us. I am only using him to prove they were together on that night. It's the woman, Joyce, that will cook his goose."

"When are you planning on her?" Madison asked, "Friday?"

"No, not on Friday. I'll ask for a continuance until Monday. I want the jury to be fresh when they hear her and there is no need to give James the whole weekend to prepare a rebuttal to her testimony."

"Good idea."

"I'll get word to her to be here on Monday," Horry said.

"Where is she?"

"Atlanta, out of sight."

"Good," was all Bigelow replied, before he got up and left.

On that same day, Ken Martinelli had been given a flight from Columbia up to the Yucatan, where he refueled, and then on into the Gulf of Mexico, crossing the end of Florida two hundred miles west of Key West.

He had a homing device onboard, which allowed him to locate a transmitter from over a hundred miles away. It was with this he found the Aerostar, due south of New Orleans, as it was making a scheduled flight from Brownsville, Texas to Tampa, Florida.

Slipping the big Lockheed under the belly of the Aerostar, they headed, almost coupled, for the west coast of Florida at 12,000 feet and 250 knots. When they were less than seventy miles out, Ken suddenly dropped down to forty feet above the gray waters of the Gulf and raced inland, cutting the coast a few miles south of Naples over the swampy islands that dot Collier County's coastline. Ken landed at Sampala Lake as usual, just at dark and unloaded half of his cargo. After refueling, he took off for North

Carolina. Twice before, he had made this same run, into the big pasture north of Rockingham.

There, men with unknown names and forgotten Mexican faces, would fire the 55-gallon drums filled with oil and diesel fuel over water. These were set two hundred feet apart, for three thousand feet, making a nice lighted runway.

At the east end of this makeshift strip was a large pole barn, which housed thousands of bales of hay when it was not being used as a clever stealth hanger. It was there Ken had taken the Rebel a week before and it was in this same barn he would leave the PV-1.

Ten miles out, he made the call on the CB radio installed below the instrument panel, and quickly thereafter, the barrels began to light up, one after the other.

He made a low pass and turned hard keeping his left wing only a hundred feet above the rolling terrain. Ken really didn't have to worry about hitting anything; there were no trees near the field, save two large hickories at the west end, but he could easily see them against the fiery barrels.

A downwind run was always hard work in the sleek old bomber. She loved going fast and fought you when you tried to make her slow down. Getting her down to flap extension speed took all his attention and finally, just as he turned left making a carrier approach, totally unknown to Ken, the men on the ground spotted the jet circling overhead.

Immediately, they began dousing the fire in the barrels and headlights of half a dozen trucks suddenly came on. Then the vehicles took off in different directions as the Mexicans attempted to escape the area.

"I think he's going to hit it," Agent Small said, as he watched the Lockheed on his infrared screen just above the camera pod protruding from the belly of the US Customs' Citation.

He was right.

When Ken came out of his steep turn, expecting to see the lighted runway ahead, all he saw were the lights of the vehicles leaving the area.

This new confusion caused him to take his eyes off the touchdown spot for just a couple of seconds as he tried to figure out what was happening. Unfortunately, it was a second too long and the left wing of the PV-1 clipped the top of the biggest hickory, which snapped, but not before it had laid claim to a small portion of that wing. The aileron departed and the big airplane simply went out of control. Two seconds later, it was nothing more than a huge ball of fire, spreading 100-octane aviation fuel over a large portion of the pasture.

Before the volunteer fire department arrived and got it under control, the fire had consumed the pole barn, which was half-full of very dry hay, and a beautiful little Murphy Rebel.

On that very day, Christina Voorhies received a message on her satellite phone to report in.

"Yes, sir?" she said, when the connection was made.

"Christina, I have some work for you to do immediately. There will be an envelope waiting for you at the Delta counter at Kennedy. Ask for Cary. Your instructions will be in it, along with your tickets to Hamburg."

"Oh, sir, I'm in the middle of a trial. I have to be in Florida on Monday to testify," she replied, then realizing the sudden problem she was creating, she said, "Hold on a moment, please," and told the man beside her in the bed what was happening.

"Give me that damn phone," he said, and took it from her hand.

"Uberto, its Nate here. Look, it is very important to me for Chrissie to be in Florida on Monday. Could you find someone else this one time?"

"I see. Yes, if you ask this of me, I will contact someone else."

"Thank you. I'll make it up to you."

When the old man laid the receiver down, he shook his head.

Nate, on the other hand, smiled and said, "Now why don't you slip down there and see what you can bring up."

That night, when Worm opened the envelope he had taken from the locker, a large smile crossed his face. *'Damn, I would almost do her for nothing.'*

The Rugg penthouse was on the fortieth floor of *The General Lee Building*. Across Peach Tree Circle, in the elevator of *The General Jackson Building*, a small man in a fatigue jacket looked lustfully at the woman who was sharing the ride with him so early this Sunday morning. "'Nice Tits," he said under his breath.

She had seen him in the lobby and thought how out of place he looked, his long stringy hair and soiled clothes reminded her of pictures she had seen of the hippies, back in the sixties and seventies. When he entered the elevator beside her, she never again looked his way, but she would remember him, and his smell.

The sun was bright, but the wind was quite strong, just as the weatherman had predicted, especially atop the building.

Removing the third exhaust vent from the roof's door exposed the hard rifle case, just where he had said it would be.

While the sniper was slipping the four, 165-grain boat-tail hollow points into the Remington action, across the way in the east tower of *The Twin Generals,* the man arose from the large bed and went to the bathroom. A few minutes later, he returned and called out, "Chrissie, we need to get going."

The woman stirred a little, and then rolled over and said, "Just a couple more minutes."

He returned to the bathroom and shaved. They had been up quite late and both had used a little too much coke.

He would give her the extra two minutes, she had earned them, but twenty minutes later after having finished shaving and showering, he saw she still had not moved an inch and he walked over, pulled the large comforter and sheet down, exposing her shapely nakedness. Then with a smile of satisfaction on his face, he drew back the large glass door that opened onto the terrace, allowing the cold wind to sweep in.

She suddenly sat up in the bed and screamed, "What the hell are you doing?"

"Isn't bothering me and I don't have a nice warm comforter around me."

"Well, you get the medal for being able to best handle the cold today," she replied hatefully as she grabbed for the lavender covering and pulled it up.

A little over a hundred yards away, the sniper laid the rifle over the folded coat and worked the bolt, loading the Federal round into the chamber. Next, the knurled knob was twisted, calculating the wind correction before the rifle was swung so the crosshairs were placed on the man. Slowly the finger squeezed on the trigger, then stopped, and the rifle was moved to the right just a few degrees so the crosshairs now centered between the breasts of the woman. Again, the trigger was carefully squeezed until the recoil of the round caused the rifle to bounce and the sight picture was lost.

Nate turned around when he heard her scream, the report of the shot being lost in the wind. Seeing her there, he suddenly realized she had been shot. He turned back in shock, looking to the rooftop across the way.

He had just focused on the small image, with long hair blowing in the wind, when he saw the barrel of the rifle bounce upward. Even before he felt anything, he knew what that meant.

Homicide Investigator Dooley Grubbs got the call around seven that night.

The hotel security officer explained to him, "The owner of the suite had requested room service to have the apartment cleaned that morning, but when the maid came to do it, she found the door still chained from the inside and left.

"Around three, when Mr. Rugg had not arrived at the airport as expected, his personal pilot called the Penthouse repeatedly. Finally, he called us and explained the situation. After that, I notified the police."

"Thank you, if I need you again I will get in touch with you," then he handed the rent-a-cop his business card and added, "Oh, Officer, if you get any more information you think I should know, please call me."

Dooley knew giving it to such a man would make him feel a part of the investigation and he would keep an ear out for anything that might help solve the double murders.

Grubbs walked into the large bedroom, looked about and shook his head. "What do you think a joint like this would cost a fellow, Casey?"

The forensic specialist looked up from his work at the sergeant, and then around at the Penthouse suite. "A hell of a lot more than you will ever be able to afford."

"Well, he can't use all that dough where he is now."

"You can say that again, Sergeant."

It was then he walked closer and looked at the woman. She was sitting up in bed with her back to the large headboard. It had been a huge mirror, but was shattered now. Her head was bent forward and her chin was resting on her upper chest. Between and slightly above her breasts was a hole. From it, a single trail of dried blood ran into the valley and disappeared beneath the satin comforter, which covered her legs and lower body. "Are you through here, Casey?"

"Let me get one more picture for my class," he said.

Dooley stepped back until after the flash, and then he returned. Placing a hand on the woman's shoulder, he leaned her over. The stiff body did not respond well and it took both of his hands to force her forward. In the center of her back was a large hole. Behind it in the backboard, were several pieces of bone and flesh, embedded in the wall.

"Well, one thing for sure, she never knew what hit her," he said, and then let go and the body slowly rolled to its right side. "We know who she is?"

"Yeah, there is a' Illinois drivers' license here," a uniformed officer said, holding the DL, along with a woman's purse. "She is Christina Voorhies from Chicago."

"She was yesterday, maybe," Dooley replied. "Where is her Sugar-Daddy?"

"Out there on the terrace."

'Looks like, unlike the woman, the man lived for some time before the black angels came and snatched his soul away. There is blood everywhere,' Dooley thought, as he walked through the big open door.

"The bullet blew his dick clean off," the officer chuckled. "A ricochet, I would say, off the balcony wall yonder," he added, pointing at the fresh scar on the top of the granite covering of the four-foot high balcony. "That shooter almost missed his mark with his first shot."

"Yeah, I reckon that's why there is so much blood," Dooley replied. "Does look like he was trying to crawl back inside when the second one caught him in the back."

It was then Detective Hoxey came in carrying a rifle case. "Found this over on the roof of *The General Jackson*. It's a Remington M-40 with a suppresser. No prints, looks like a professional hit to me."

"Yeah," was all Dooley said.

When Joyce failed to arrive at the courthouse on Monday, Dorsey became nervous and soon was on the phone to Madison Horry. "Where the hell are you?" he yelled, "The Judge is on my case about the delay."

"She isn't here. I don't know where she is," he replied. "Hell, I can't even get in touch with Nate."

Blue, of course, knew where her husband was. The Atlanta Police Department had called her the night before to inform her of her husband's death. They also mentioned a woman was killed along with him, but they didn't disclose her identity. Blue immediately called Hilton James with the news. The next morning when Joyce didn't arrive to testify, Hilton began to suspect who the dead woman must be. By one o'clock when the trial was to once again begin, and Dorsey still had no witness to put on the stand, James asked the court for a directed verdict, based on the fact no evidence being brought forth connecting his client with the murder. This was highly disputed by the prosecution.

"Your honor, as soon as Miss Joyce arrives, we will most definitely have all the evidence we need."

"Well, where is she?"

"I don't know your honor. She was fully aware she was to be here this morning. I talked to her Friday and she left me with all the confidence in the world she would be here."

"If I may, your honor," James interrupted, "I might shed some light on the subject."

"Please tell us you know where she is," the judge said.

"I believe I do, and if someone would contact the sheriff's office, I think there should be a telephoto of a Christina Voorhies there, from the Atlanta Police Department. If it is not there, it will be soon."

"All right," the judge said, and turned to the bailiff. "See what you can find out, Officer."

The Deputy nodded his head as he spoke, "Yes, sir," and then he left the room.

"Will you enlighten us on one thing, Mr. James? Just what does this Christina Voorhies have to do with this case?" asked Bigelow.

"I believe Christina Voorhies and Elvira Joyce are one and the same. She has been lying to the court about her true identity, and everything else, I assure you."

"That's utter nonsense," Dorsey injected.

"We'll see when the picture arrives," the judge replied, and recessed the trial for one more hour.

By three o'clock the jurors had been dismissed, Hilton James had his directed verdict of acquittal, and Wallace Roberts was walking from the courthouse a free man. Beside him with her arm wrapped around his, walked Blue, and on his other side was Hilton James.

"I just don't know how to thank you both. They had me deep in a tunnel and I couldn't see no light at the end," Wall said.

"You never were in real danger. If we had to, we could have subpoenaed the pilot who flew you to Colorado that night. As a last resort, we could have placed Blue on the stand, but that would have been a last resort, for sure," Hilton said.

When they reached the parked cars at the curb Hilton James stopped. "Well, Wall, do you want me to drive you somewhere?"

"I'll be driving him," Blue said.

"I kind a' figured that. So, what's next for you two?" Hilton asked.

"Well, I guess I'll try and get my job back at the Co-Op."

"Like hell you will! I plan to hire you for as long as you want to work for me," she said, squeezing Wall's arm.

"Kind a' figured that, too," the big man said. Then turning, he nodded his head and added, "Be seeing ya'."

That night they slept in her bed in the Rugg Mansion. Although they had shared Nate's bed once, it was his first time in her bed, and he felt completely out of place.

He did enjoy their swim in the pool, and the sex afterward. It was sort of a fulfillment of the fantasy he had dreamed of from the first moment he had laid eyes on her. However, all of this was just not Wall Roberts.

"I'd like to go to Wyoming. I want to hunt mule deer and the season starts tomorrow, October 26, and only lasts the week."

"Great. I want to be right by your side," she said, and then she kissed him hard on the lips. "I might shoot one myself."

Chapter Twenty
Big Wonderful Wyoming

Dooley Grubbs was no fool and it did not take him any longer to find the connection between Nate Rugg and the Pentagon than it did connecting Rugg to the Chicago Mob. During the third week in November, he said to his boss, "I tell you, Captain, this one may have to go unsolved. There is considerable evidence it was a professional hit, probably by the mob. The Voorhies woman's prints were found in a motel room near Tucson, Arizona, where a professional hit was made back in 1993, and the FBI has a photograph of her eating lunch last year with one Uberto Spindetto, a known mob boss. I gotta hunch she was no longer in favor with them and Rugg was just in the wrong place at the wrong time."

"Sounds reasonable to me."

"However, there is also a possibility it was a CIA operation," the detective added, as he opened his file on the Rugg murder and they reviewed the many pages together. "I know they aren't supposed to work operations in the US, but we both know they do pretty much as they please."

An hour later, Captain Snyder nodded his head. "We don't want to stir up anything that might be a government operation. You're right, file it 'On Going,' and bury it deep."

Two hundred and fifty miles northeast at the main office of Teague Racing, a man in a business suit laid the tape on the desk in front of him. "I think you will appreciate this, Mr. Teague."

"Is it what I think it is?"

"Yes sir. Took some doing, but it is a good copy, and they appreciated the tip," the man said, satisfied with his work.

"My wife and I must view it tonight," Teague said, nodding his head.

"Remember, it's infrared and it maybe hard to see a lot of it, but there is no question about what happened to the pilot of that old airplane. I mean you can see it hit those trees and then there is this huge fireball."

"Thank you," Cullen said, and handed the man a fat envelope. "I think you will find this sufficient."

The contact opened the business size envelope and looked inside. A smile came to his face and he replied, "Thank you very much, Mr. Teague, and, ah, I hope you win this month."

"I've already won this month."

Lucy Teague had no knowledge of the Lockheed crash. During the last contact she had with Ken, they had set this night to rendezvous at the lake house, although he told her he would be late arriving. She agreed to drive on up there ahead of time. One could only imagine the expression on her face when she heard the rumble of a big block approaching the rear of the cabin, instead of an airplane out front. Looking out, she almost lost her bladder when she spotted her husband step from the Ford.

'Oh my God! What if Ken arrives while he's here?'

"What are you doing here? I thought you were down in Daytona for Biketoberfest this weekend."

"Oh, I was, but I finished my business there and decided to come up and see the old place where we first made our life together. I rather thought it would be more run down than it is. By the way, what are you doing up here? "

"Oh, I just wanted to come and clean up the place, how do you like it?"

"Looks great, so do you for that matter. If I didn't know better, I'd think you were expecting me."

She was a bucket of nerves, Cullen wasn't at all acting in the manner he had for the last few years. He wasn't solemn and he wasn't short with her. He was confident, almost the old Cullen she had first found so alluring.

Although she was still scared to death about Ken arriving that evening, her husband had taken her to bed and screwed her like he had not done in years, and she was beginning to feel guilty about the divorce she had so recently considered.

It wasn't until he suggested they watch a skin flick did she see something she had not before realized in him. Never had he done such a thing. He had always been above such, and she likewise had, save a couple of films Ken showed her of people screwing on an airplane, which, she had to admit, had been a huge turn on for her. Now her husband was offering the same. It wasn't until she recognized the scene was of the very bed she was now in, did she realize what was taking place.

Immediately, she became nauseous and started for the bathroom, but he grabbed her arm, forcing her back to the bed beside him.

"Watch!" he demanded.

She looked back, but couldn't keep her eyes on the TV. They were blurred from tears and she placed her hands over them and lowered her head.

It was painful, but it was not the pain that hurt the most when he backedhanded her hard on her left cheek. Never before had he laid an angry hand on her, even through all of their fights. The fact that he hit her was the hurt she felt most, followed by his next statement.

"You will watch every minute of this, every man on my racing team has watched it, and you will, too," he shouted, as he grabbed her chin and squeezing tightly, turned her face back to the TV at the end of the bed.

For the next twenty-five minutes, she sat in horror, as the film of her sex with a strange man was exploited. Finally, the tape ended with her atop Ken screaming her lungs out as she climaxed. Then the screen turned to snow and the sound to very loud static.

Lucy now knew her marriage was over. She knew she could never get anything of the Teague fortune with evidence like this against her, but at least she had Ken. *'He will take care of me.'*

She started to rise, but again her husband grabbed her arm and stopped her. "That, my dear, was only the first half of this show."

'Oh God, what else has he got on me?' she wondered.

Cullen rose and walked naked over to the VCR player, removed the tape before pitching it to her. "This copy is yours. I have the original for the divorce court, should you be so foolish as to require me to use it." Then he placed the next tape in the Panasonic player. "This one should really get your motor running."

As promised, the tape was not clear, it was that awful green image of infrared heat, rather than detail. However, anyone who had the slightest knowledge of aviation would recognize the big twin engine Lockheed making its downwind run, parallel to the lighted drums.

"You see, my dear, he has the right engine running a little too rich, just look at the brighter exhaust on that side.

"There - did you see a quick backfire when he retarded the throttles? This dude is more flyboy than he is mechanic. A true aviator would never allow the synchronization between the engines become that great. Obviously a novice," her husband offered.

"Now watch closely, see the lights going out. That's his buddies running away. Watch closely, he's about to hit that tree."

She was sick. She had still not realized the significance of the film, but she knew she was about to see one or more people die and her stomach was ready to lose the wine she had consumed before their sex. However, for some reason, she could not tear her eyes away from the screen now.

The left wingtip soon twisted back; a split second after it contacted the strong limb, and then the big airplane spun around two complete circles before slamming into the North Carolina ground and burst into flames.

"Watch closely as it slides into that barn," he demanded.

She sat there with the sheet over her legs, but exposed above the waist, watching as the only structure in the film also burst into flames.

"Do you know what's in that barn?"

She did not answer. *'How could I know? What has this to do with me anyway?'*

"In that barn is that little airplane you and your lover used to fly up here, and my dear, in that ball of flame is your lover boy, burned to a crisp."

When he said that, she lost her stomach and spewed soured wine all over her bed, before rushing into the bathroom.

Half an hour later, she emerged expecting him to chew her out, or maybe even beat her. Instead, she found him gone, and it surprised her that she had not heard his pipes when he drove away.

She did find on top of the TV, a two-page legal document ordering her to respond to the divorce he had requested. In it, she was to receive everything she had brought into the marriage, and nothing more.

There was a handwritten note attached:

If you know what's good for you, you will sign this and waive a court hearing. I don't wish to see you spend time in prison for being an accomplice to the drug smuggling operations you and Ken Martinelli were engaged in.

She had no knowledge of how Ken had made his living, other than he was a pilot for some big company in Florida. Still, she knew Cullen had the political influence to have her connected, so she signed the document, gathered her few possessions, and drove away.

It was on the last day of the deer season when Wall and Blue finally set out to rendezvous with Deputy Sanders.

He agreed to get them permission to hunt a large portion of land on the ranch where he had grown up. It was out of Casper, on the high plateau east of Hat Six Road.

His father had been a top hand for *The Hat Six* outfit at the time of Nick's birth and old man Brooks liked the hard-working man and his whole family. He had recommended the Sheriff hire Nick, ten years before, and the name of Brooks carried a lot of weight in Natrona County, Wyoming.

Nick knew the area well. He and his brother hunted coyotes from their snow machines for their pelts every January and made good money at it, although not nearly as much as they had before the animal rights people came into so much power.

He knew where there was a large herd of big Muleys holed up in a stand of timber that covered a couple thousand acres in a depression on the plateau. Since the snow had not been heavy so far this fall, he was sure they would still be there.

Nick pointed out the area on a topographical map right after they arrived, but he couldn't get off work until that morning. Still, he was sure they would get a shot at a nice buck.

The day they landed, Blue asked Wall to stop at Jim Good's museum, and of course, he did. He always did as she asked.

"Hi, Jim," she said, as the older man approached them from his office, and she held out her hand for him to see.

"Well, this calls for a celebration and you two are just in time for my second pot of the world famous Jim Good coffee."

"That sounds like a winner," Wall admitted.

"Great, come into the office."

"We're going to tell him today?" she whispered, as she passed Jim, and then snickered. He only nodded his head in reply.

"What's going on?" Wall asked seeing the exchange.

"Well, we have a secret we were going to keep for a while longer, but I just can't."

"What, has my new bride been running around on me already?" he said back, teasingly.

"Hardly," Jim answered twisting his head.

"No, here look at this!" she said picking up the small maroon logbook from the desk. "I'm learning to fly. I almost have this man convinced to let me take my check ride."

"What?"

"Yep, I will soon be known as Co-Pilot of Super Cub 41577."

"Did you take that long cross-country while you were back down south?" Jim asked.

Suddenly, she felt weak, and placed her fingers on the desk for a moment to steady herself. "No, I rented the 172 like you suggested, but I chickened out at the last minute," she said, hoping her lie would not be detected by either of them.

"Well, that's probably best anyway. I really don't like for my students to do cross-countries to places we have never landed."

"How long are you going to be here this time?"

"Not sure, until my husband kills his first mule deer, and who knows after that."

"Good, we'll get you checked out right away then, if the weather holds out. It's really unusual for us to have such a warm snap this time of the year. I was over the mountain just yesterday, and most of last week's snow has melted. But that won't last long, not in Big Wonderful Wyoming," Jim said.

She smiled at the man that had become her very own flight instructor, and then pulling on Wall's arm, she said, "Come on, Honey, I want to show you how well I can do a wheel landing."

"Be careful, Mr. Roberts, she scares the hell out of me," Jim teased.

That morning they flew over the mountain circling their cabin, and then drifted over to the place Nick had shown them on the map. Sure enough, they spotted several muleys browsing along the edge of the timber. "God, they are so big," he said into the intercom.

"And beautiful," she added.

The idea to get married had been a fluke thing. They were 23,000 feet over Kansas City when she asked him, and he just shook his head and said, "Sure."

She then called Frank Alvarez on the intercom phone and had him divert to Las Vegas. They were married that night. The two pilots stood as their witnesses and they were back in the air enroute to Casper within three hours after landing at Vegas.

Blue had not been happier since the days of her youth. Here she was, high in the Rocky Mountains, hunting with a man she loved more than anything else in the world, just like she was in the fall of '76 when she killed her first Muley. Only this time, the man was her husband, instead of her father.

The snow started sometime after midnight and was still coming down by the time they met with Nick, although not heavily.

"This snow might be just what we need to drive them off the mountain and down where it won't be so deep," the big deputy said, as he looked at the timber ahead some three hundred yards through his binoculars.

It was cold, but not cutting, and Wall was beginning to really get into the idea of the powder when Nick said, "Yeah, I see some does coming out, heading towards the rim of the mountain."

He lowered his glasses and pointed to the line of gray bodies moving through the blanket of white. They watched until Blue saw him first. "Look! There is a really big fellow!"

Swinging to where she was pointing, they also saw the big buck. In fact, they saw several big bucks emerging from the timber, although taking a different trail than had the does.

"I guess the rut is over, or they would have stayed with the does," Nick offered. Then he pointed and said, "That third one is really a good one. Go 400 pounds or better and it looks like he's carrying a tree on his head."

They both looked over the deer their friend had pointed out and Wall agreed. "I think I will take him."

Carefully, Wall sat and watched the big fellow through his scope for a long time. The front bucks were moving in the general

Cub making low pass over Roberts cabin.
Jacuzzi room to the left of the photograph.

direction of the hunters until they reached a fair-sized boulder. Then they started cutting away on a trail that would increase the distance between them.

"You need to take him before he gets to that rock," Nick said, not taking his eyes from the binoculars. He waited and waited and thought, *'If he doesn't shoot soon it will be too___.'* At that moment, the thought was interrupted by the tremendous boom of the big Weatherby Magnum spitting forth its projectile.

Wall lowered the Winslow to his lap and looked. The big deer was on his side, thrashing around with one of his front legs, but that lasted less than half a minute and then all was still.

The other deer were nowhere in sight. However, there were several trails in the snow giving evidence of their routes of departure.

"Come on, let's go check him out," Nick said standing.

"You boys go ahead," she said, picking up the camera, "I want to video it from here."

They both laughed and shook hands before laying down their rifles and walking out to the Muley.

Blue had the camera up and running as they walked away, but suddenly it stopped humming and she looked at it, wondering what had happened, it was then she saw the huge mule deer slipping out of the timber following the doe trail. She wanted to stop them, but they were too far away and she didn't dare yell.

Instead, she carefully laid the Canon down and reached for the Winslow, but then thought better of it. She had seen the punishing recoil when Wall had sighted it in, and she really wanted no part of that. Instead, she took the old Model Seventy Nick had left there on his backpack and slid the bolt back just enough to make sure there was a round in the chamber, then closed it again.

She removed her down vest and laid it out in front of her, as she remembered her father doing for her. Then sliding down into a prone position she sighted through the 3X9 Leopold.

The stock was a little long for her, as Nick had added a recoil pad, but she adjusted to it. Judging the distance to be a little over three hundred yards, she released the safety and raised the crosshairs until the horizontal line rode right along the buck's backbone, and then she squeezed the trigger. The 180 grain aught-six Hornady plowed into him three inches behind his right shoulder and passed through both his lungs and snipped off the top of his heart before exiting his other side and traveling on towards Converse County.

The big muley rose up on his hind feet and jumped around, twisting in the air, back towards the timber from where he had come, but he was dead when his feet came back to the frozen earth, and he never moved again.

Both men jumped at the report. Nick immediately recognized the sound of his old Winchester and was totally in awe of why she would be shooting it. There was just enough of a rise between them and her deer that they could not see what she had shot at.

"Go ahead and look your Muley over, I will go back and make sure everything's all right," Nick said, but Wall stopped him, "Let's do it the other way. You check out my deer, and I will go and check on her."

"Hell, your buck ain't going nowhere, we'll both go back and see that she is okay."

"Good grief, that was a long shot," Nick said, looking at the big gray mound lying in the snow. Later he paced it off and decided it had been three hundred and forty yards.

"You sure made a lucky shot, Mrs. Roberts," he said, shaking his head, but Blue corrected him, "No, I'm a damn good shot, Sergeant Sanders."

"Yes, you are," Wall agreed.

"My father taught me and he was a damn good shot," she replied, matter of factly.

They field dressed the animals where they lay and then took them back on the snowmobiles to Nick's pickup. After dropping them off at the meat processing plant on West Yellowstone Avenue, Nick said, "I really think you should enter that big one in the Boone & Crocket competition. They are both good, but that one she shot has the biggest rack I have ever seen."

"Maybe, after we get them back from the taxidermist. They have to dry anyway," Wall countered.

"I think it will look great having those two big heads on the same mount up over your fireplace."

"Yeah, I agree," Wall said, and then stretched forth his hand to the deputy. "Never would have happened were it not for you. Thank you very much."

"Been my pleasure, Mr. Roberts."

"Look, I had much rather be known as Wall."

"Okay, Wall it is."

When she shook his hand, she left three bills in his palm. "Oh no, Mrs. Roberts, I didn't take you folks up there for money."

"If you are going to call him Wall, you better start calling me Blue, although Mrs. Roberts does have a nice ring," she said, and then turned and opened the door of the Grand Cherokee and sat down before he could argue about the tip.

Later that night while they were sitting in the Jacuzzi drinking Asti Spumante and watching the snow fall, Wall said, "You know I just can't believe all of this."

"All of what, my love?"

"All of this," he repeated waving his arm around, "This, this cabin, this place, you."

"Well, believe it, because I am never going to let you get away from me, and now that Nate is out of the way, you, my husband are a billionaire."

"That's just it. I don't even know what a billionaire is. I mean I know it's a person with more money that anyone needs, but I'm just a simple man. I have no comprehension of how to be a billionaire."

She turned to him with a sway to her head and he realized she had a lot more to drink than he had. "I was married to a man who knew how to be the perfect billionaire, and I hated him. I love you because you are a simple man. You are my man, my cowboy, and I love you for it," she said, and then stood up and walked over and refilled her glass, almost losing her balance as she did, but the force of the water rushing past her, kept her up right.

"Still, just a few days ago I was looking at the possibility of spending the rest of my life in prison, if I wasn't fried in the chair," he said. He almost stood to steady her, but she saw him and realizing what he was about to do, waved him off and sat down across from him, slid her foot between his legs and wiggled her toes.

"Hey," he said. Then he reached down, took her foot in his hand, lifted it to his mouth, and kissed each of her toes before he continued. "You know, I was really scared I would be convicted of a crime I had nothing to do with."

"You were never going to be convicted," she said, and again wiggled her toes teasingly at him. "I would never let that happen."

"I know you would have come forward and testified for me, but what scared me was Hilton James."

"Hilton James?"

"Well, not him himself, but I knew he was really worried the jury would believe that woman over you, and that was what scared me about him."

"Yeah, he convinced me of that, too," she said, and then nonchalantly added, "that's why I had to stop them."

Wall almost didn't realize what she had said, but then it hit home, "You stopped them?"

"I did. I told Nate I would kill him if he hurt you and he just laughed," she slurred, looking down into the swirling blue water, and then back to her glass from which she took another drink.

"What are you saying, Blue?"

"Nothing, nothing. But I will never let anyone hurt you. Never."

"It was you. You shot them!" he said.

"I'm a good shot," she said, nodding her head agreeing with her own statement, "Aren't I?" she then sort of drifted off..., "Blew that bastard's cock clean off and put one right between his new whore's tits," she added, as coolly as if she were talking about the mule deer she had killed that day.

"He was hiding behind the wall and trying to crawl back inside to the phone. I only had a thin sight picture, but I got him. Thought I'd missed when I saw that puff of dust come off the top of the wall, but it just touched it and then went home, straight between his shoulder blades."

Then finishing her drink, she said, "Come my sweet husband, it's my birthday, screw my eyeballs out."

It was the first night they had ever spent together that they did not have sex.

The next day, she slept until after the noon hour and when she finally came out, she had a terrible hangover. Immediately, she detected his mood.

"What's wrong?"

"What's wrong?" he shouted back.

"Yes, what's wrong?" she shouted at him. And then she placed her hands on her head and said, "Oh, do I ever have a headache."

"I'll tell you what's wrong," he said. "Last night you told me it was you who killed Nate and Joyce, or the Voorhies woman, or whoever she was."

"I did?" she said back looking up at him.

"Yes, you did."

Blue took a deep breath and shook her head, "Well, I must have been drunk."

"Hell yes, you were drunk."

"Well, you know drunks say all kind of crazy things," she replied, and then headed for the bathroom.

Later that day he told her, he wanted to go back to Florida. She didn't like it, but she dared not refuse him.

Two weeks later, he went to Atlanta and asked to speak to the detective who was working the murder of Nate Rugg and asked to see the investigation reports. He was refused on the grounds of it being an on-going case.

It was then he remembered something Blue had once told him.

About six that night, a man in uniform knocked on the door of his room at the Holiday Inn, "Mr. Roberts?"

"Yes."

"I believe this is what you wanted to see," the man said, and handed him a file.

Wall looked at it quickly and then placed ten one hundred dollar bills in his hand and said, "You will not remember me, will you?"

"No sir. I never saw you in my life," the officer replied, before turning and walking away.

He only wanted to see two things, where the victims had been shot, and what was the conclusion of the police. After reading both, he closed the file and placed a match to it and watched the flame as he held it until he had to place it in the empty trashcan to keep from burning his fingers.

The next day, he was back in Florida moving out of the Rugg Mansion and back to his little rented house in Hansen.

Blue tried everything she knew to get him to come back to her, but he only said it once, and that was it. "Your Pa taught you to shoot and mine taught me that a land without laws is the fertile soil where tyranny will sprout.

"I don't always agree with the law, but I must live by it. I love you Blue, more than life itself, but I wouldn't be Wall Roberts if I condoned what you did."

"But, I did it for you," she pleaded.

"Yes. I know that is so true. That's the tragedy of it all, but to condone a murder would change me, and I know you would learn to hate the man I would become."

During the next few months, Blue did a few critical things. She sold all of the Rugg holdings in the Carolinas, the Georgia penthouse in Atlanta, and everything she owned in Florida, except her mother-in-law's home in Madison. Then she moved back to Colorado.

She saw to it Ellen Huntington was released from the hospital and returned to Hester's home. She set up a fund so Ellen would always have the care she needed, and lastly, she had Hilton James create enough legal entanglement that would keep Wall from ever being able to divorce her.

"Do you want me to call in those letters we placed out there?"

She thought a few seconds and then shook her head, "No. I want someday everyone to know the evilness of Nate Rugg," she replied to Hilton and patted his hand between hers. "I thank you so much for all you have done."

"Are you sure, you don't just want to be rid of Wall all together?"

"No," she said shaking her head. "He loves me and someday he will come back to me."

She was wrong.

Three years later, Virginia Blue was riding in the high country near where Old Red had broken down and was thrown from her horse. She died of a broken neck.

Wall had never considered a divorce; he knew he would never marry again, so he saw no point in it.

He did get his old job back, for a while, but when it became known he had inherited the Rugg fortune, so many pestered him about borrowing money, he finally moved away, and left no forwarding address. However, not before he took Dixie Marie to the Fourth of July Races in Daytona. It turned out that weekend was the only time he slept with her. For some reason, it just didn't seem right.

Epilogue

Hilton James, and he alone, knew to send the papers, which required Wall's signature, to Casper Mountain Route, Box 41.

Every year until her death, Nell Cobb would purposely go to the little family cemetery there on the ranch on the second of November to see if once again, the many bouquets of beautiful blue flowers would have mysteriously arrived during the night covering the graves of Roy 'Doggy' Belle, Dorothy Marie Belle, and their daughter, Virginia Blue Belle Roberts.

I was in Elmer's Genealogy Library, in downtown Madison, some time back when I heard someone ask Sandra Norris, "Whatever became of Wall Roberts?"

She shook her head and replied, "I don't think anyone really knows, for sure."

I smiled at her answer, because I have heard it said that far away on many a crispy sunrise, the still mountain air is arrested by the roar of a Lycoming engine, and the little red squirrels run frantically about barking at the yellow airplane that skims the timber of that high country, flirting dangerously with the lurking down drafts.

For only the howl of the coyote could come close to expressing the loneliness of the simple man who lives in that little log cabin, a mile south of the Hogadon Ski Lodge.

Publisher's note.

We hope you have enjoyed T.H. Bear's *Murder in Madison County* as much as we did during our work producing his thrilling story of mystery, crime, spirituality, and integrity. T.H. Bear has always created wonderful characters and placed them into stories that caused his readers to stay up late into the night trying to finish the tale in one sitting.

We highly recommend T.H. Bear's three previous books published by BluewaterPress LLC. His epic story, *The Owl Hoot Trail*, includes the first book, *Gold in the Red Desert*, followed by *The Withlacoochee Renegades*, and ends with, *The Long Trail*.

In *Gold in the Red Desert*, T. H. Bear introduces his readers to Reb Brown, a returning prisoner of war from the Federal Prison at Point Lookout, Maryland. Within months of his homecoming, the authorities falsely charge Reb with a capital crime and he must flee his home state of Georgia, just ahead of a lynch-man's posse.

The Owl Hoot Trail leads him from a murder committed among the cypress and sweet gum trees of South Georgia to a murder among the sagebrush and prickly pear on the Red Desert of central Wyoming, at a time when the cry of "Gold!" was raging throughout the Sweetwater Region.

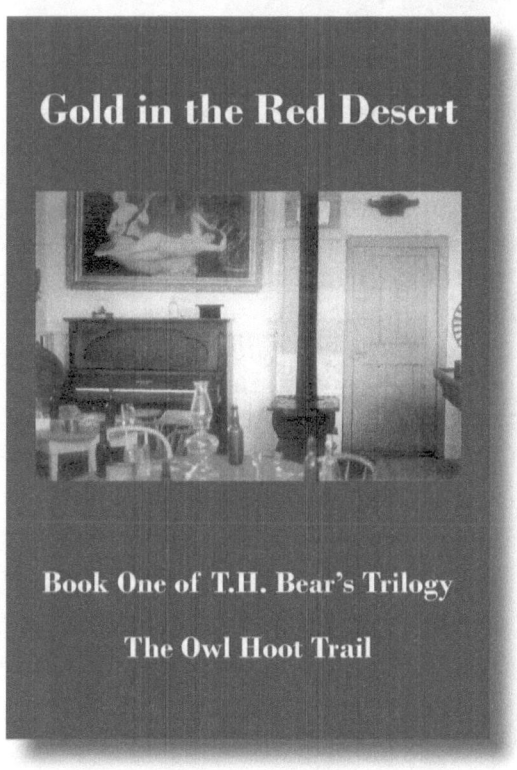

The Withlacoochee Renegades

Book Two of T.H. Bear's Trilogy

The Owl Hoot Trail

The reader found in *Book One of The Owl Hoot Trail: Gold in the Red Desert*, Clifford Brown had fled his home state of Georgia ahead of a murder warrant for a man who had actually been killed by a corrupt appointed official.

His travels allowed him to be in the right place at the right time, to witness another murder, also by dishonest men in power, although the second killing took place on the great plains of the Wyoming Territory.

During the following year, he is the one person responsible for the righting of this wrong and the return of stolen property to its rightful owner. There, he also falls in love with a beautiful raven-haired woman who becomes his wife.

Book Two, The Withlacoochee Renegades, is the story of their return to Georgia during times many considered more horrible than the war itself, "The Unholy Reconstruction Period," where Corruption outnumbered Christianity in the Occupational Government.

All of these titles are available online through
www.bluewaterpress.com

The Last, and Best Book
of the *Owl Hoot Trail Trilogy*

The Long Trail is the Final Book in the Saga of T.H. Bear's Trilogy, *The Owl Hoot Trail.*

In Book Three, we follow Cliff as he pursues his arch enemy, John M. Tidwell, the man who murdered countless of the home folk who were Reb's friends.

In dogged pursuit, Reb will not falter until he reaches his goal to go face to face with John Tidwell and to do justice for those he loved, those he fought with throughout the time he led the Withlocoochee Renegades.

As with all of T.H. Bear's books, the story is intense and moving, leaving the reader no choice but to work at finishing the story as quickly as possible.

T.H. Bear is an author of Historical Novels, Cowboy Action adventure tales, Murder Mystery thrillers and is just plain the damnedest story teller since Louis L'Amour or Zane Gray graced our hearts and minds through the window of our eyes.